THE HARDY BOYS

UNDERCOVER BROTHERS™

PAPERCUTZ™

THE HARDY BOYS®

#5

UNDERCOVER BROTHERS™

Sea You, Sea Me

SCOTT LOBDELL • Writer
DANIEL RENDON • Artist
preview art by SIDNEY LIMA
Based on the series by
FRANKLIN W. DIXON

PAPERCUTZ™
New York

Sea You, Sea Me
SCOTT LOBDELL – Writer
DANIEL RENDON — Artist
MARK LERER – Letterer
LAURIE E. SMITH — Colorist
JIM SALICRUP
Editor-in-Chief

ISBN-10: 1-59707-022-X paperback edition
ISBN-13: 978-1-59707-022-5 paperback edition
ISBN-10: 1-59707-023-8 hardcover edition
ISBN-13: 978-1-59707-023-2 hardcover edition

Printed in China.
Distributed by Holtzbrinck Publishers.

10 9 8 7 6 5 4 3 2 1

CHAPTER ONE: "EN GARDE!"

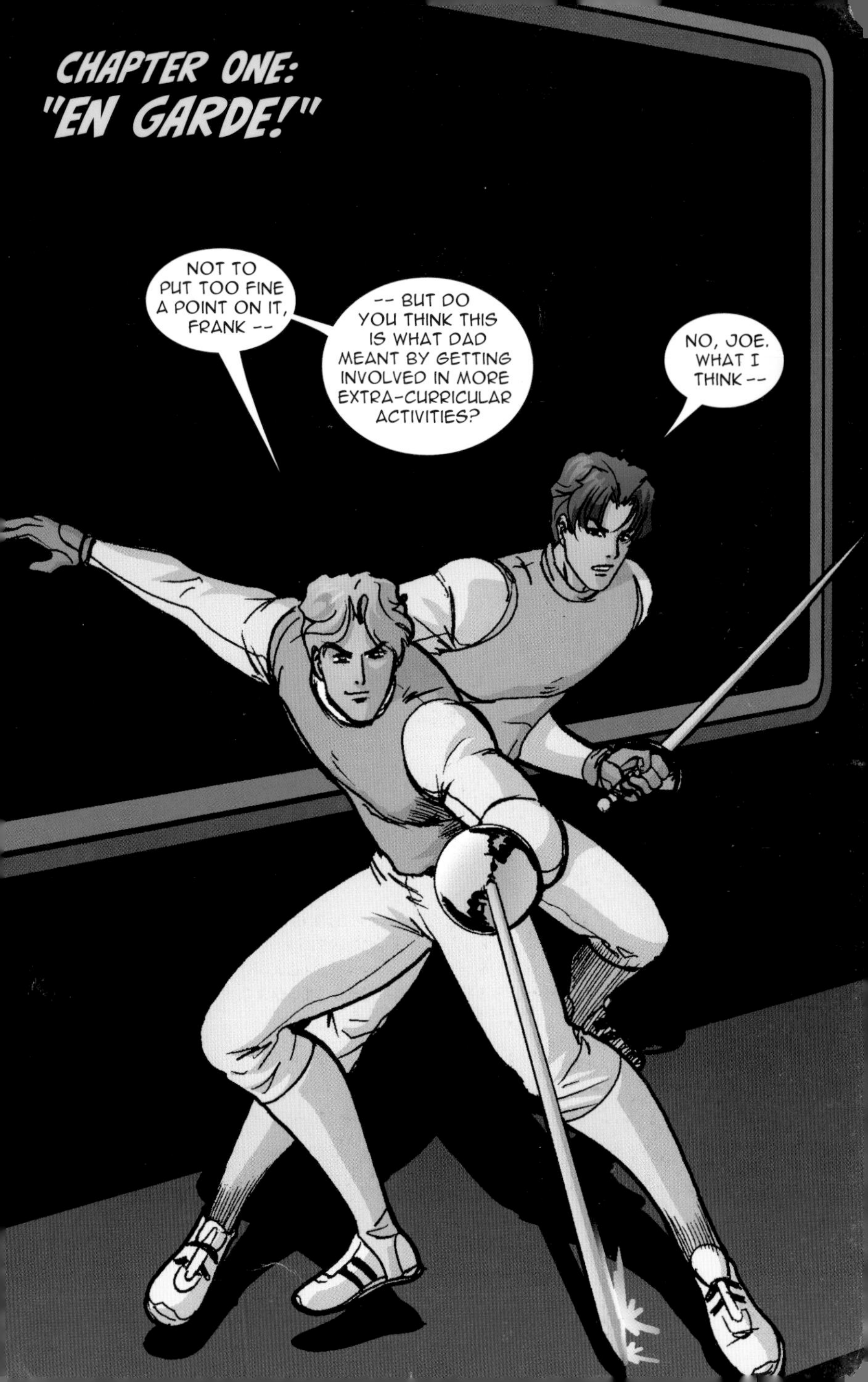
NOT TO PUT TOO FINE A POINT ON IT, FRANK --
-- BUT DO YOU THINK THIS IS WHAT DAD MEANT BY GETTING INVOLVED IN MORE EXTRA-CURRICULAR ACTIVITIES?
NO, JOE. WHAT I THINK --

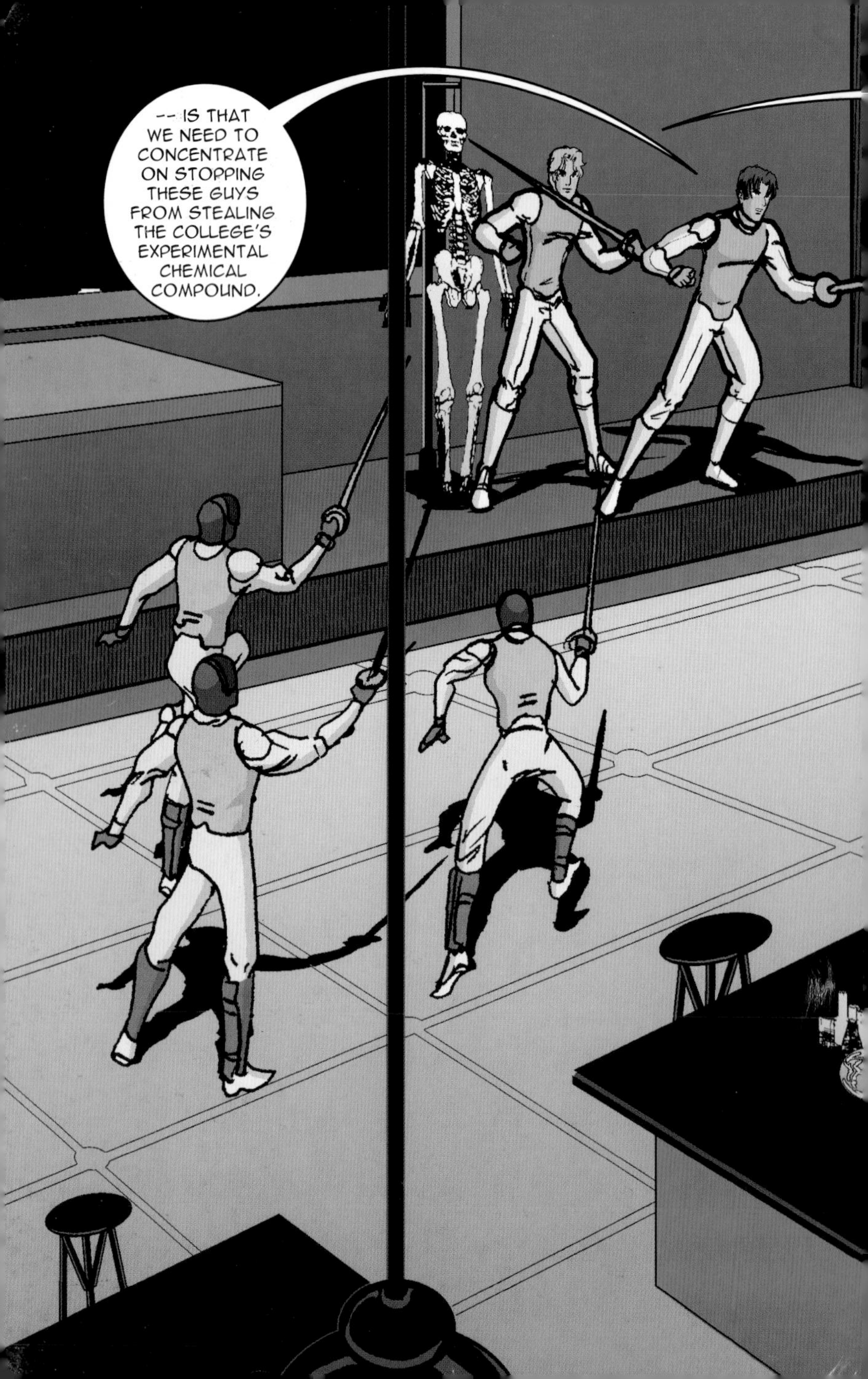
-- IS THAT WE NEED TO CONCENTRATE ON STOPPING THESE GUYS FROM STEALING THE COLLEGE'S EXPERIMENTAL CHEMICAL COMPOUND.

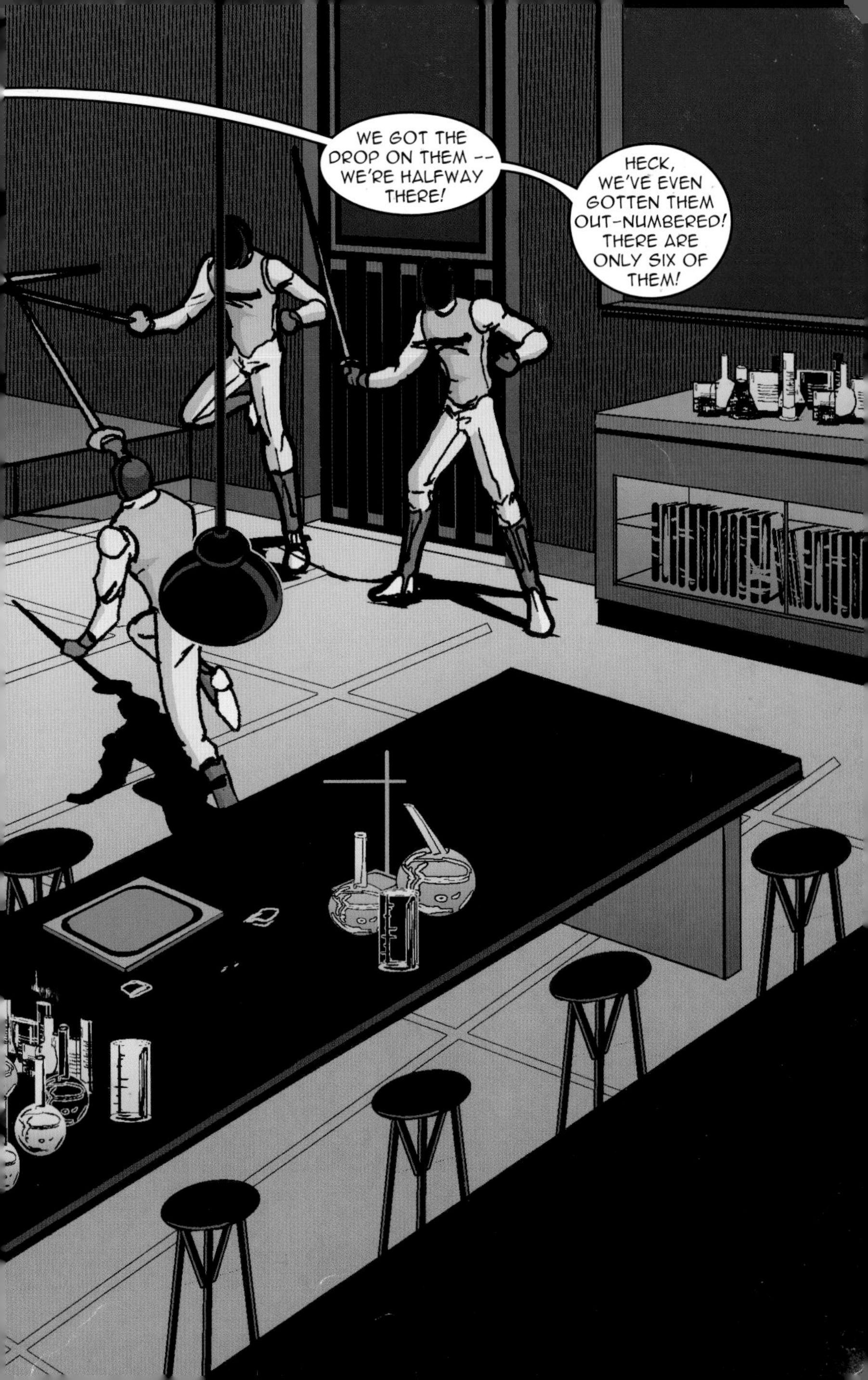
WE GOT THE DROP ON THEM -- WE'RE HALFWAY THERE!
HECK, WE'VE EVEN GOTTEN THEM OUT-NUMBERED! THERE ARE ONLY SIX OF THEM!

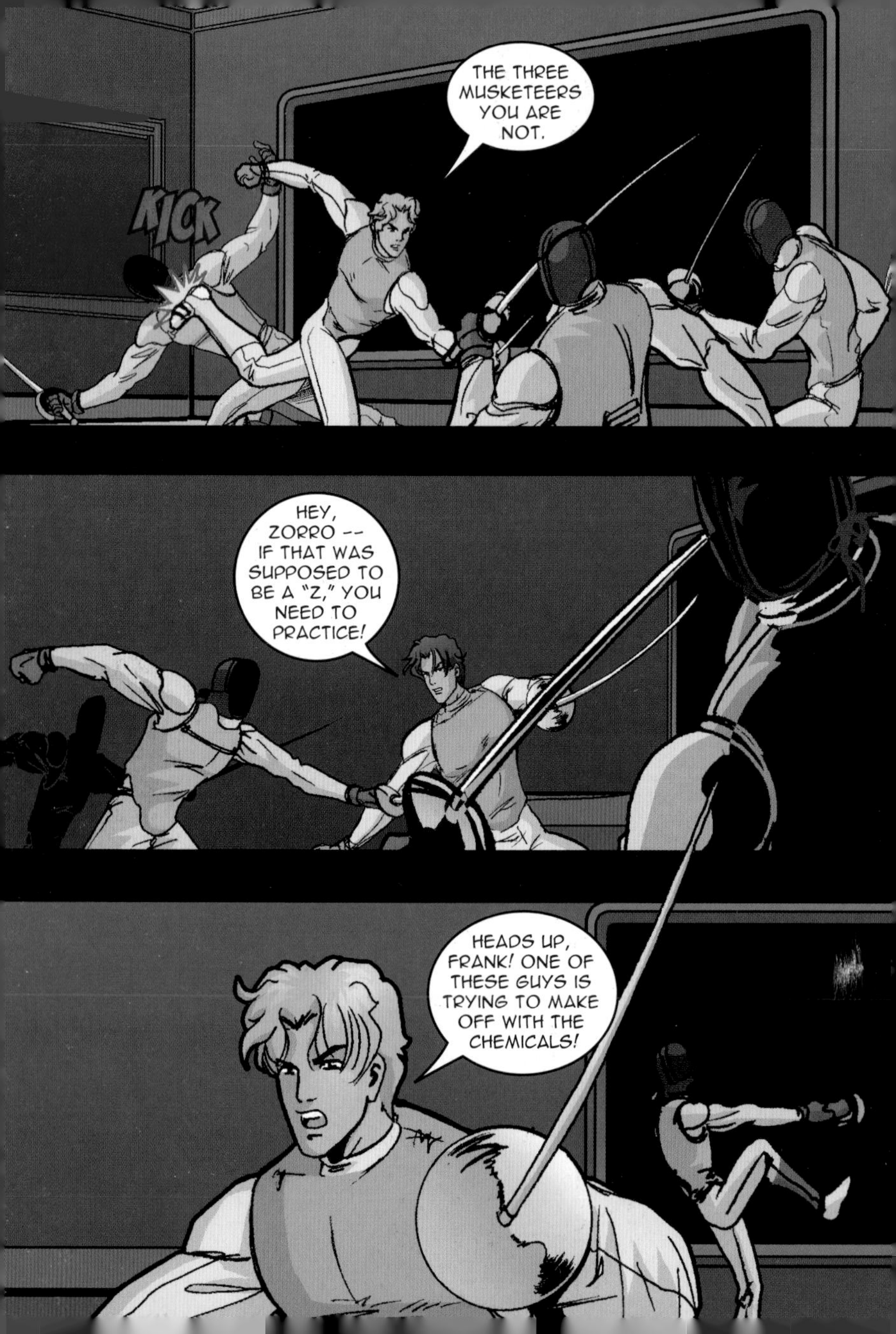
THE THREE MUSKETEERS YOU ARE NOT.
KICK
HEY, ZORRO -- IF THAT WAS SUPPOSED TO BE A "Z," YOU NEED TO PRACTICE!
HEADS UP, FRANK! ONE OF THESE GUYS IS TRYING TO MAKE OFF WITH THE CHEMICALS!

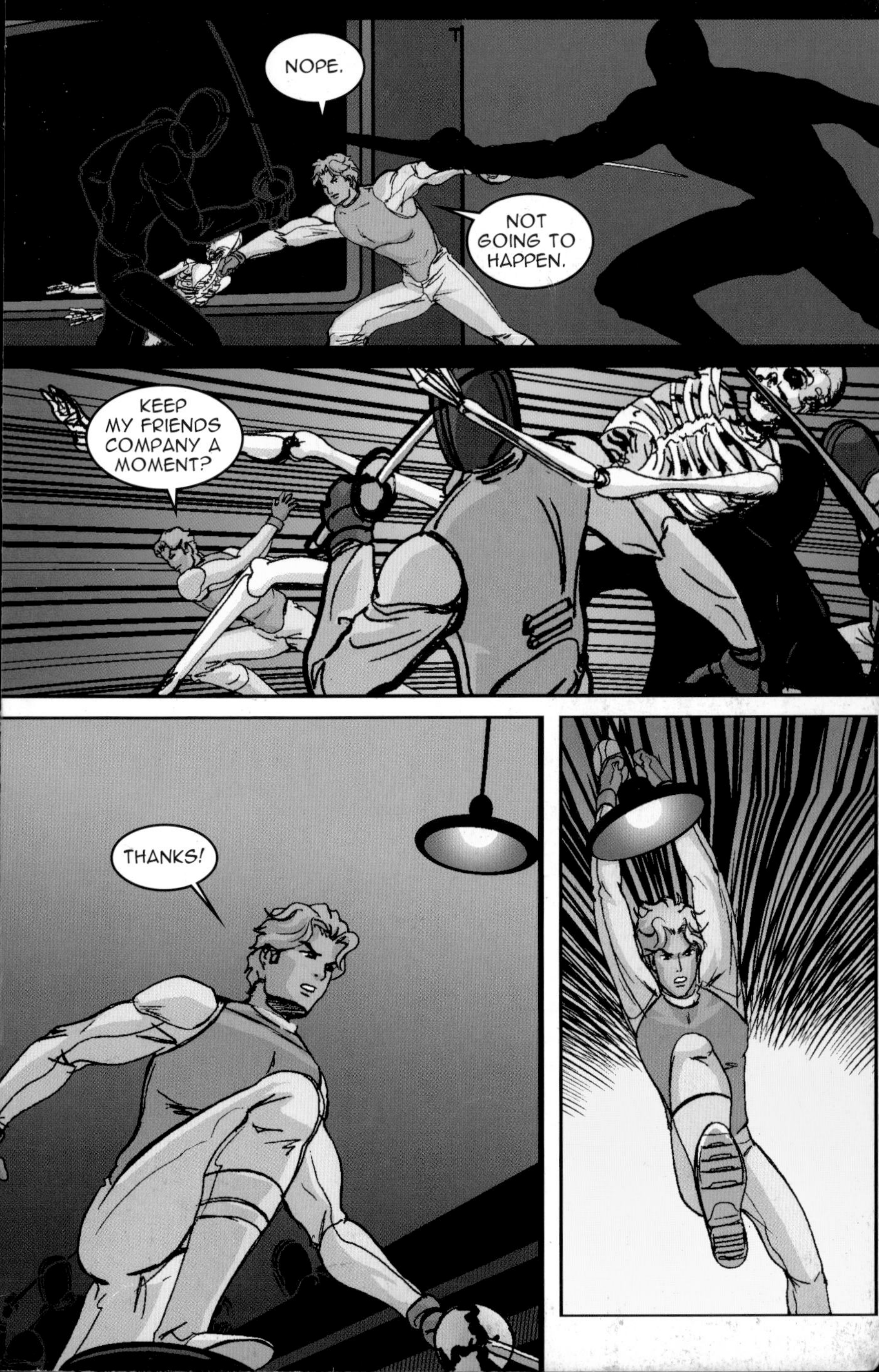
NOPE.
NOT GOING TO HAPPEN.
KEEP MY FRIENDS COMPANY A MOMENT?
THANKS!

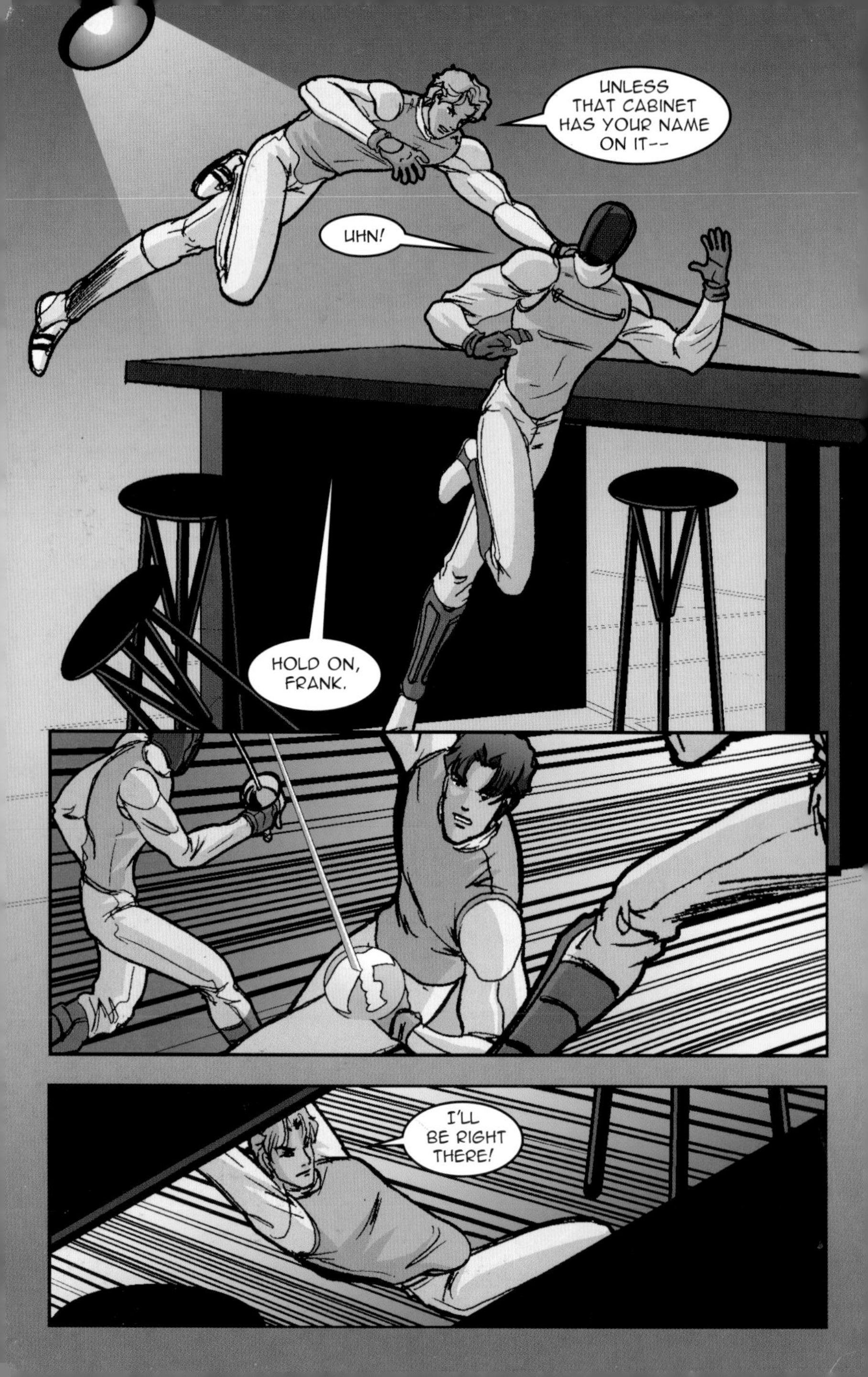
UNLESS THAT CABINET HAS YOUR NAME ON IT--
UHN!
HOLD ON, FRANK.
I'LL BE RIGHT THERE!

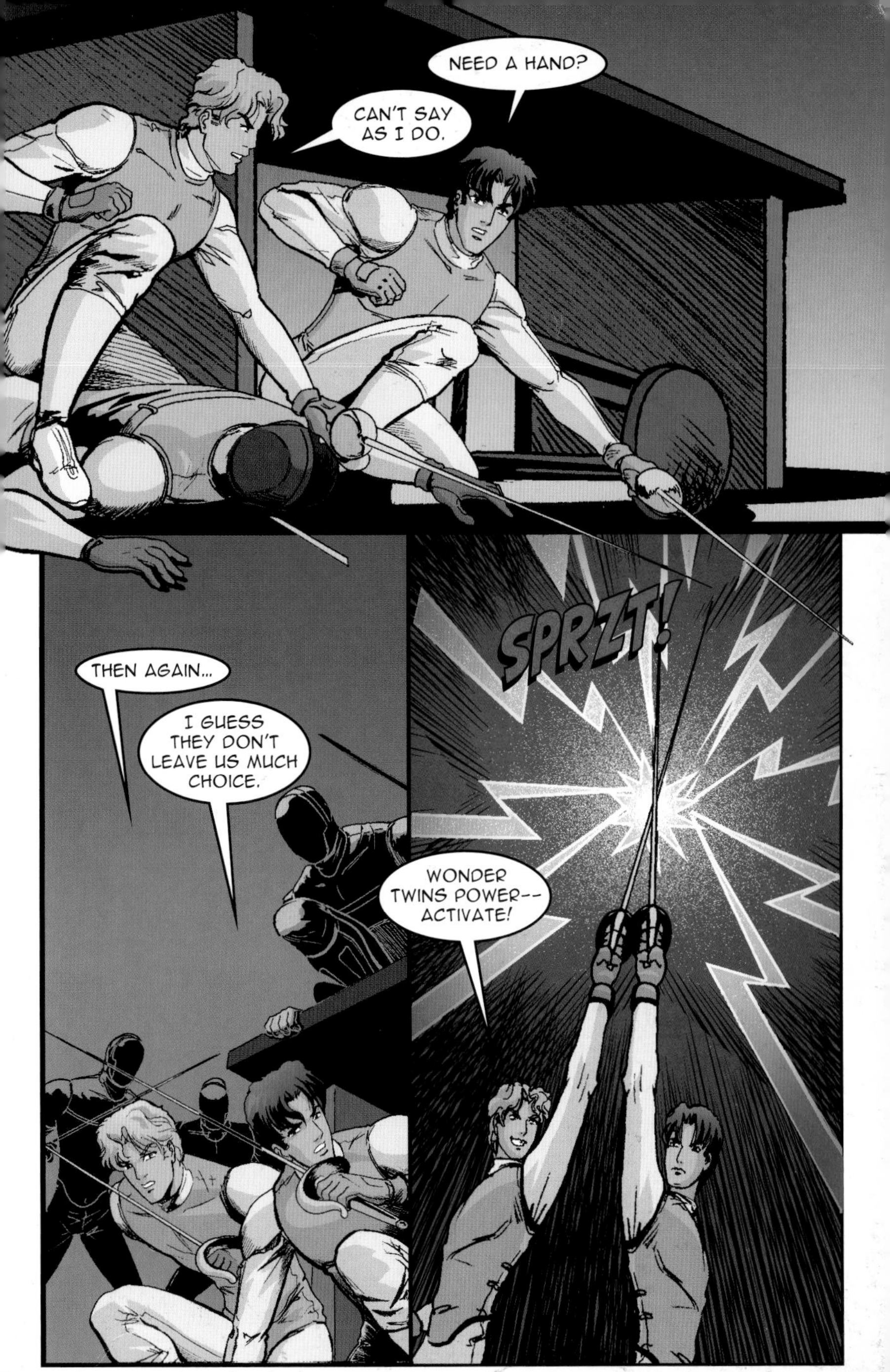
NEED A HAND?
CAN'T SAY AS I DO.
THEN AGAIN...
I GUESS THEY DON'T LEAVE US MUCH CHOICE.
SPRZT!
WONDER TWINS POWER-- ACTIVATE!

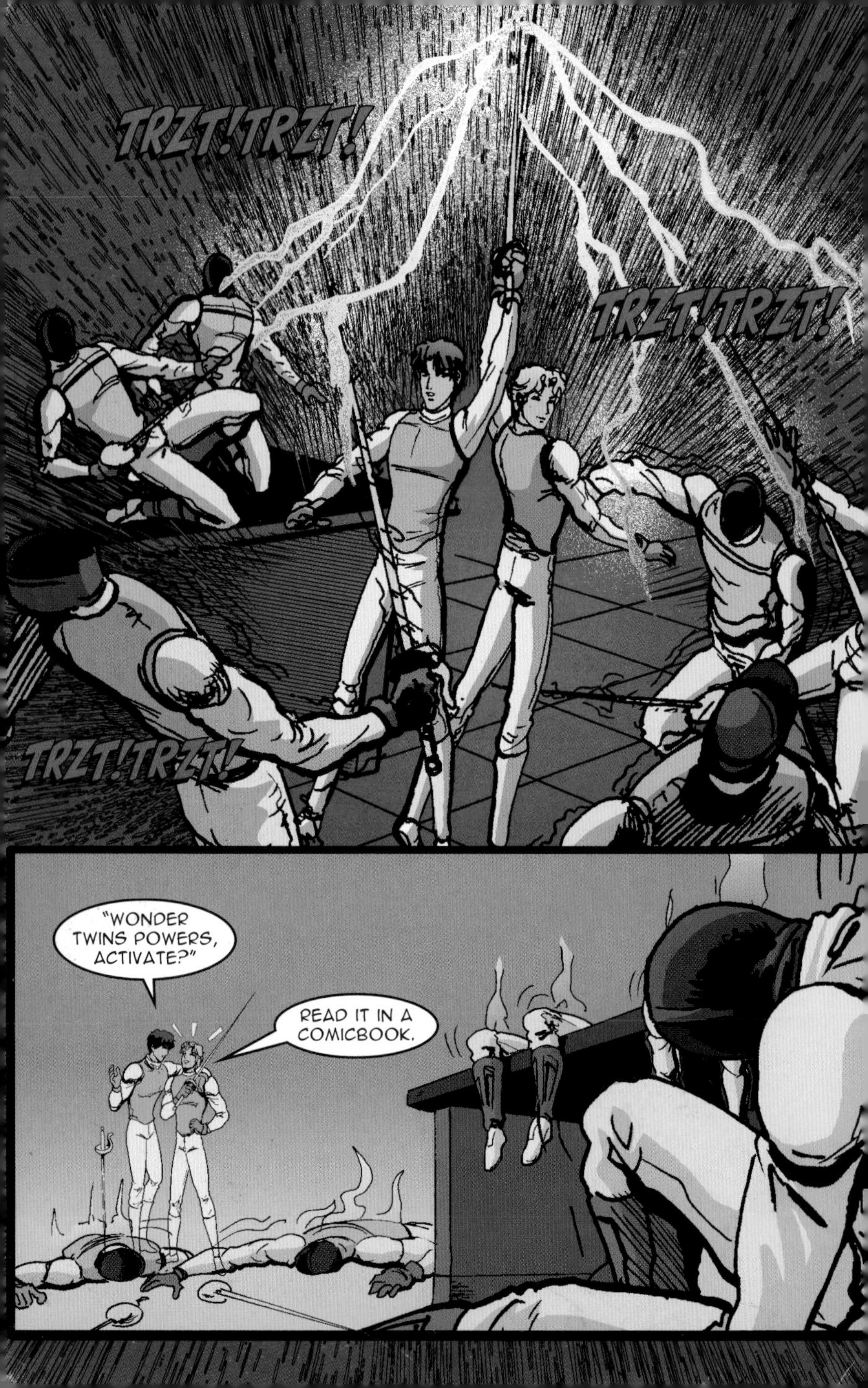
TRZT!TRZT!
TRZT!TRZT!
TRZT!TRZT!
"WONDER TWINS POWERS, ACTIVATE?"
READ IT IN A COMICBOOK.

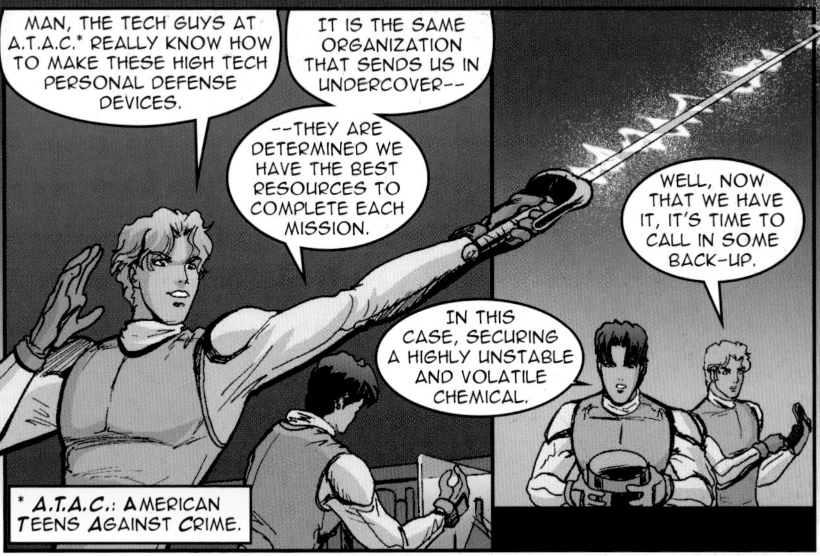
MAN, THE TECH GUYS AT A.T.A.C.* REALLY KNOW HOW TO MAKE THESE HIGH TECH PERSONAL DEFENSE DEVICES.
IT IS THE SAME ORGANIZATION THAT SENDS US IN UNDERCOVER--
--THEY ARE DETERMINED WE HAVE THE BEST RESOURCES TO COMPLETE EACH MISSION.
* A.T.A.C.: AMERICAN TEENS AGAINST CRIME.
WELL, NOW THAT WE HAVE IT, IT'S TIME TO CALL IN SOME BACK-UP.
IN THIS CASE, SECURING A HIGHLY UNSTABLE AND VOLATILE CHEMICAL.

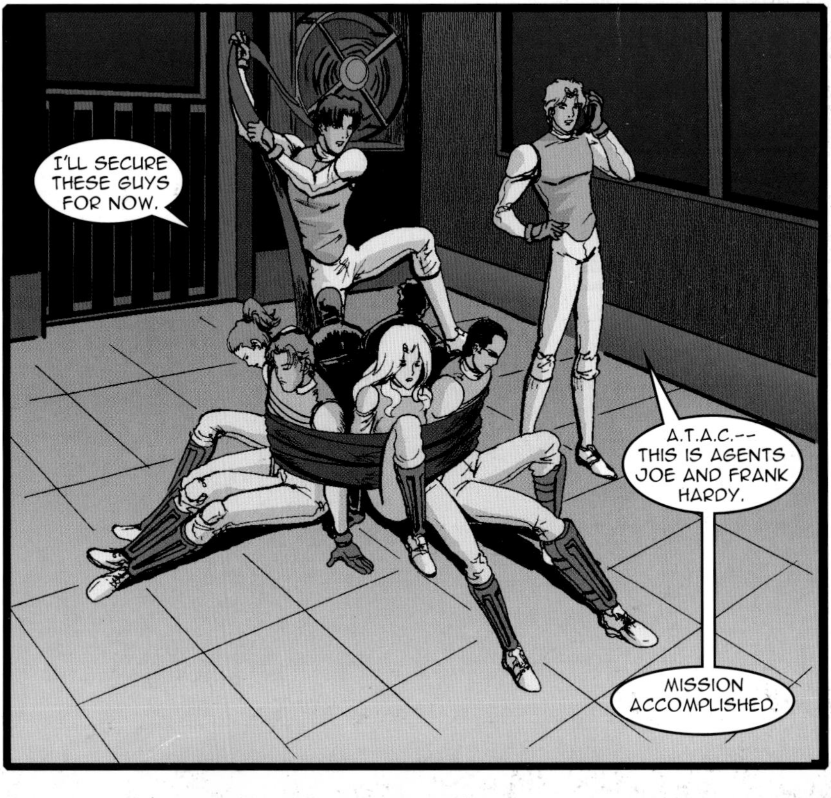
I'LL SECURE THESE GUYS FOR NOW.
A.T.A.C.-- THIS IS AGENTS JOE AND FRANK HARDY.
MISSION ACCOMPLISHED.

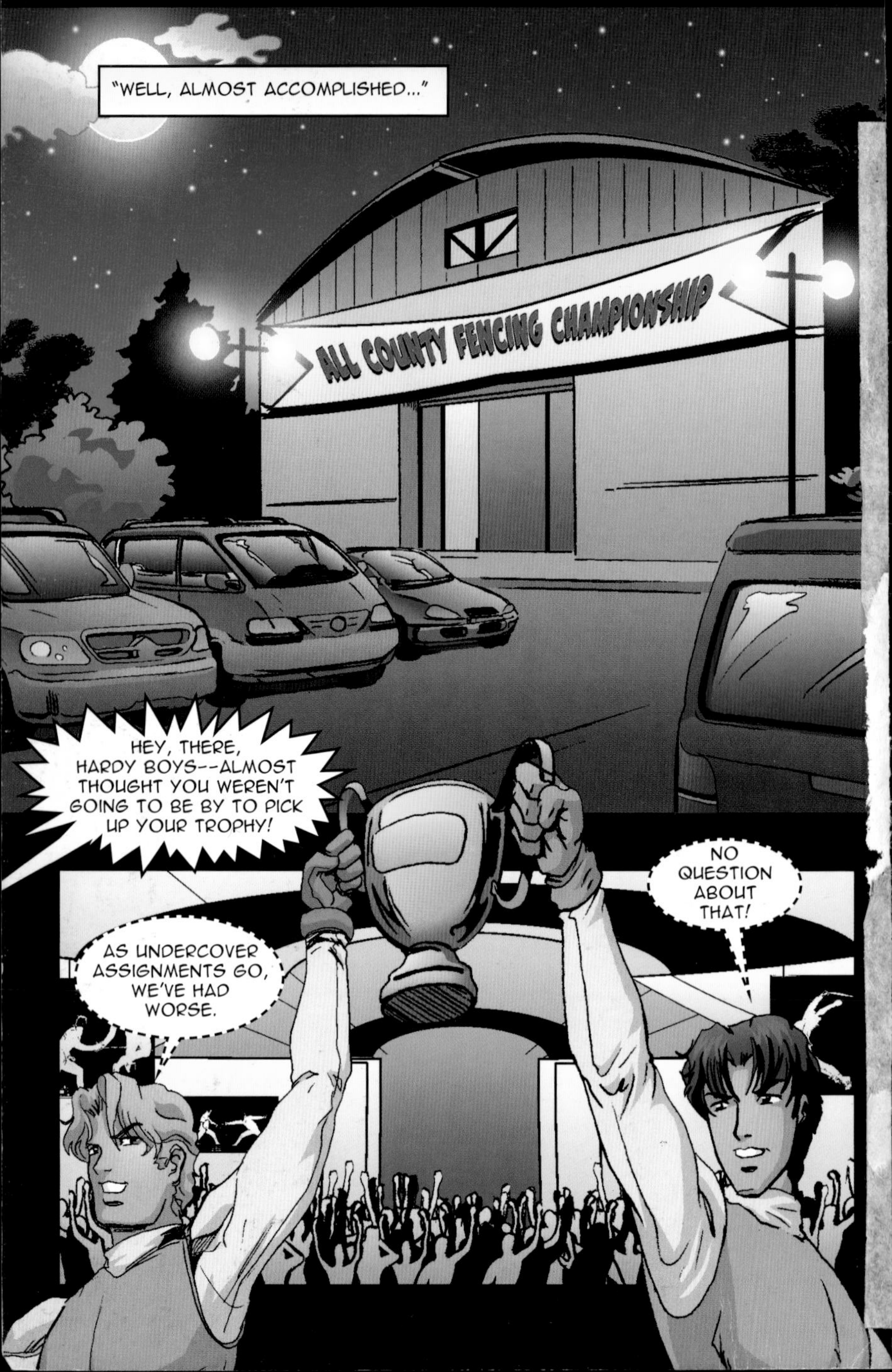
"WELL, ALMOST ACCOMPLISHED..."
ALL COUNTY FENCING CHAMPIONSHIP
HEY, THERE, HARDY BOYS--ALMOST THOUGHT YOU WEREN'T GOING TO BE BY TO PICK UP YOUR TROPHY!
AS UNDERCOVER ASSIGNMENTS GO, WE'VE HAD WORSE.
NO QUESTION ABOUT THAT!

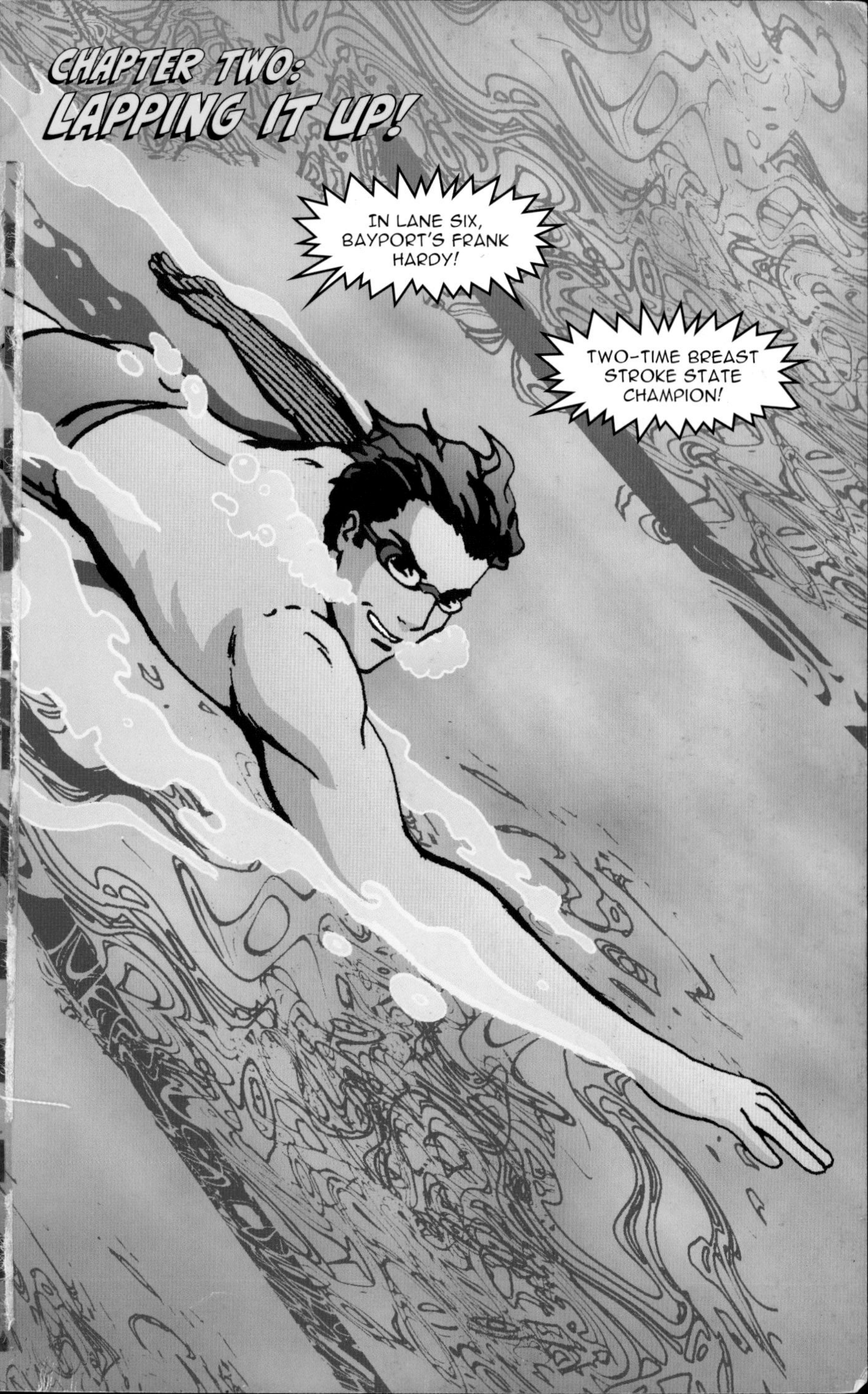
CHAPTER TWO:
LAPPING IT UP!
IN LANE SIX, BAYPORT'S FRANK HARDY!
TWO-TIME BREAST STROKE STATE CHAMPION!

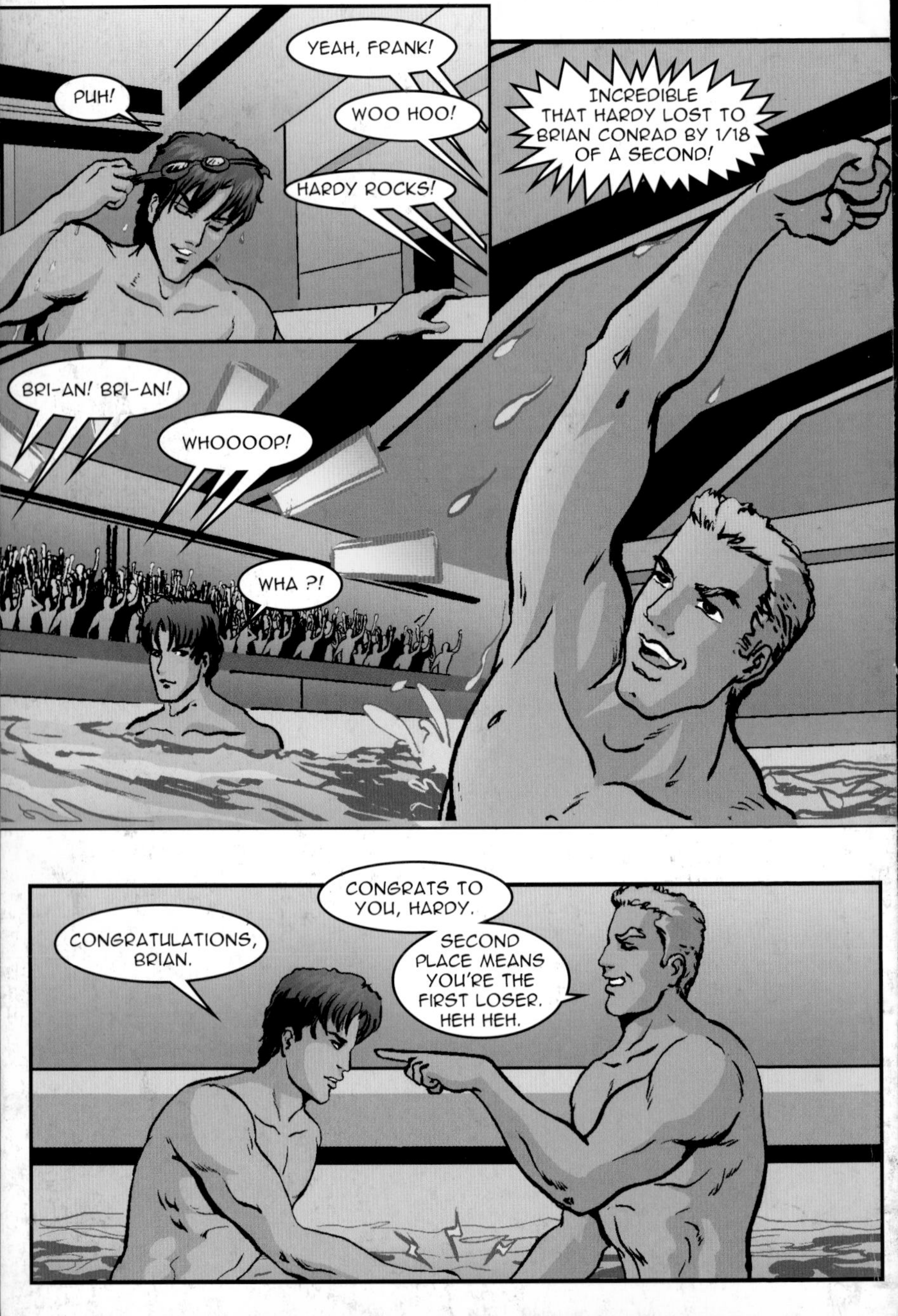
YEAH, FRANK!
PUH!
WOO HOO!
HARDY ROCKS!
INCREDIBLE THAT HARDY LOST TO BRIAN CONRAD BY 1/18 OF A SECOND!
BRI-AN! BRI-AN!
WHOOOOP!
WHA ?!
CONGRATULATIONS, BRIAN.
CONGRATS TO YOU, HARDY.
SECOND PLACE MEANS YOU'RE THE FIRST LOSER. HEH HEH.

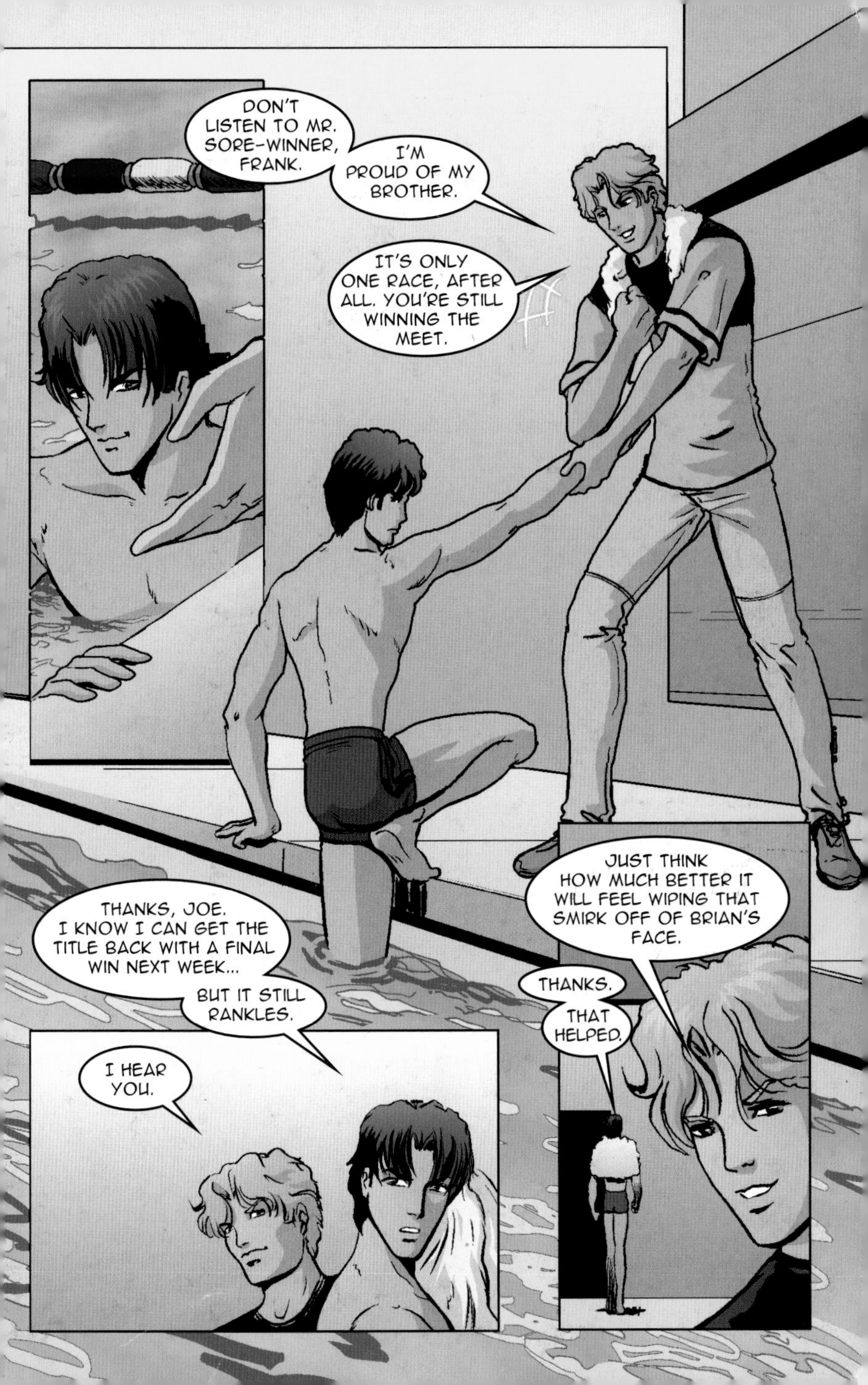
DON'T LISTEN TO MR. SORE-WINNER, FRANK.
I'M PROUD OF MY BROTHER.
IT'S ONLY ONE RACE, AFTER ALL. YOU'RE STILL WINNING THE MEET.
THANKS, JOE. I KNOW I CAN GET THE TITLE BACK WITH A FINAL WIN NEXT WEEK...
BUT IT STILL RANKLES.
I HEAR YOU.
JUST THINK HOW MUCH BETTER IT WILL FEEL WIPING THAT SMIRK OFF OF BRIAN'S FACE.
THANKS.
THAT HELPED.

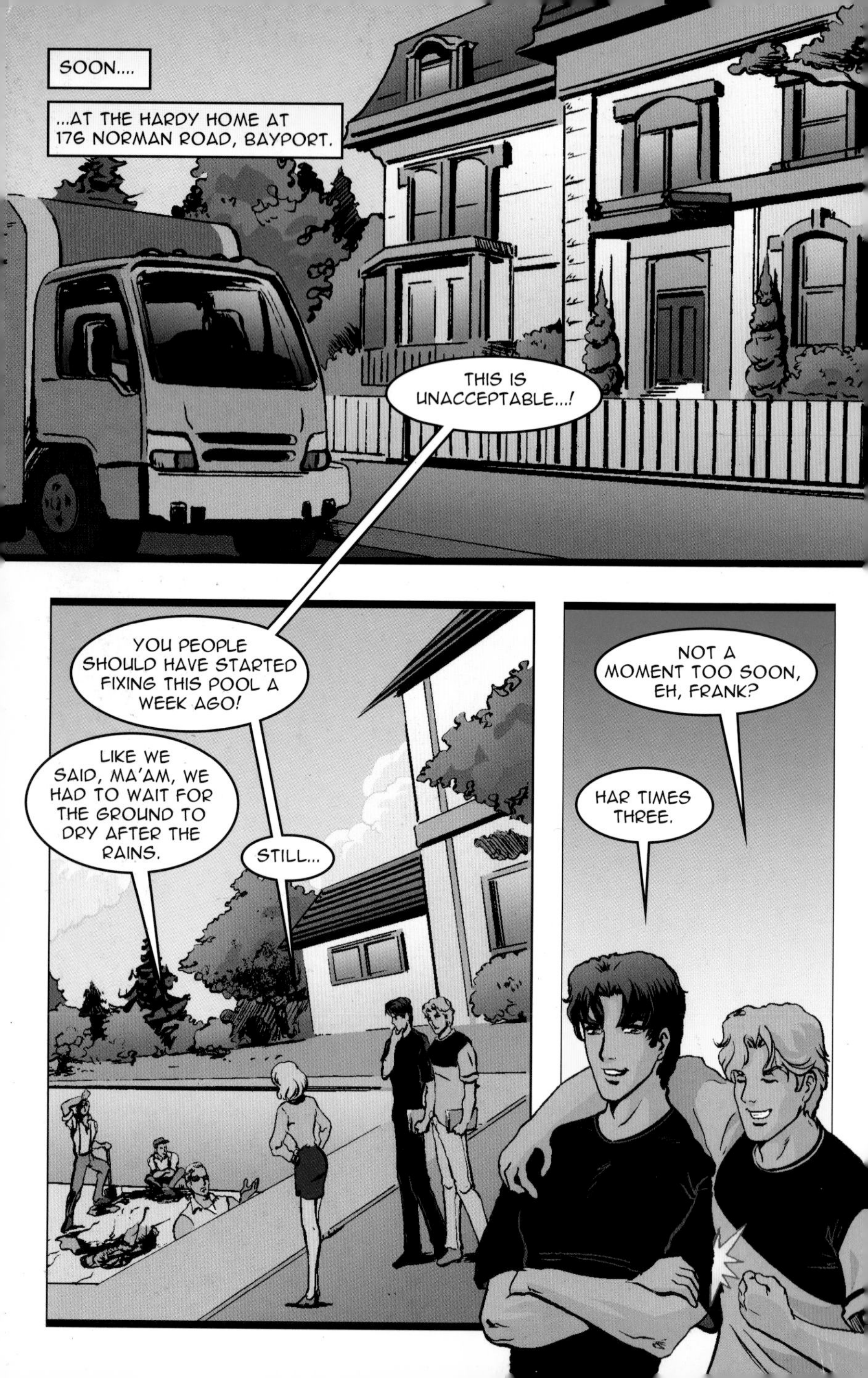
SOON....
...AT THE HARDY HOME AT 176 NORMAN ROAD, BAYPORT.
THIS IS UNACCEPTABLE...!
YOU PEOPLE SHOULD HAVE STARTED FIXING THIS POOL A WEEK AGO!
LIKE WE SAID, MA'AM, WE HAD TO WAIT FOR THE GROUND TO DRY AFTER THE RAINS.
STILL...
NOT A MOMENT TOO SOON, EH, FRANK?
HAR TIMES THREE.

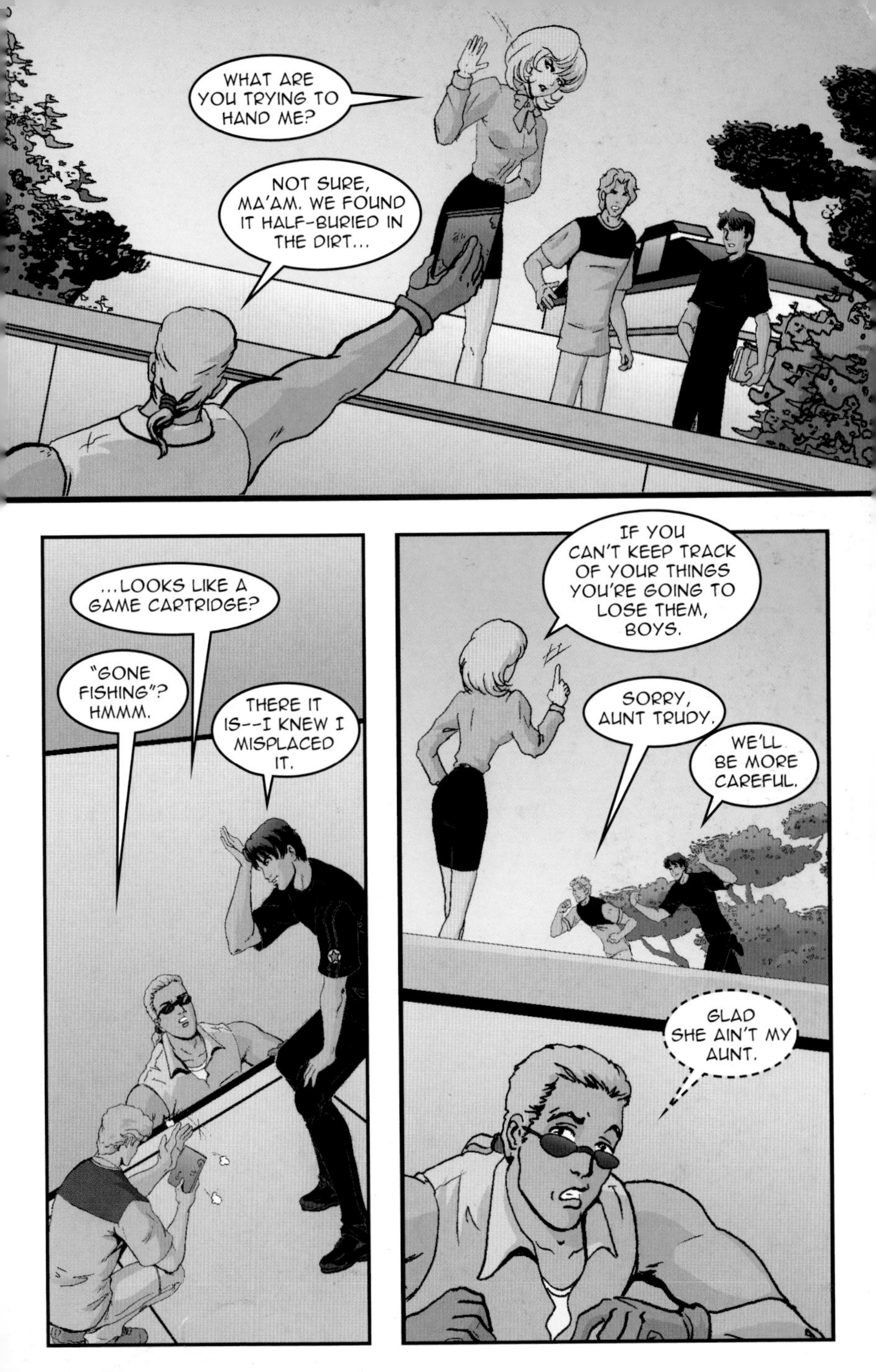
WHAT ARE YOU TRYING TO HAND ME?
NOT SURE, MA'AM. WE FOUND IT HALF-BURIED IN THE DIRT...
...LOOKS LIKE A GAME CARTRIDGE?
"GONE FISHING"? HMMM.
THERE IT IS--I KNEW I MISPLACED IT.
IF YOU CAN'T KEEP TRACK OF YOUR THINGS YOU'RE GOING TO LOSE THEM, BOYS.
SORRY, AUNT TRUDY.
WE'LL BE MORE CAREFUL.
GLAD SHE AIN'T MY AUNT.

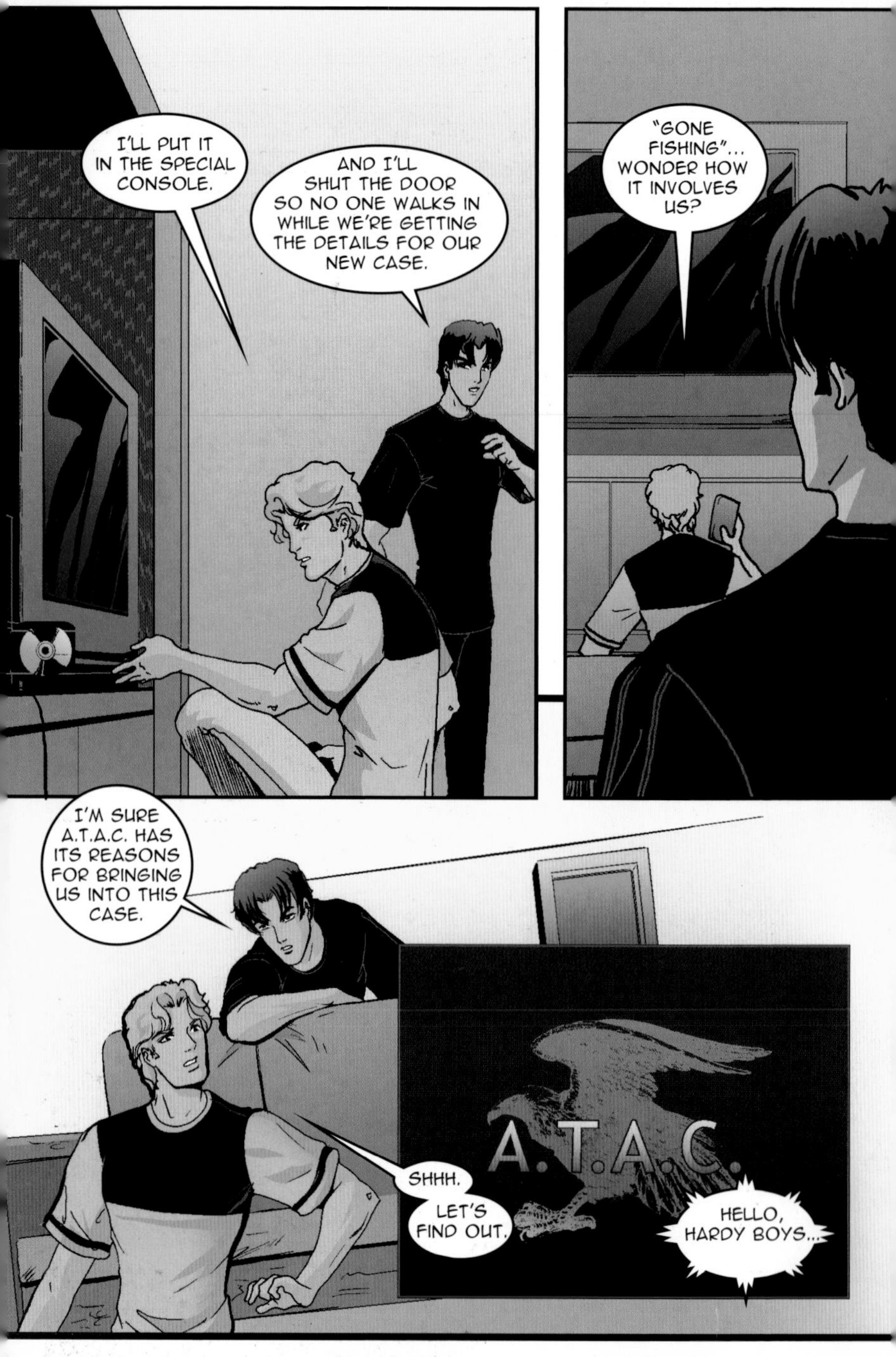
I'LL PUT IT IN THE SPECIAL CONSOLE.
AND I'LL SHUT THE DOOR SO NO ONE WALKS IN WHILE WE'RE GETTING THE DETAILS FOR OUR NEW CASE.
"GONE FISHING"... WONDER HOW IT INVOLVES US?
I'M SURE A.T.A.C. HAS ITS REASONS FOR BRINGING US INTO THIS CASE.
A.T.A.C.
SHHH.
LET'S FIND OUT.
HELLO, HARDY BOYS...

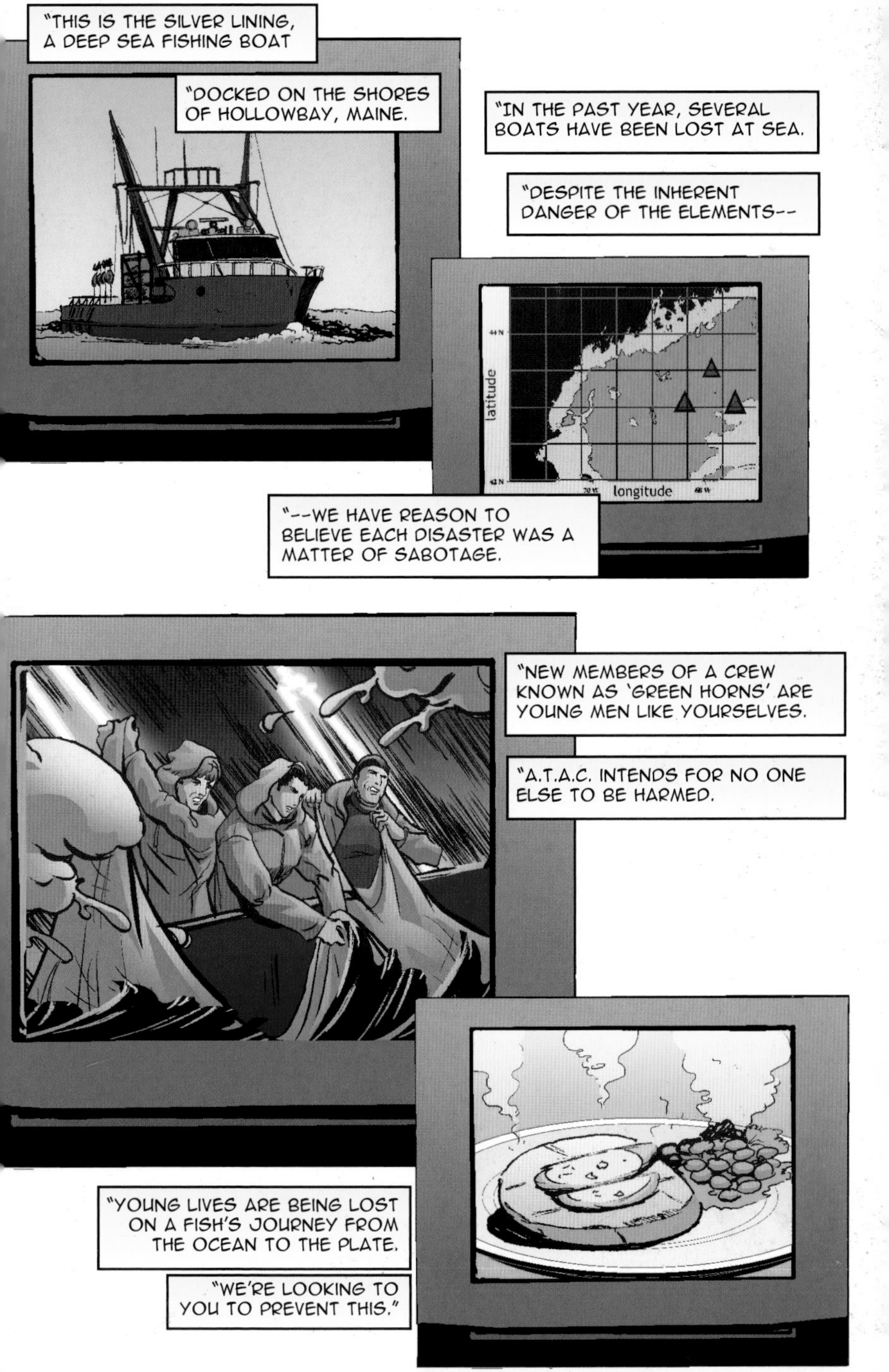
"THIS IS THE SILVER LINING, A DEEP SEA FISHING BOAT
"DOCKED ON THE SHORES OF HOLLOWBAY, MAINE.
"IN THE PAST YEAR, SEVERAL BOATS HAVE BEEN LOST AT SEA.
"DESPITE THE INHERENT DANGER OF THE ELEMENTS--
44 N
latitude
42 N
longitude
"--WE HAVE REASON TO BELIEVE EACH DISASTER WAS A MATTER OF SABOTAGE.
"NEW MEMBERS OF A CREW KNOWN AS 'GREEN HORNS' ARE YOUNG MEN LIKE YOURSELVES.
"A.T.A.C. INTENDS FOR NO ONE ELSE TO BE HARMED.
"YOUNG LIVES ARE BEING LOST ON A FISH'S JOURNEY FROM THE OCEAN TO THE PLATE.
"WE'RE LOOKING TO YOU TO PREVENT THIS."

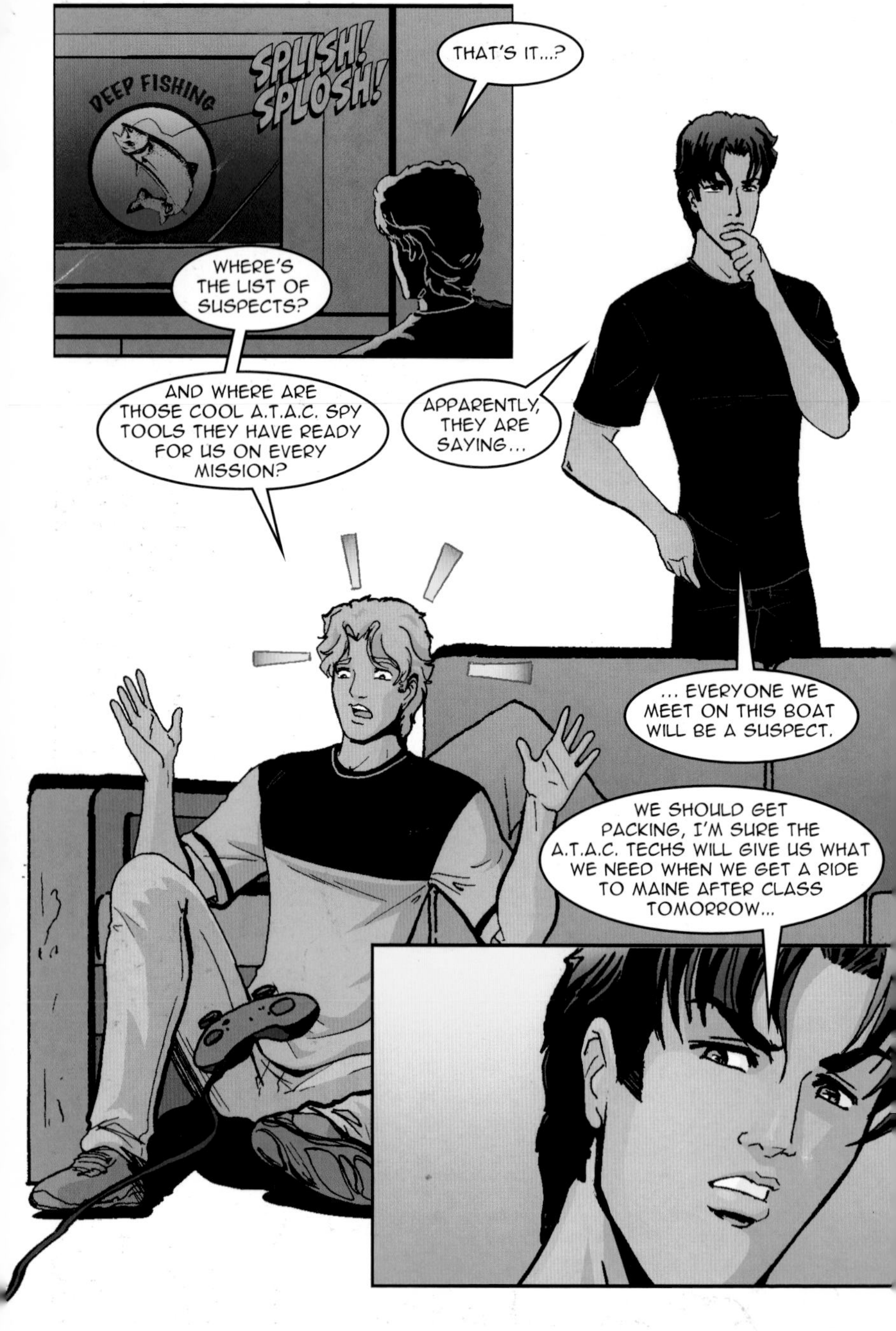
DEEP FISHING
SPLISH! SPLOSH!
THAT'S IT...?
WHERE'S THE LIST OF SUSPECTS?
AND WHERE ARE THOSE COOL A.T.A.C. SPY TOOLS THEY HAVE READY FOR US ON EVERY MISSION?
APPARENTLY, THEY ARE SAYING...
... EVERYONE WE MEET ON THIS BOAT WILL BE A SUSPECT.
WE SHOULD GET PACKING, I'M SURE THE A.T.A.C. TECHS WILL GIVE US WHAT WE NEED WHEN WE GET A RIDE TO MAINE AFTER CLASS TOMORROW...

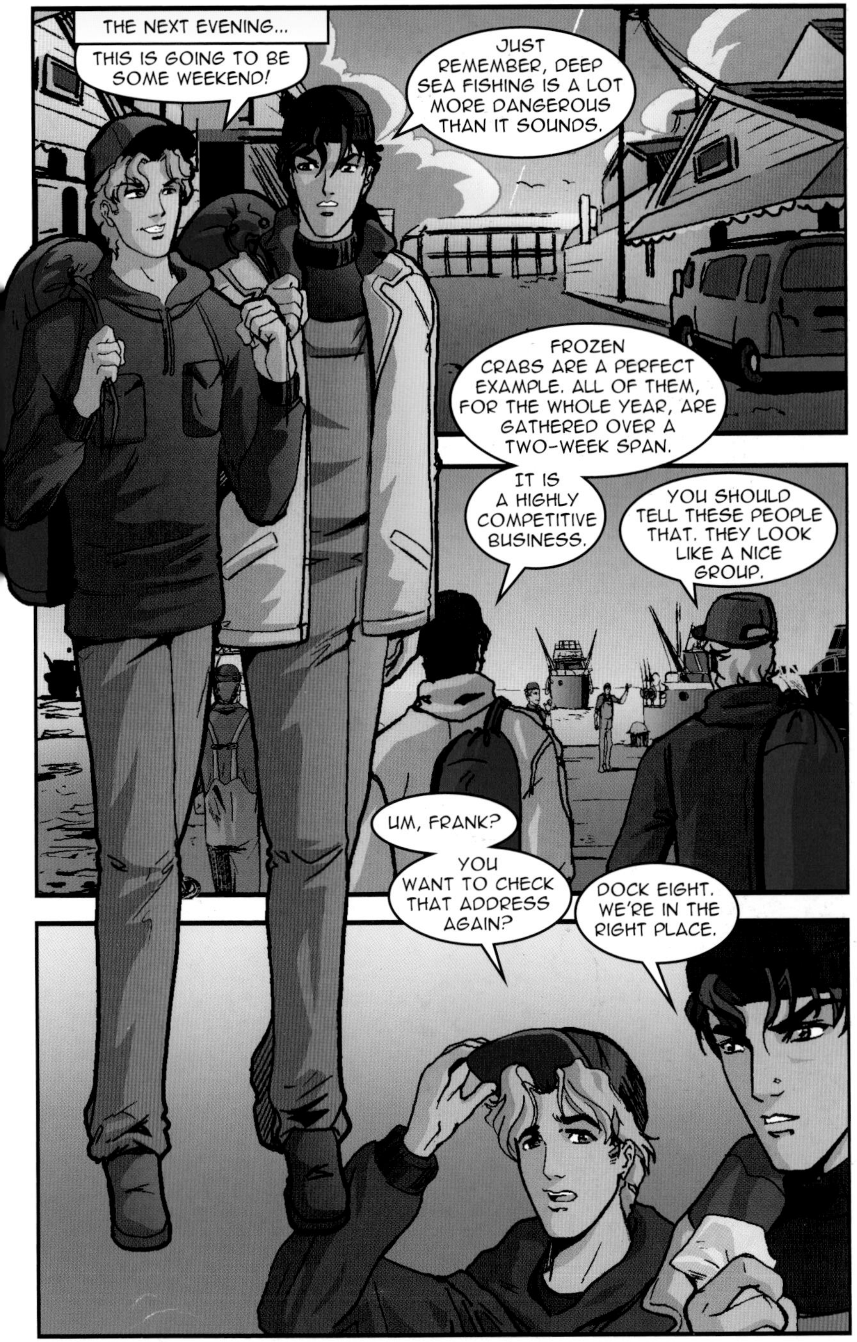
THE NEXT EVENING...
THIS IS GOING TO BE SOME WEEKEND!
JUST REMEMBER, DEEP SEA FISHING IS A LOT MORE DANGEROUS THAN IT SOUNDS.
FROZEN CRABS ARE A PERFECT EXAMPLE. ALL OF THEM, FOR THE WHOLE YEAR, ARE GATHERED OVER A TWO-WEEK SPAN.
IT IS A HIGHLY COMPETITIVE BUSINESS.
YOU SHOULD TELL THESE PEOPLE THAT. THEY LOOK LIKE A NICE GROUP.
UM, FRANK?
YOU WANT TO CHECK THAT ADDRESS AGAIN?
DOCK EIGHT. WE'RE IN THE RIGHT PLACE.

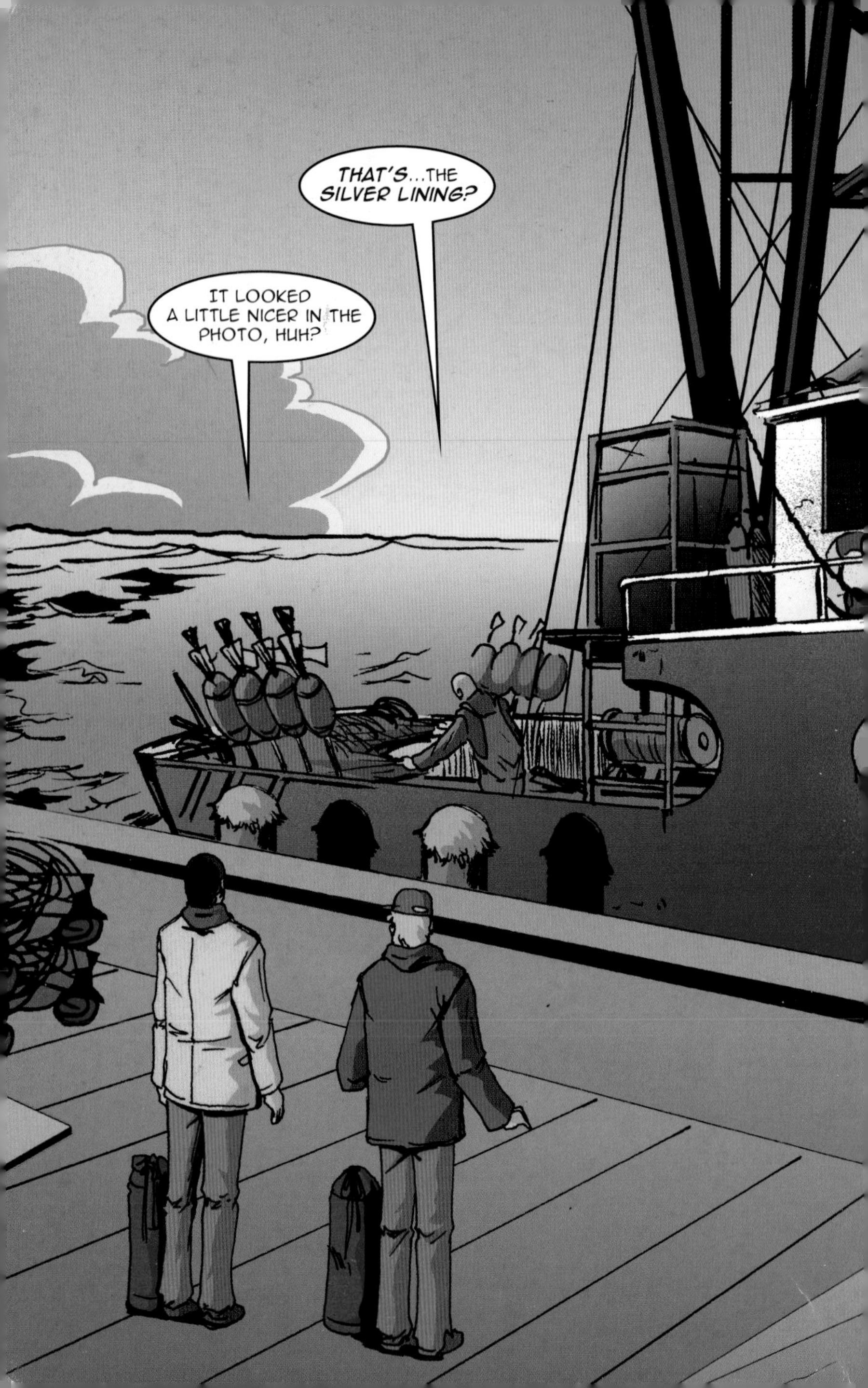
THAT'S...THE SILVER LINING?
IT LOOKED A LITTLE NICER IN THE PHOTO, HUH?

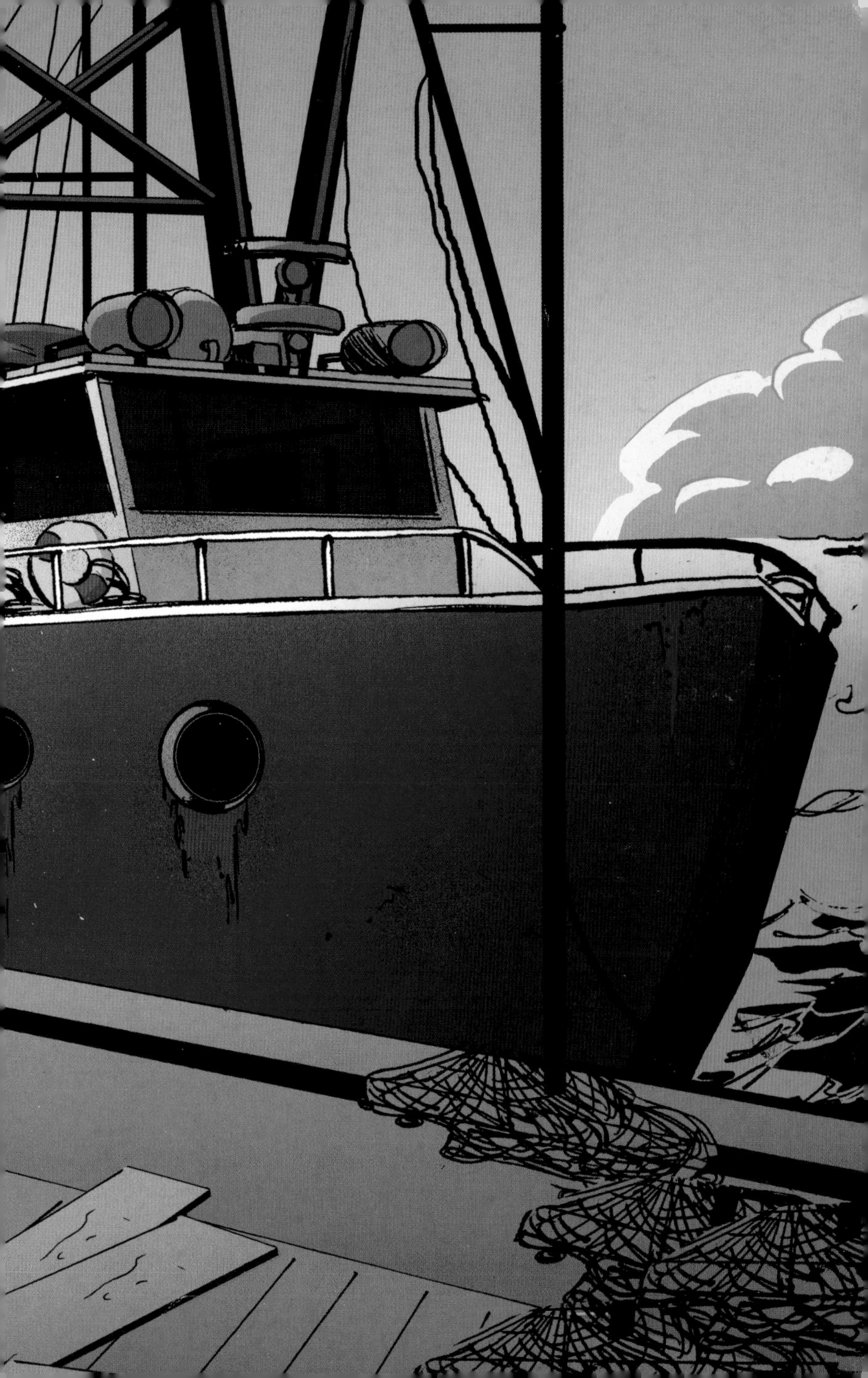

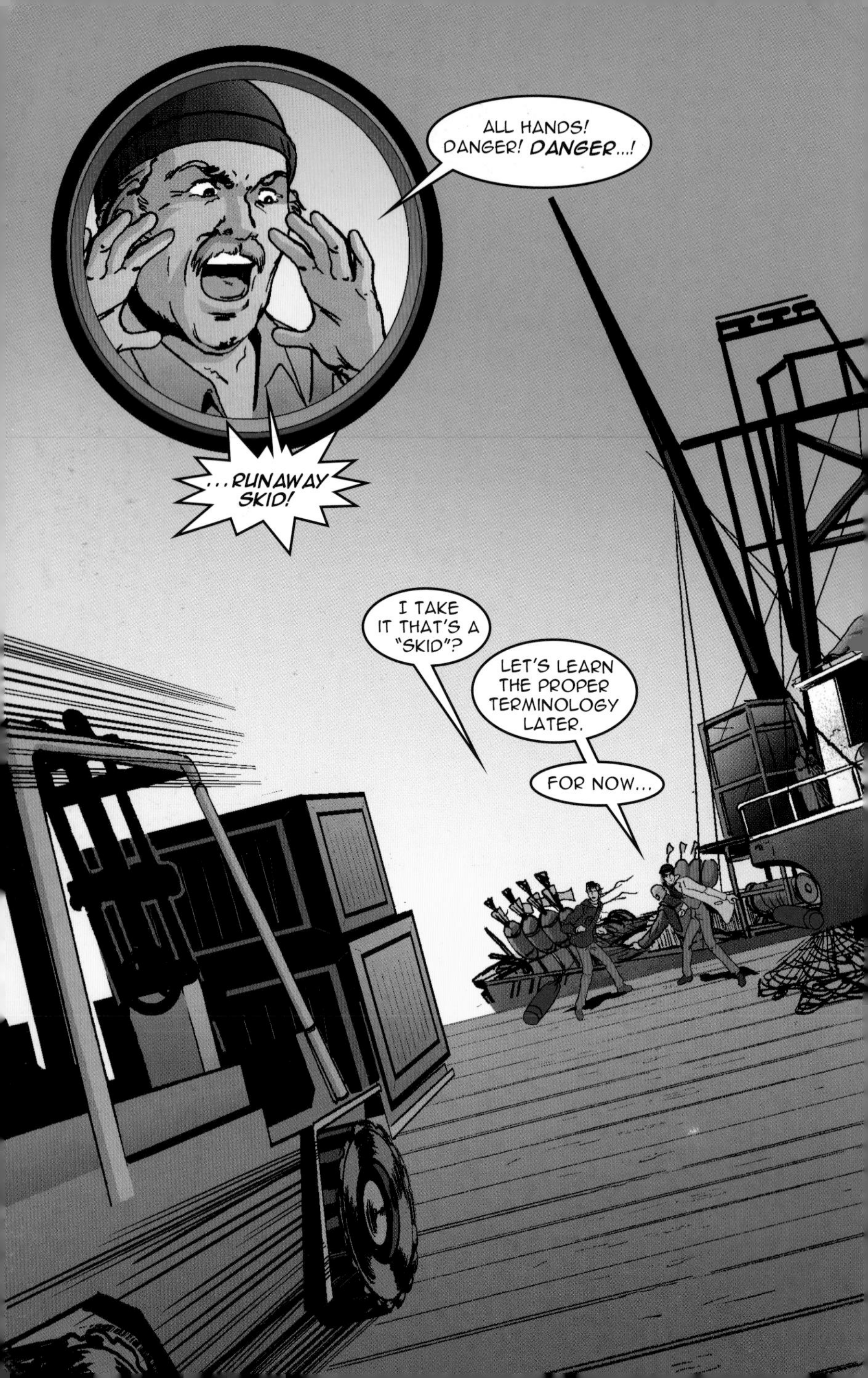
ALL HANDS! DANGER! DANGER...!
...RUNAWAY SKID!
I TAKE IT THAT'S A "SKID"?
LET'S LEARN THE PROPER TERMINOLOGY LATER.
FOR NOW...

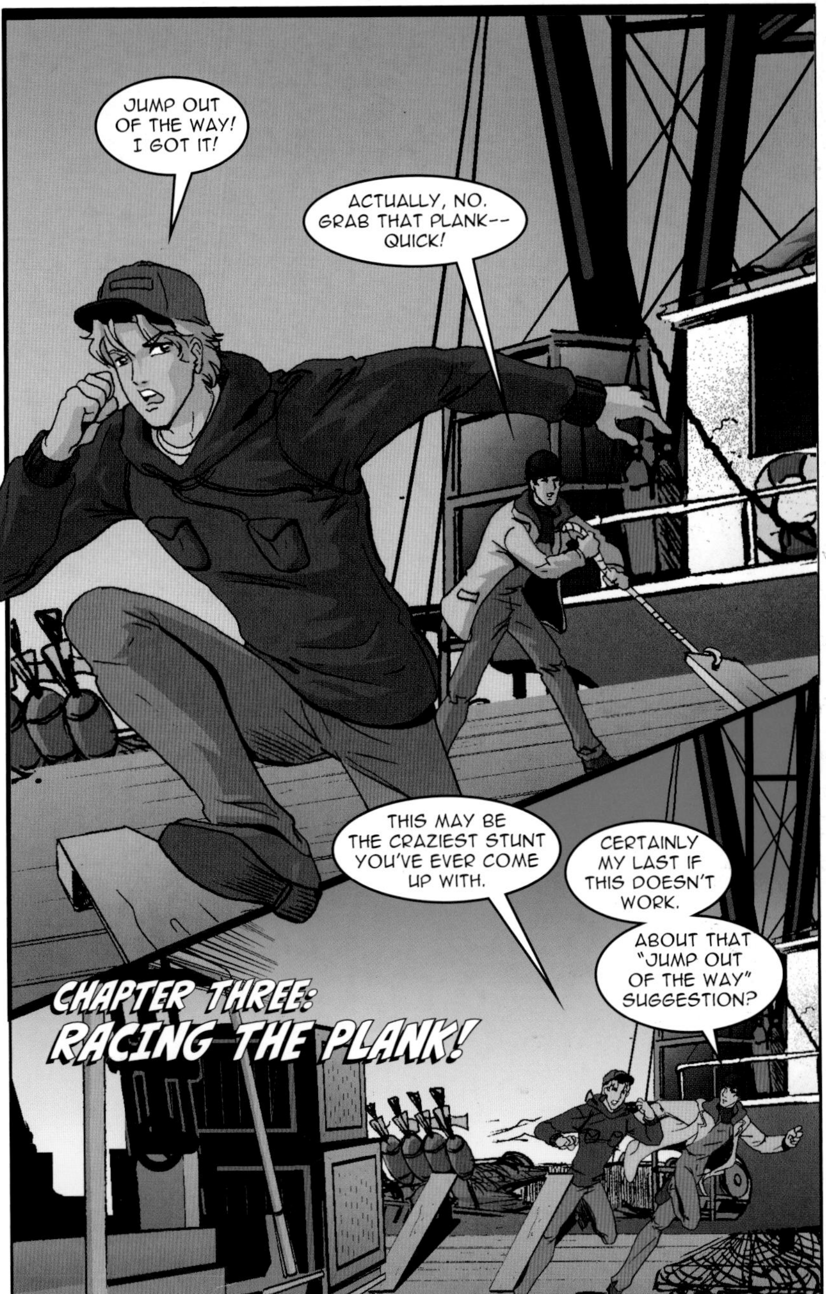
JUMP OUT OF THE WAY! I GOT IT!
ACTUALLY, NO. GRAB THAT PLANK-- QUICK!
THIS MAY BE THE CRAZIEST STUNT YOU'VE EVER COME UP WITH.
CERTAINLY MY LAST IF THIS DOESN'T WORK.
ABOUT THAT "JUMP OUT OF THE WAY" SUGGESTION?
CHAPTER THREE:
RACING THE PLANK!

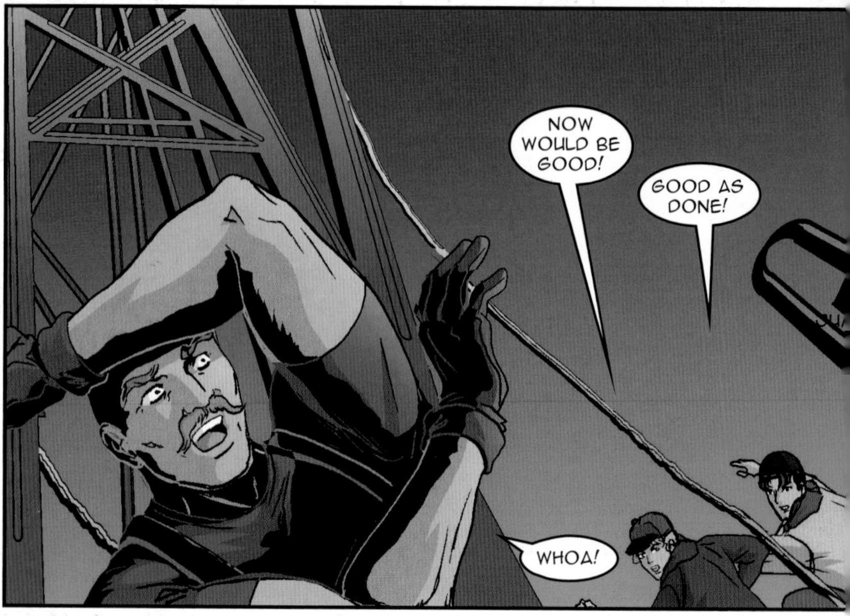
NOW WOULD BE GOOD!
GOOD AS DONE!
WHOA!

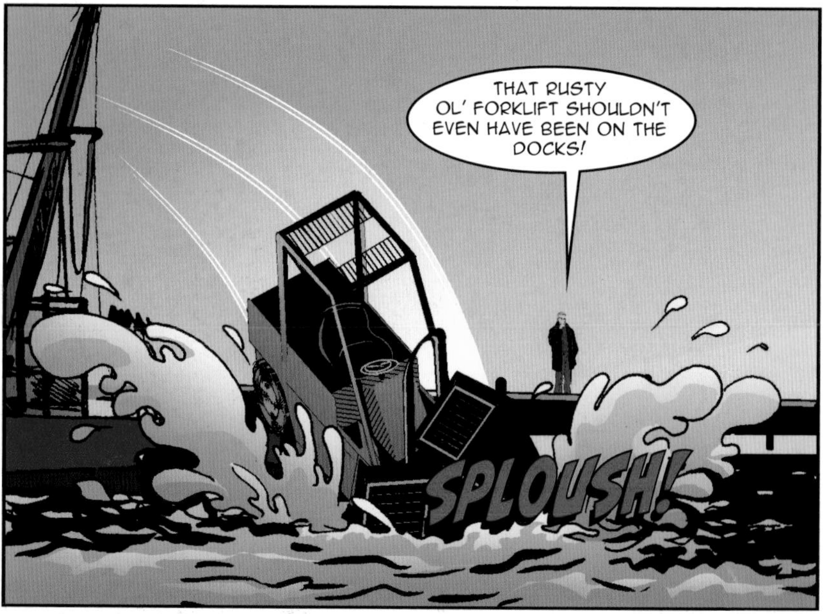
THAT RUSTY OL' FORKLIFT SHOULDN'T EVEN HAVE BEEN ON THE DOCKS!
SPLOUSH!

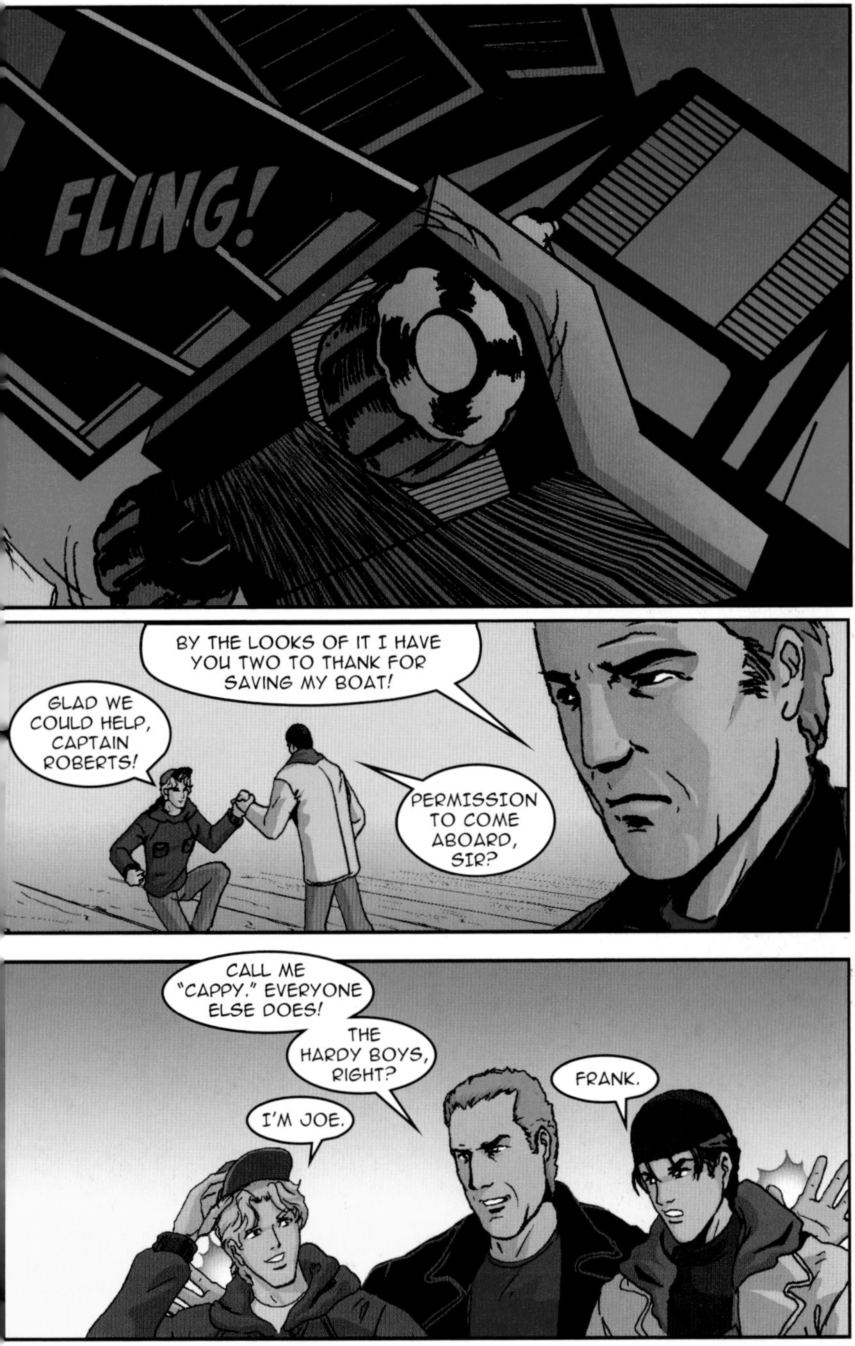
FLING!
BY THE LOOKS OF IT I HAVE YOU TWO TO THANK FOR SAVING MY BOAT!
GLAD WE COULD HELP, CAPTAIN ROBERTS!
PERMISSION TO COME ABOARD, SIR?
CALL ME "CAPPY." EVERYONE ELSE DOES!
THE HARDY BOYS, RIGHT?
I'M JOE.
FRANK.

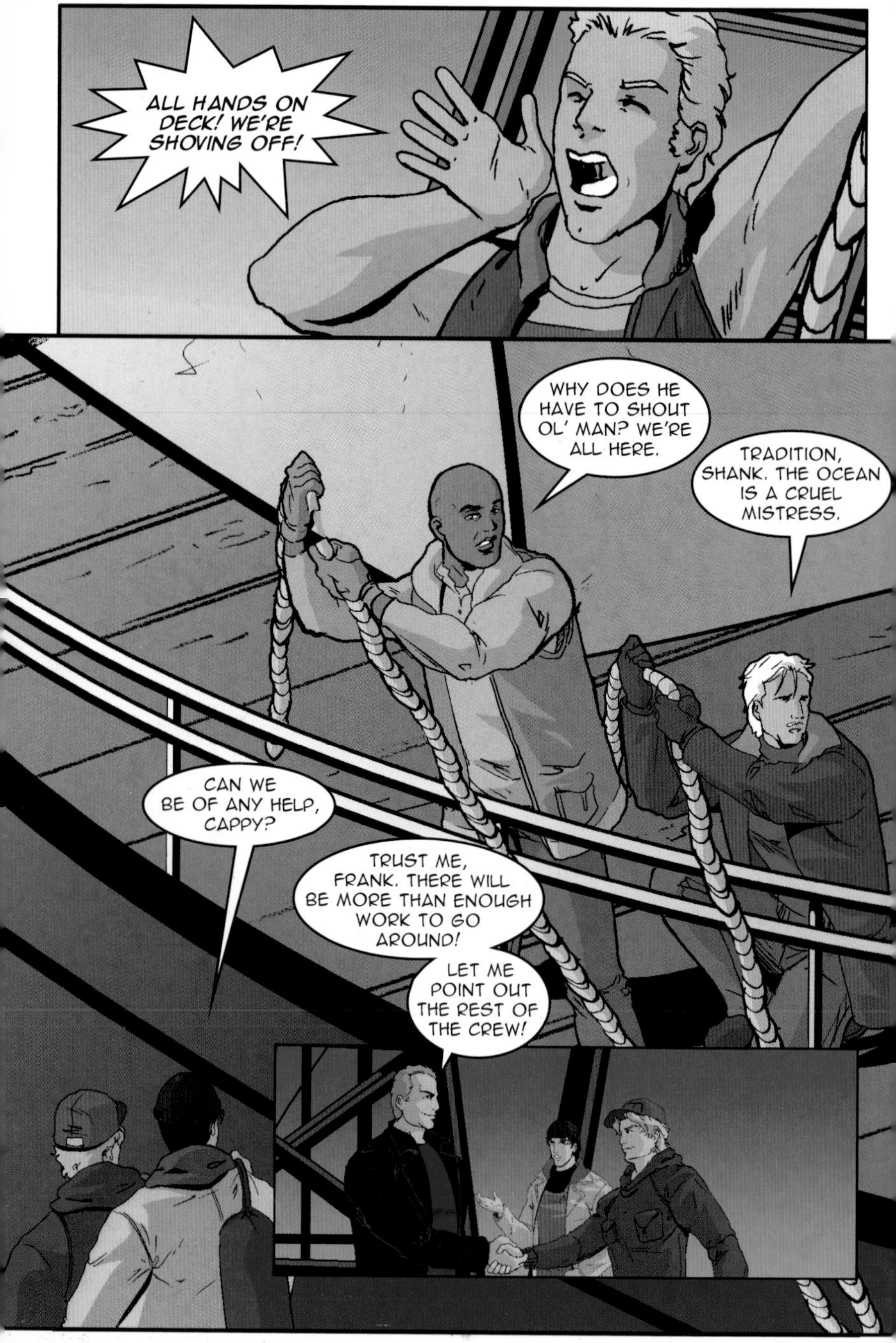
ALL HANDS ON DECK! WE'RE SHOVING OFF!
WHY DOES HE HAVE TO SHOUT OL' MAN? WE'RE ALL HERE.
TRADITION, SHANK. THE OCEAN IS A CRUEL MISTRESS.
CAN WE BE OF ANY HELP, CAPPY?
TRUST ME, FRANK. THERE WILL BE MORE THAN ENOUGH WORK TO GO AROUND!
LET ME POINT OUT THE REST OF THE CREW!

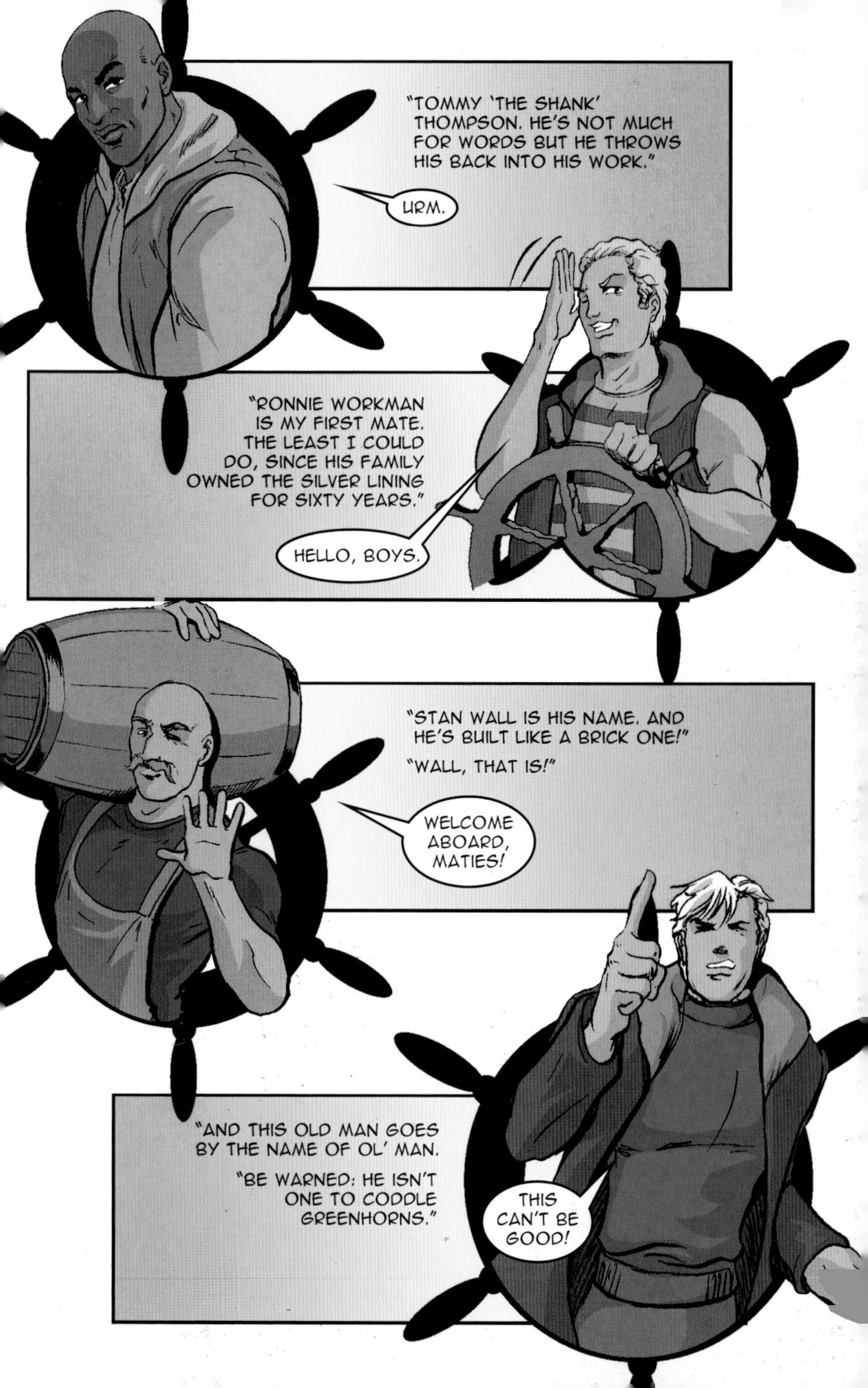
"TOMMY 'THE SHANK' THOMPSON. HE'S NOT MUCH FOR WORDS BUT HE THROWS HIS BACK INTO HIS WORK."
URM.
"RONNIE WORKMAN IS MY FIRST MATE. THE LEAST I COULD DO, SINCE HIS FAMILY OWNED THE SILVER LINING FOR SIXTY YEARS."
HELLO, BOYS.
"STAN WALL IS HIS NAME. AND HE'S BUILT LIKE A BRICK ONE!"
"WALL, THAT IS!"
WELCOME ABOARD, MATIES!
"AND THIS OLD MAN GOES BY THE NAME OF OL' MAN.
"BE WARNED: HE ISN'T ONE TO CODDLE GREENHORNS."
THIS CAN'T BE GOOD!

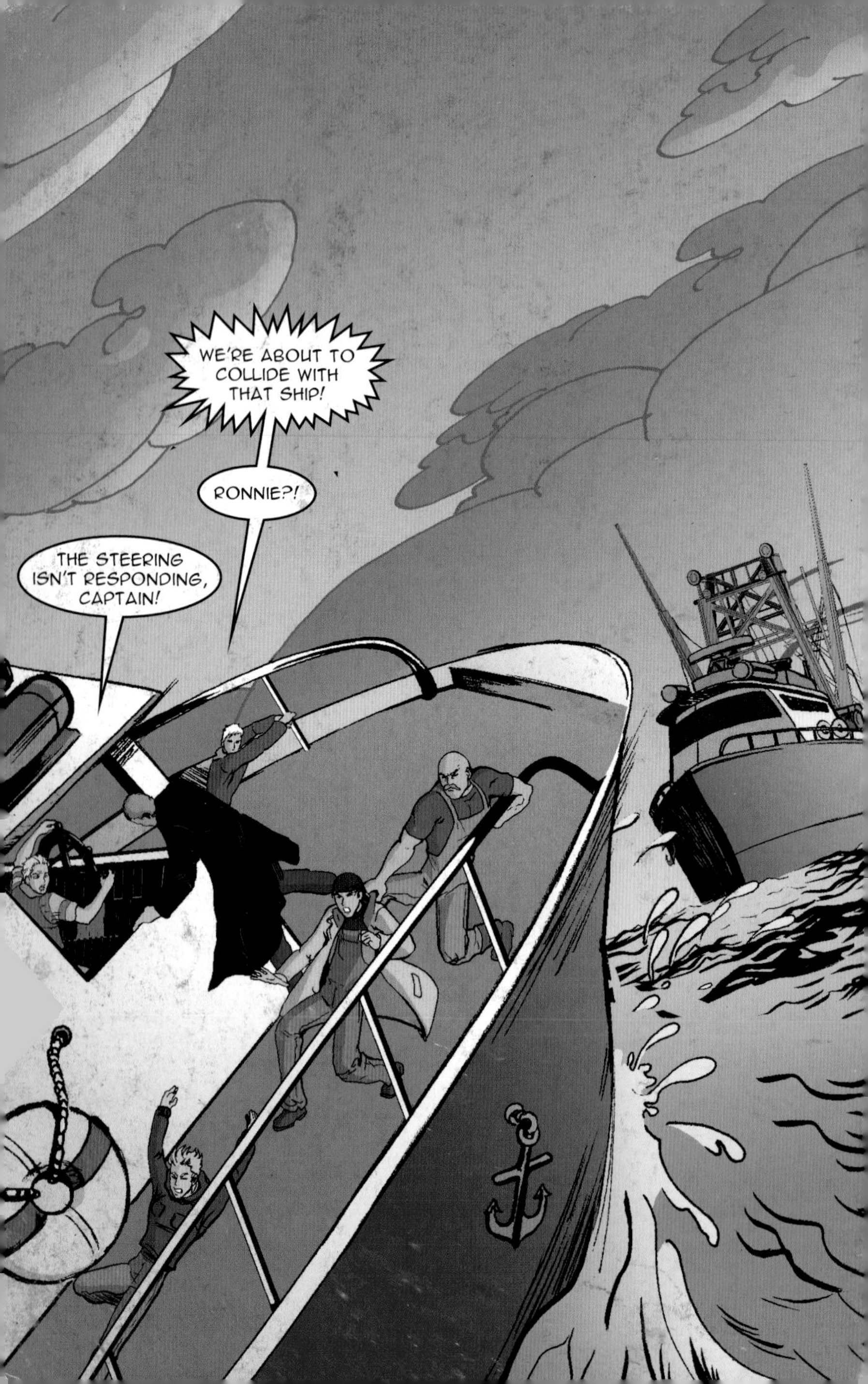
WE'RE ABOUT TO COLLIDE WITH THAT SHIP!
RONNIE?!
THE STEERING ISN'T RESPONDING, CAPTAIN!

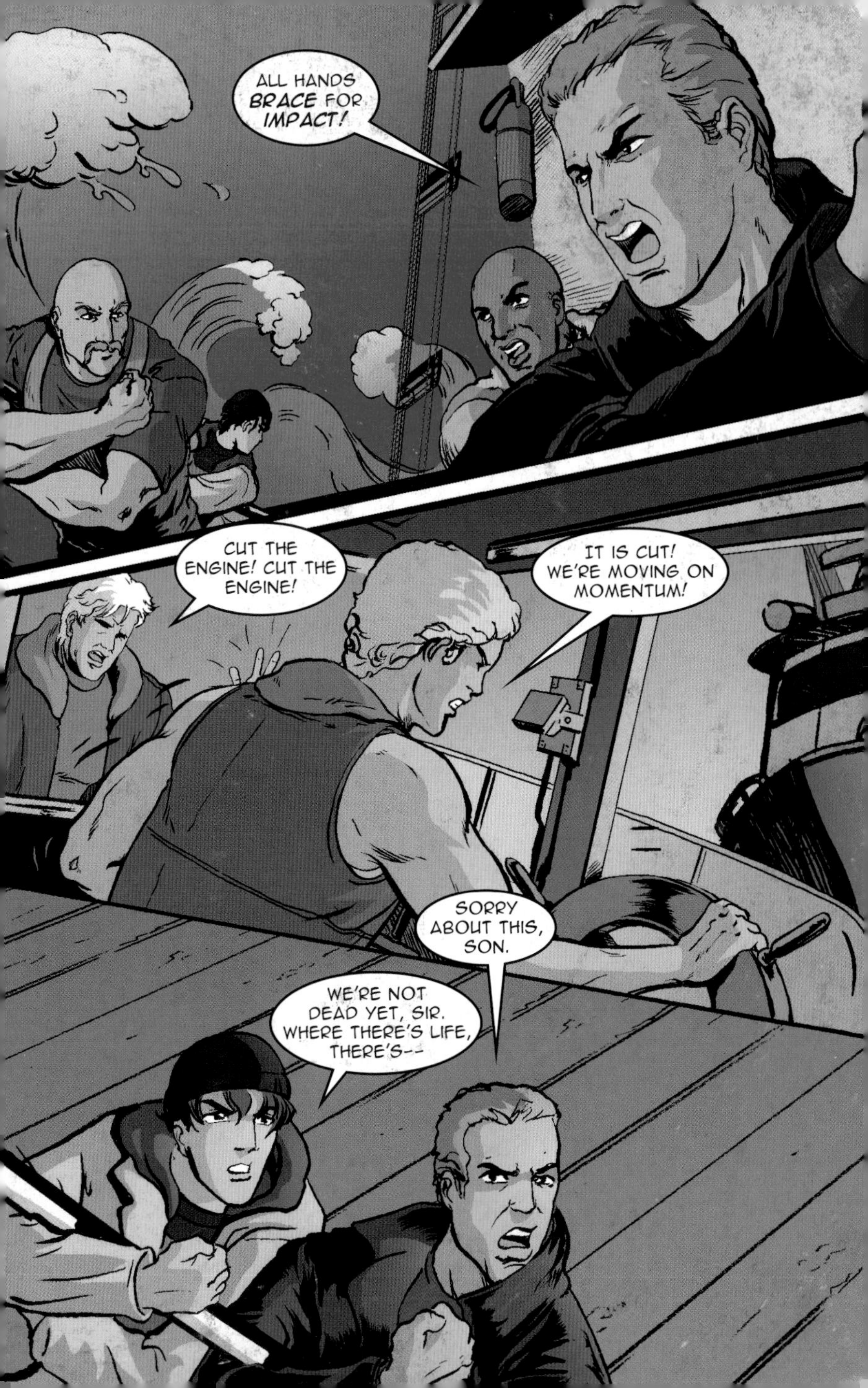
ALL HANDS BRACE FOR IMPACT!
CUT THE ENGINE! CUT THE ENGINE!
IT IS CUT! WE'RE MOVING ON MOMENTUM!
SORRY ABOUT THIS, SON.
WE'RE NOT DEAD YET, SIR. WHERE THERE'S LIFE, THERE'S--

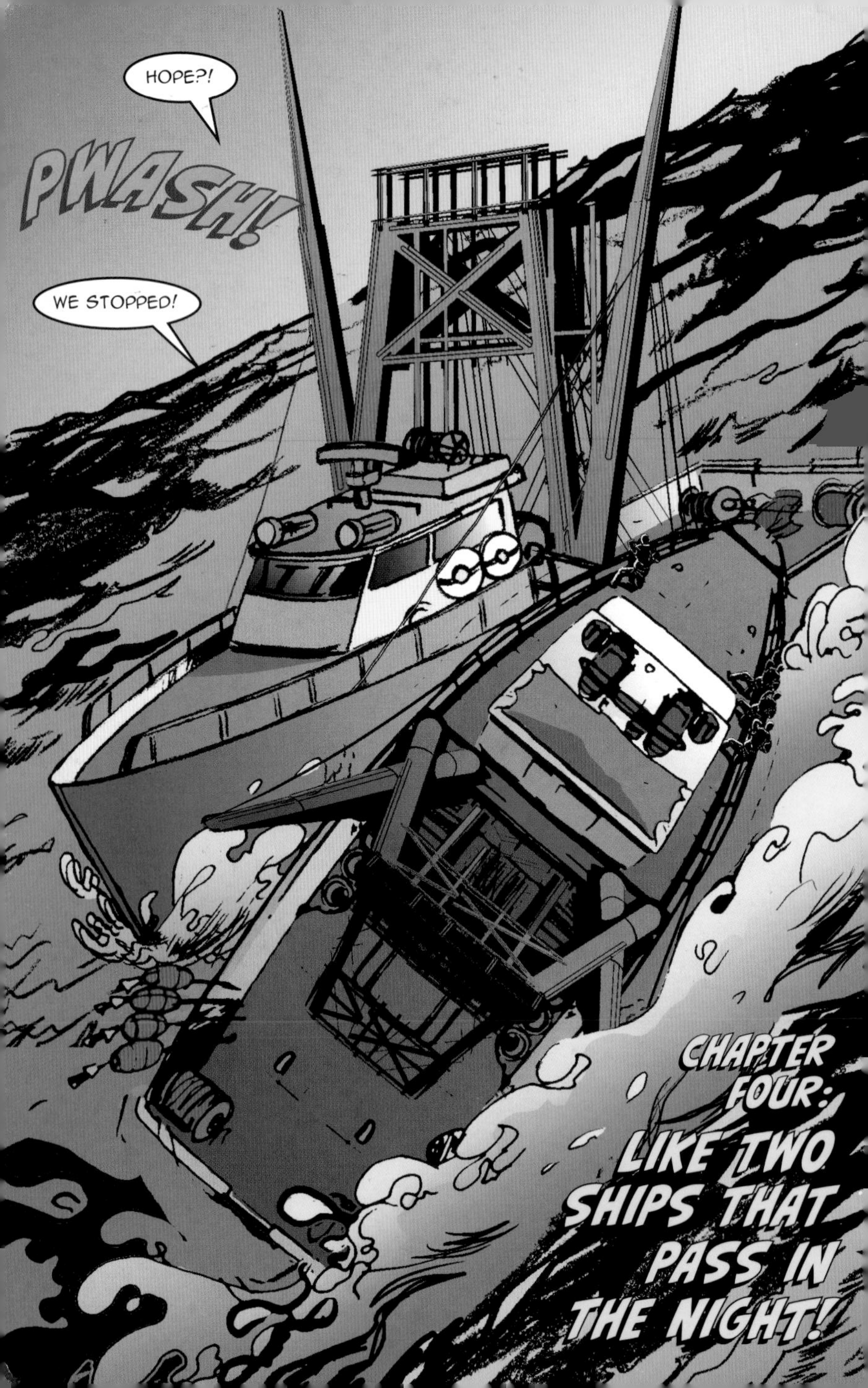
HOPE?!
PWASH!
WE STOPPED!
CHAPTER FOUR:
LIKE TWO SHIPS THAT PASS IN THE NIGHT!

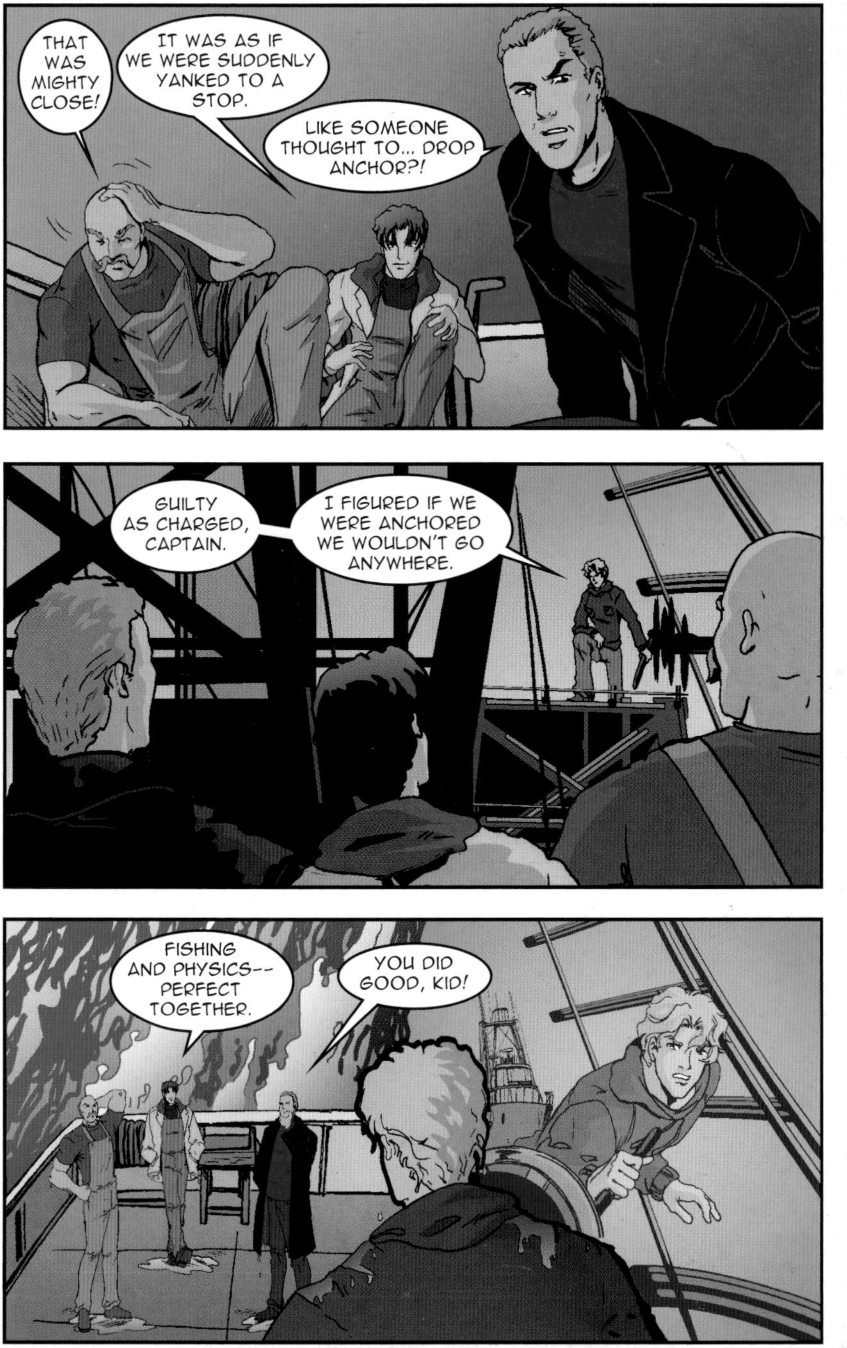
THAT WAS MIGHTY CLOSE!
IT WAS AS IF WE WERE SUDDENLY YANKED TO A STOP.
LIKE SOMEONE THOUGHT TO... DROP ANCHOR?!
GUILTY AS CHARGED, CAPTAIN.
I FIGURED IF WE WERE ANCHORED WE WOULDN'T GO ANYWHERE.
FISHING AND PHYSICS-- PERFECT TOGETHER.
YOU DID GOOD, KID!

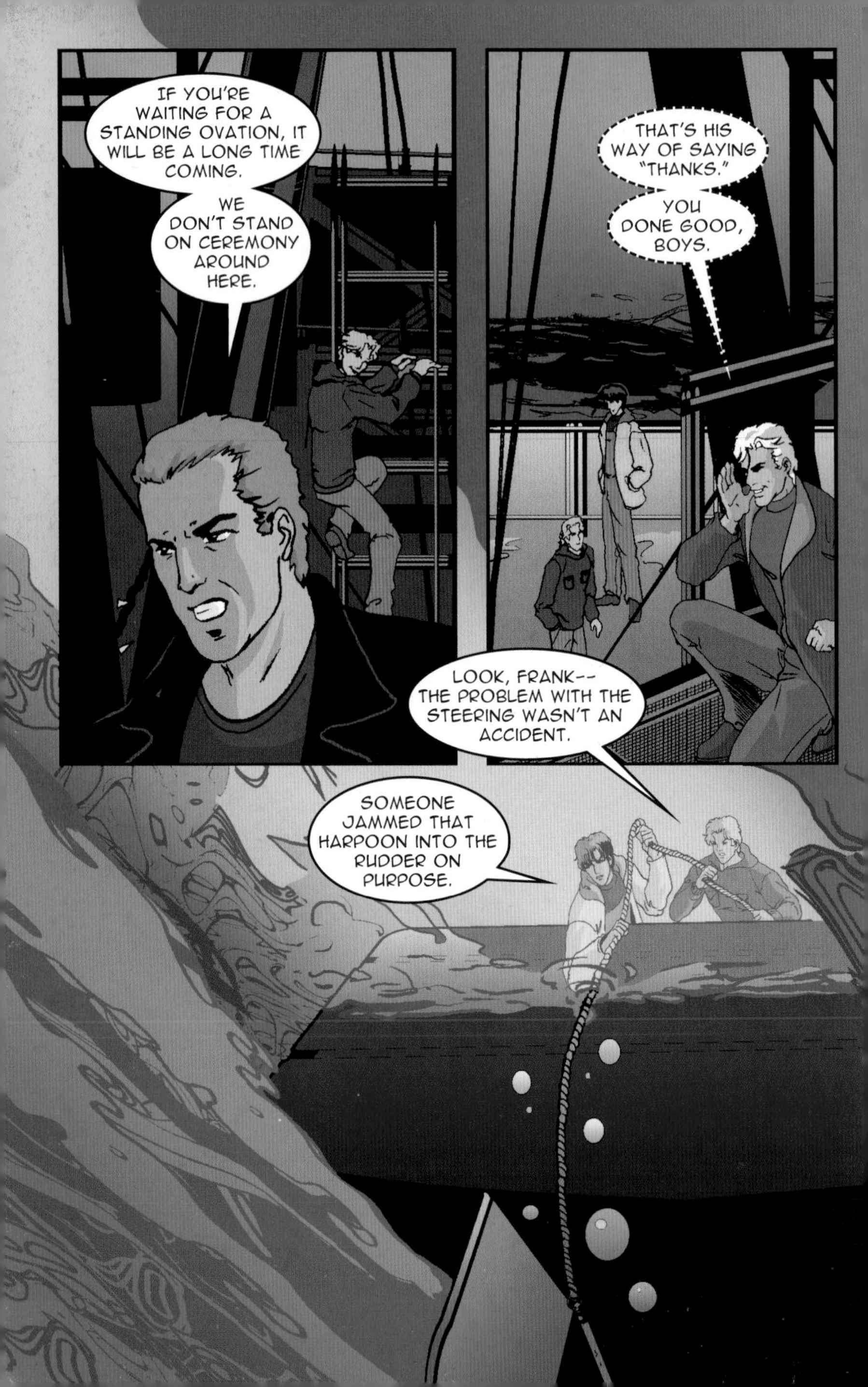
IF YOU'RE WAITING FOR A STANDING OVATION, IT WILL BE A LONG TIME COMING.
WE DON'T STAND ON CEREMONY AROUND HERE.
THAT'S HIS WAY OF SAYING "THANKS."
YOU DONE GOOD, BOYS.
LOOK, FRANK-- THE PROBLEM WITH THE STEERING WASN'T AN ACCIDENT.
SOMEONE JAMMED THAT HARPOON INTO THE RUDDER ON PURPOSE.

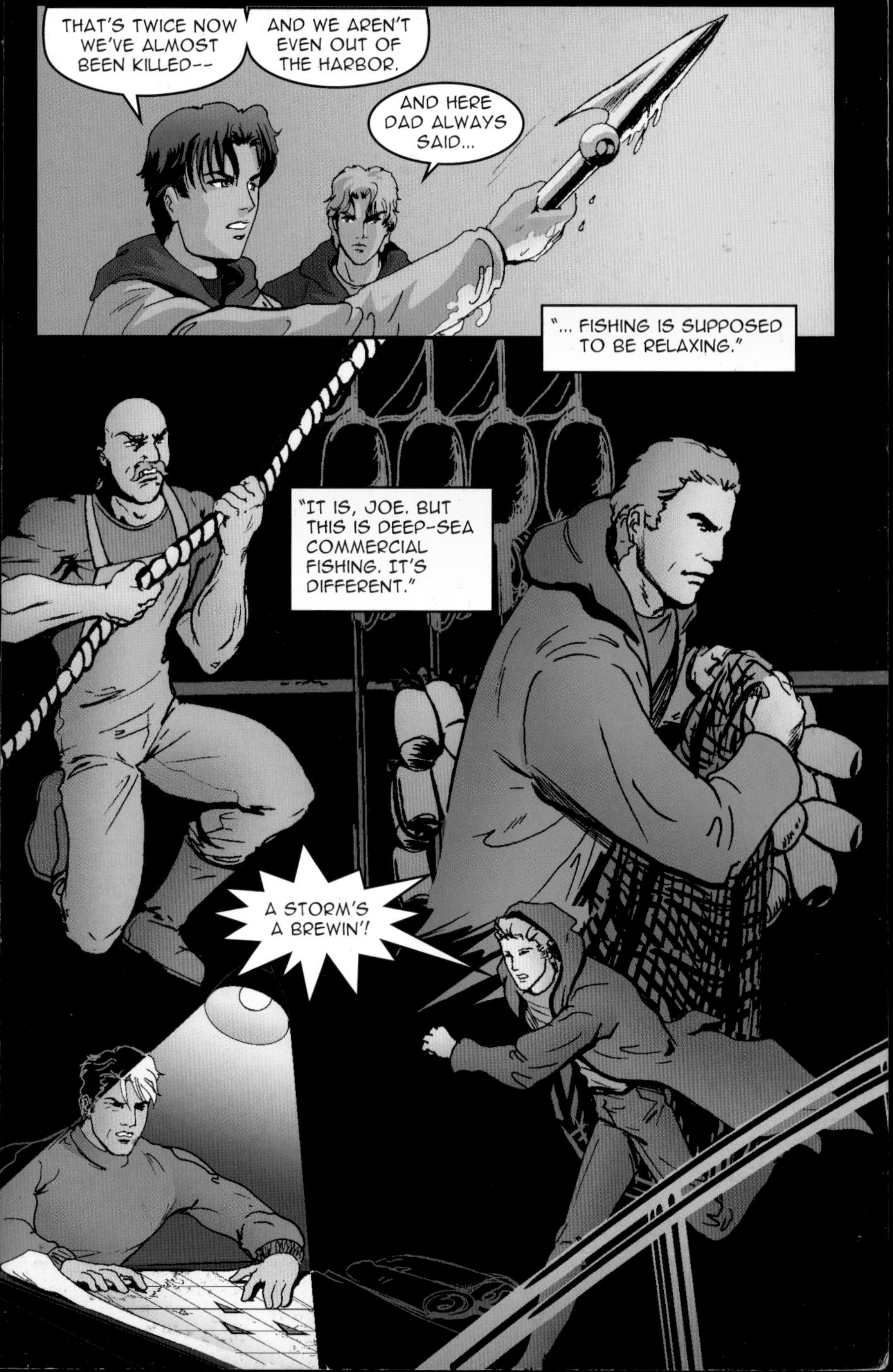
THAT'S TWICE NOW WE'VE ALMOST BEEN KILLED--
AND WE AREN'T EVEN OUT OF THE HARBOR.
AND HERE DAD ALWAYS SAID...
"... FISHING IS SUPPOSED TO BE RELAXING."
"IT IS, JOE. BUT THIS IS DEEP-SEA COMMERCIAL FISHING. IT'S DIFFERENT."
A STORM'S A BREWIN'!

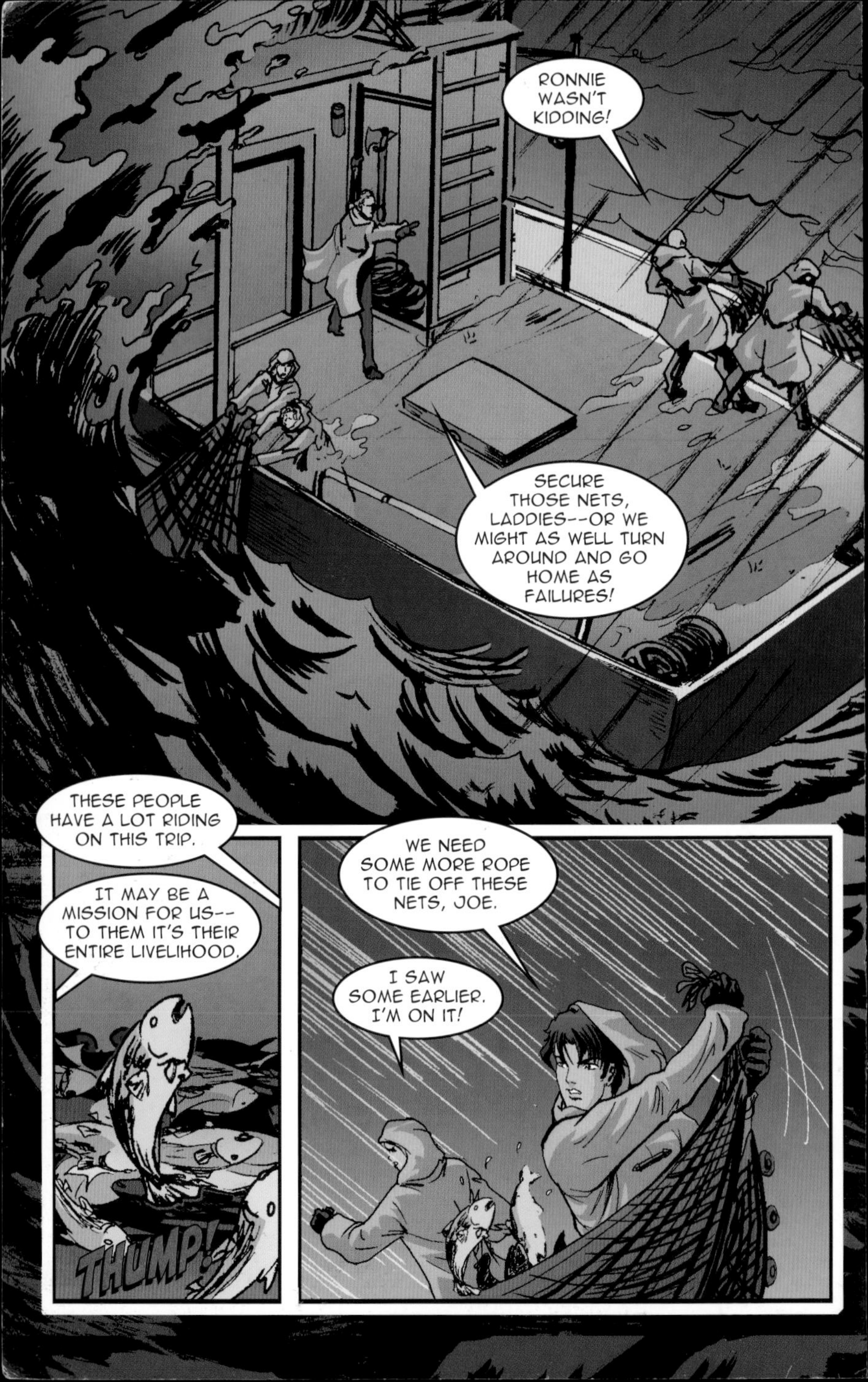
RONNIE WASN'T KIDDING!
SECURE THOSE NETS, LADDIES--OR WE MIGHT AS WELL TURN AROUND AND GO HOME AS FAILURES!
THESE PEOPLE HAVE A LOT RIDING ON THIS TRIP.
IT MAY BE A MISSION FOR US--TO THEM IT'S THEIR ENTIRE LIVELIHOOD.
THUMP!
WE NEED SOME MORE ROPE TO TIE OFF THESE NETS, JOE.
I SAW SOME EARLIER. I'M ON IT!

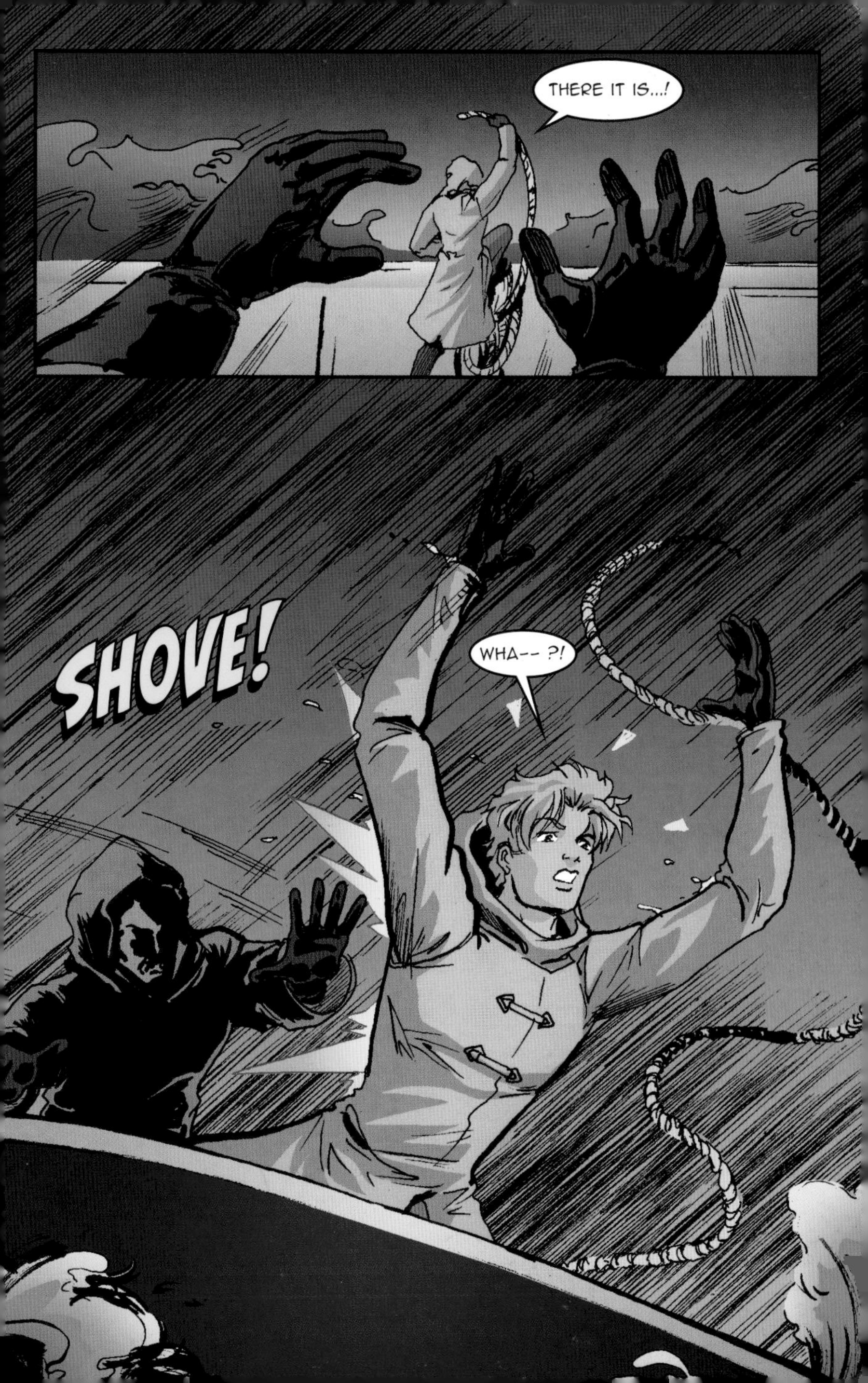
THERE IT IS...!
SHOVE!
WHA-- ?!

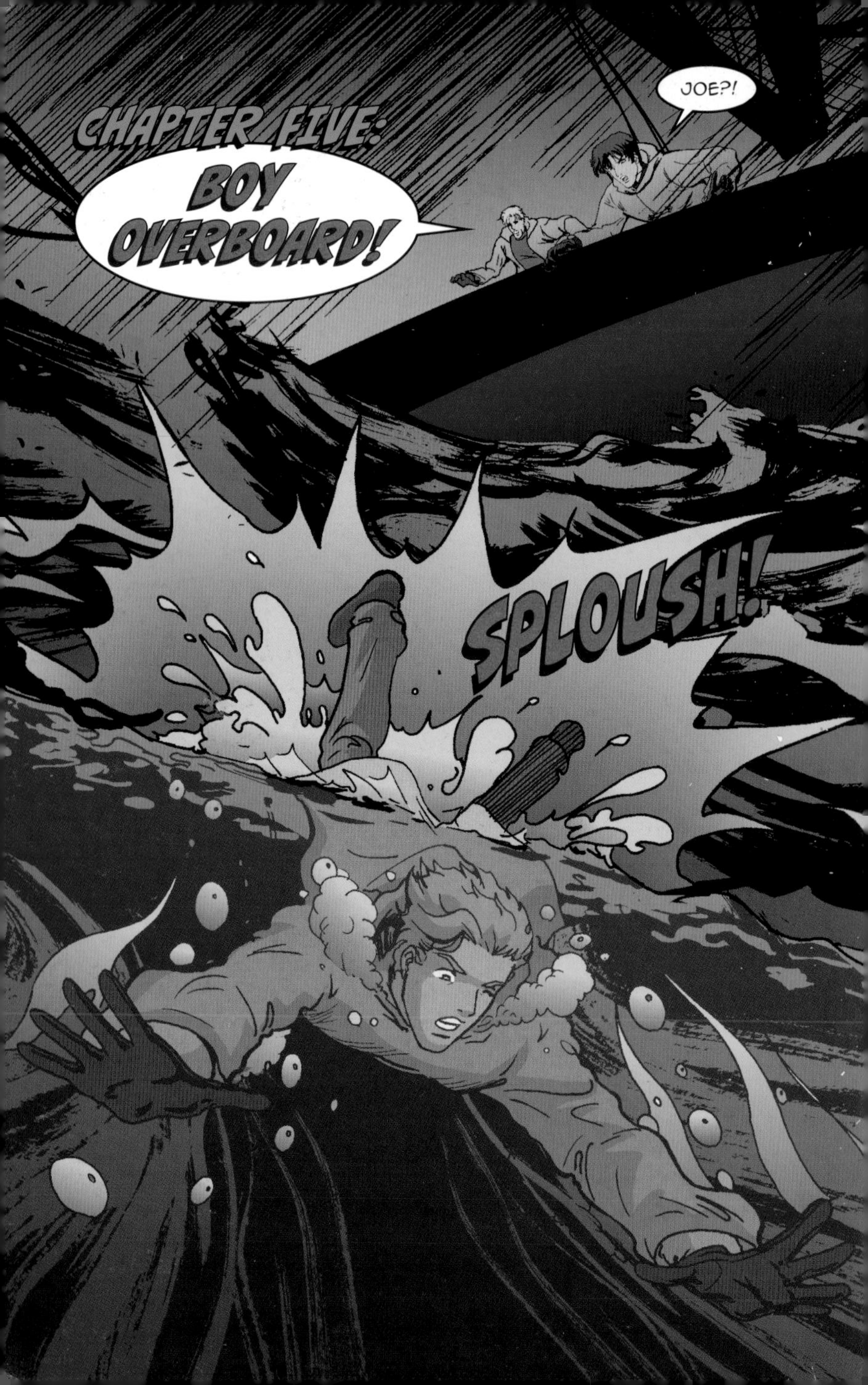
CHAPTER FIVE:
BOY OVERBOARD!
JOE?!
SPLOUSH!

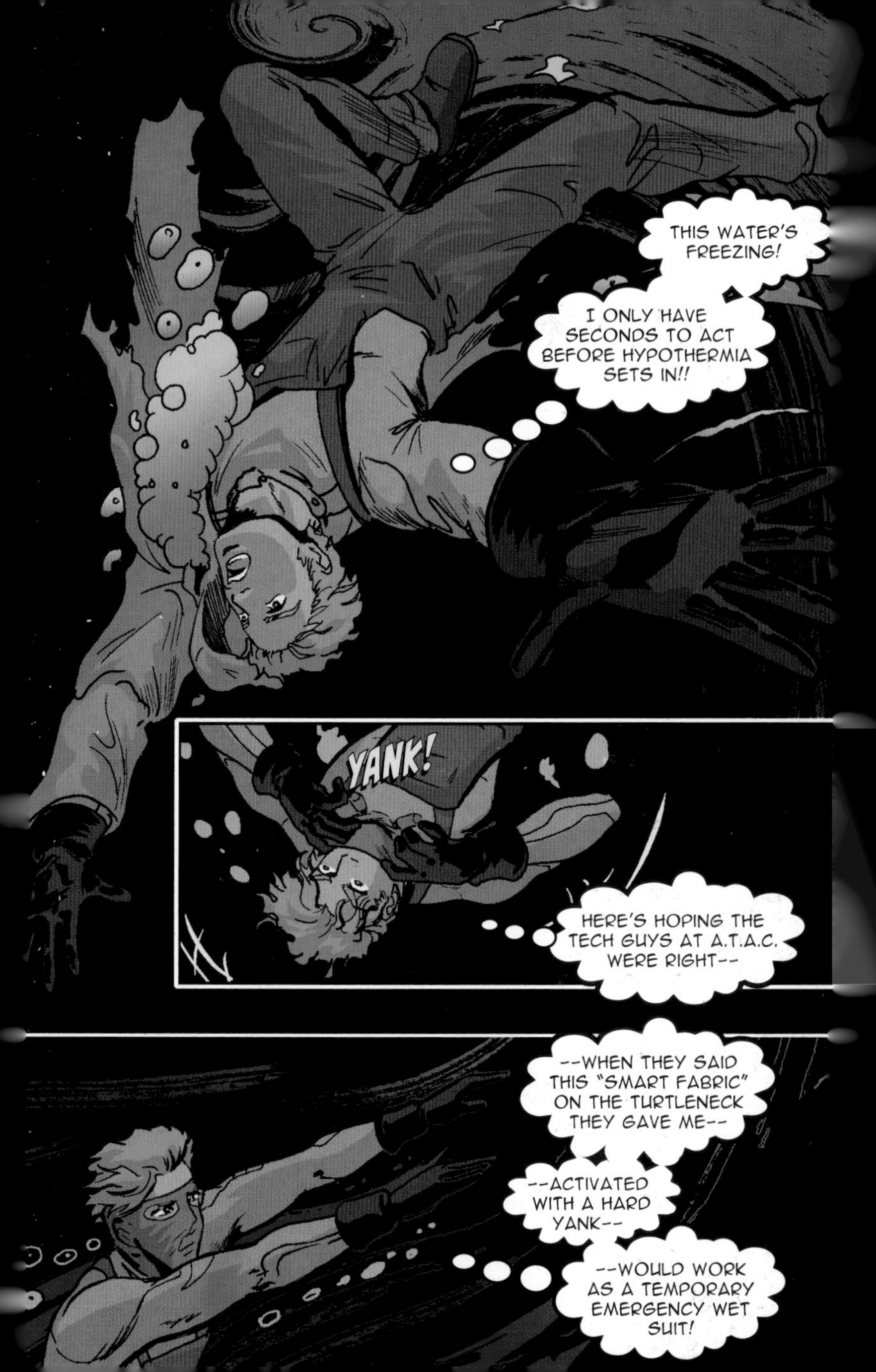
THIS WATER'S FREEZING!
I ONLY HAVE SECONDS TO ACT BEFORE HYPOTHERMIA SETS IN!!
YANK!
HERE'S HOPING THE TECH GUYS AT A.T.A.C. WERE RIGHT--
--WHEN THEY SAID THIS "SMART FABRIC" ON THE TURTLENECK THEY GAVE ME--
--ACTIVATED WITH A HARD YANK--
--WOULD WORK AS A TEMPORARY EMERGENCY WET SUIT!

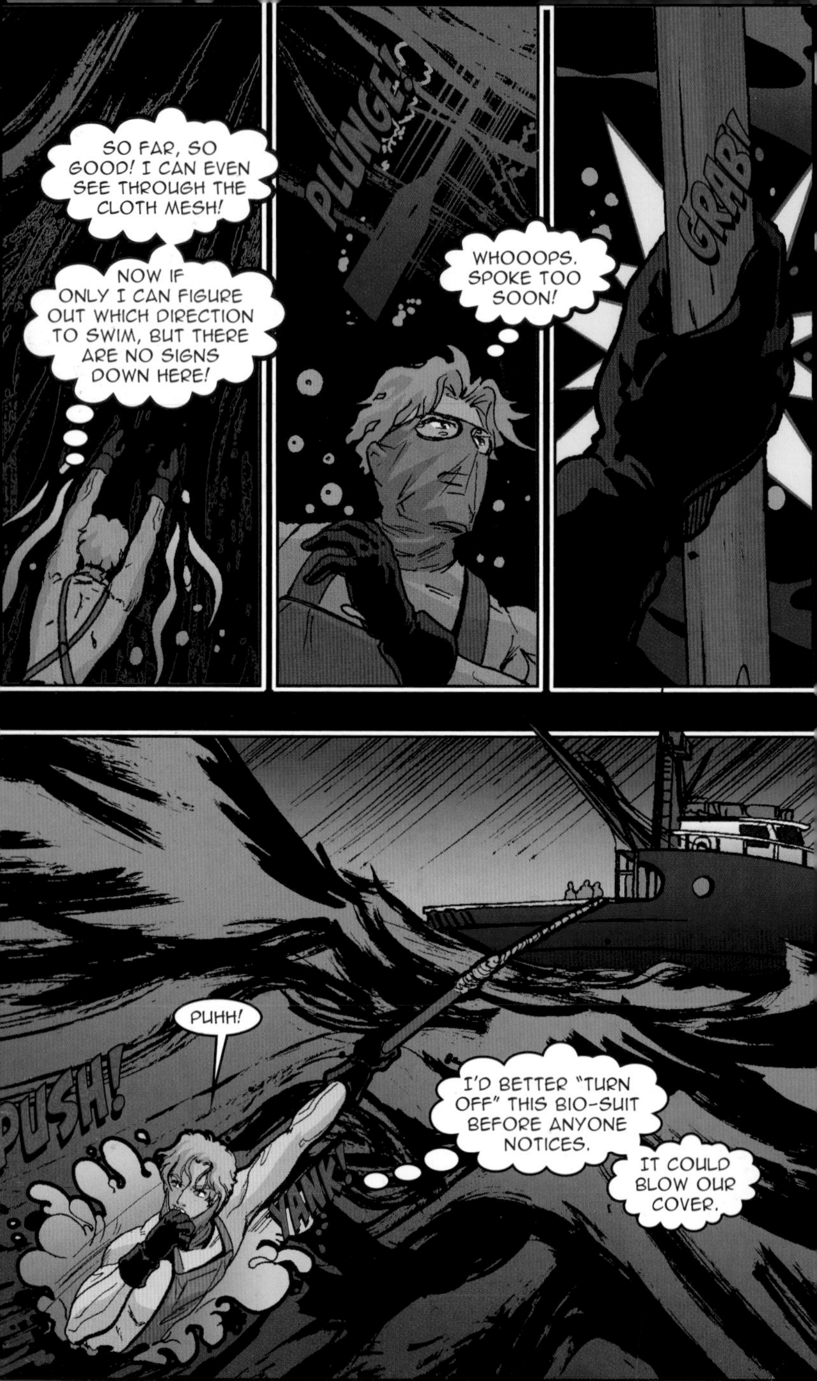
SO FAR, SO GOOD! I CAN EVEN SEE THROUGH THE CLOTH MESH!
NOW IF ONLY I CAN FIGURE OUT WHICH DIRECTION TO SWIM, BUT THERE ARE NO SIGNS DOWN HERE!
PLUNGE!
WHOOOPS. SPOKE TOO SOON!
GRAB!
PUHH!
PUSH!
YANK!
I'D BETTER "TURN OFF" THIS BIO-SUIT BEFORE ANYONE NOTICES.
IT COULD BLOW OUR COVER.

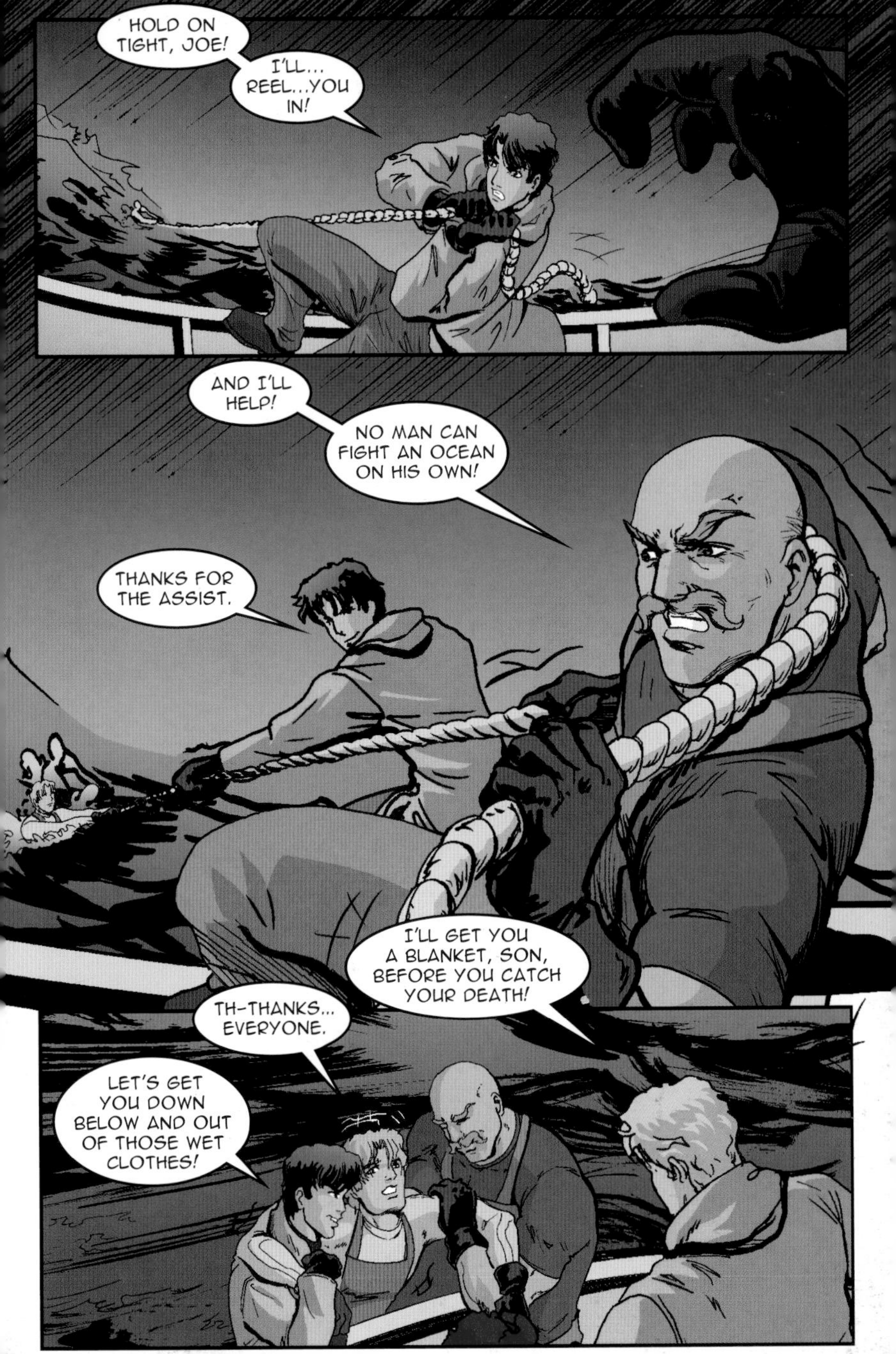
HOLD ON TIGHT, JOE!
I'LL... REEL...YOU IN!
AND I'LL HELP!
NO MAN CAN FIGHT AN OCEAN ON HIS OWN!
THANKS FOR THE ASSIST.
I'LL GET YOU A BLANKET, SON, BEFORE YOU CATCH YOUR DEATH!
TH-THANKS... EVERYONE.
LET'S GET YOU DOWN BELOW AND OUT OF THOSE WET CLOTHES!

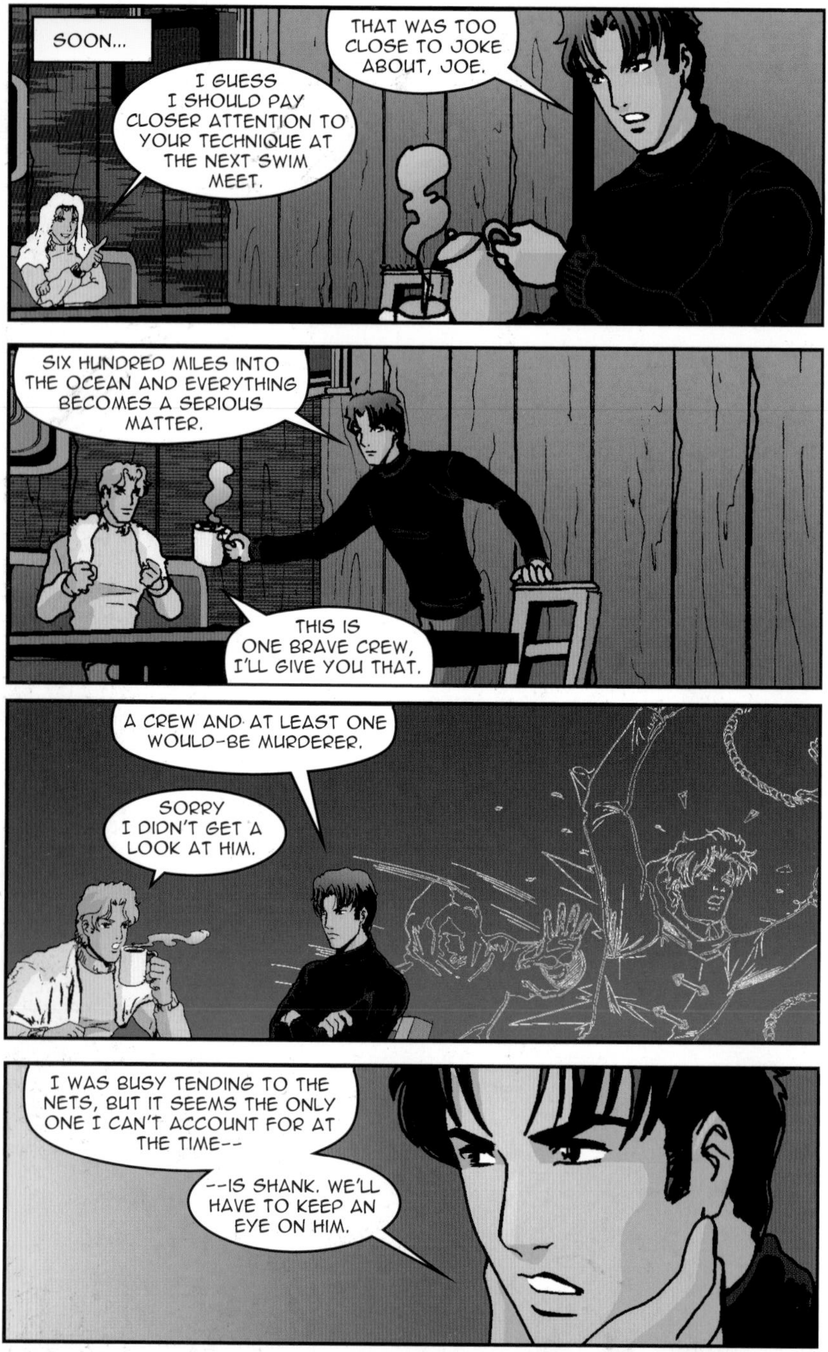
SOON...
I GUESS I SHOULD PAY CLOSER ATTENTION TO YOUR TECHNIQUE AT THE NEXT SWIM MEET.
THAT WAS TOO CLOSE TO JOKE ABOUT, JOE.
SIX HUNDRED MILES INTO THE OCEAN AND EVERYTHING BECOMES A SERIOUS MATTER.
THIS IS ONE BRAVE CREW, I'LL GIVE YOU THAT.
A CREW AND AT LEAST ONE WOULD-BE MURDERER.
SORRY I DIDN'T GET A LOOK AT HIM.
I WAS BUSY TENDING TO THE NETS, BUT IT SEEMS THE ONLY ONE I CAN'T ACCOUNT FOR AT THE TIME--
--IS SHANK. WE'LL HAVE TO KEEP AN EYE ON HIM.

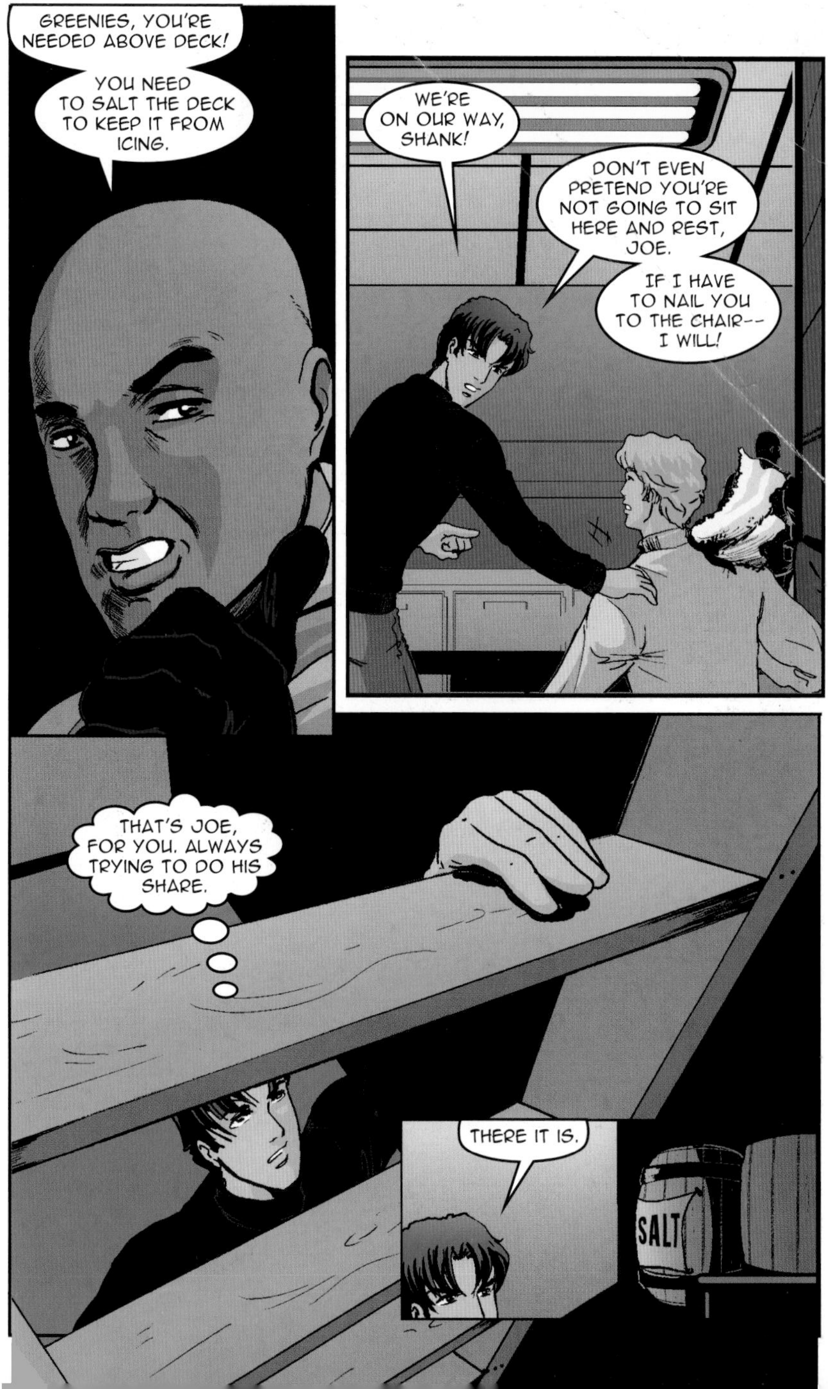
GREENIES, YOU'RE NEEDED ABOVE DECK!
YOU NEED TO SALT THE DECK TO KEEP IT FROM ICING.
WE'RE ON OUR WAY, SHANK!
DON'T EVEN PRETEND YOU'RE NOT GOING TO SIT HERE AND REST, JOE.
IF I HAVE TO NAIL YOU TO THE CHAIR-- I WILL!
THAT'S JOE, FOR YOU. ALWAYS TRYING TO DO HIS SHARE.
THERE IT IS.
SALT

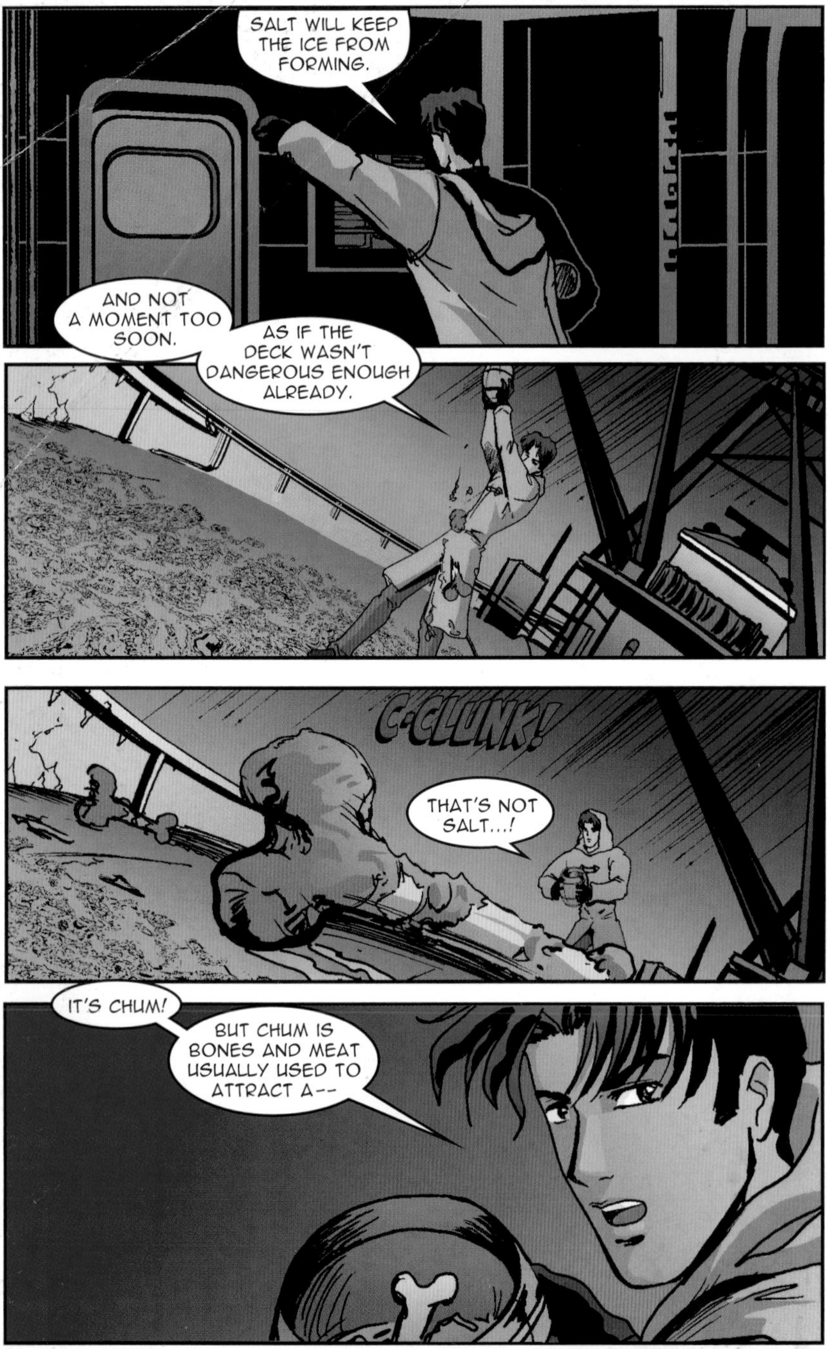
SALT WILL KEEP THE ICE FROM FORMING.
AND NOT A MOMENT TOO SOON.
AS IF THE DECK WASN'T DANGEROUS ENOUGH ALREADY.
C-CLUNK!
THAT'S NOT SALT...!
IT'S CHUM!
BUT CHUM IS BONES AND MEAT USUALLY USED TO ATTRACT A--

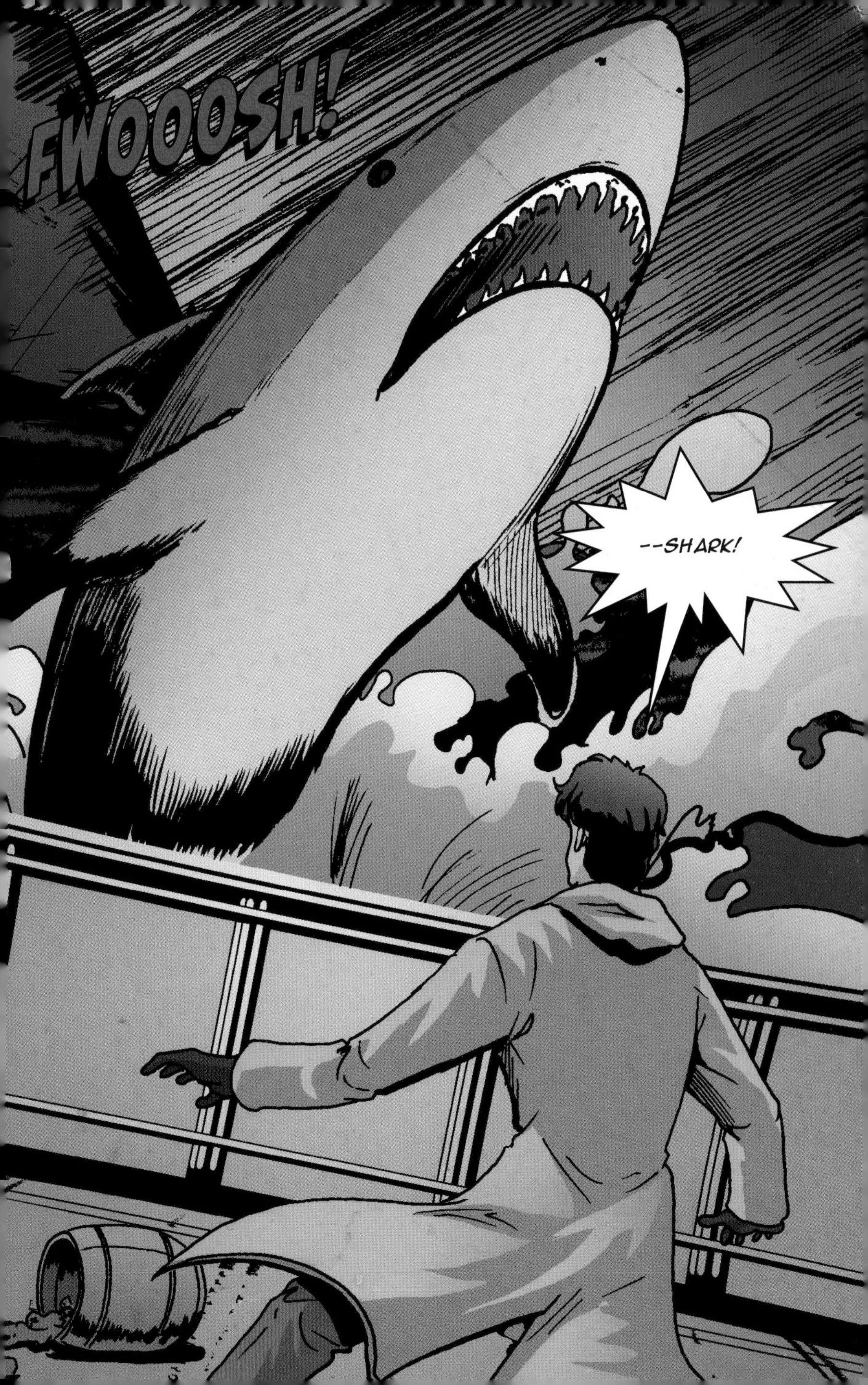
FWOOOSH!
--SHARK!

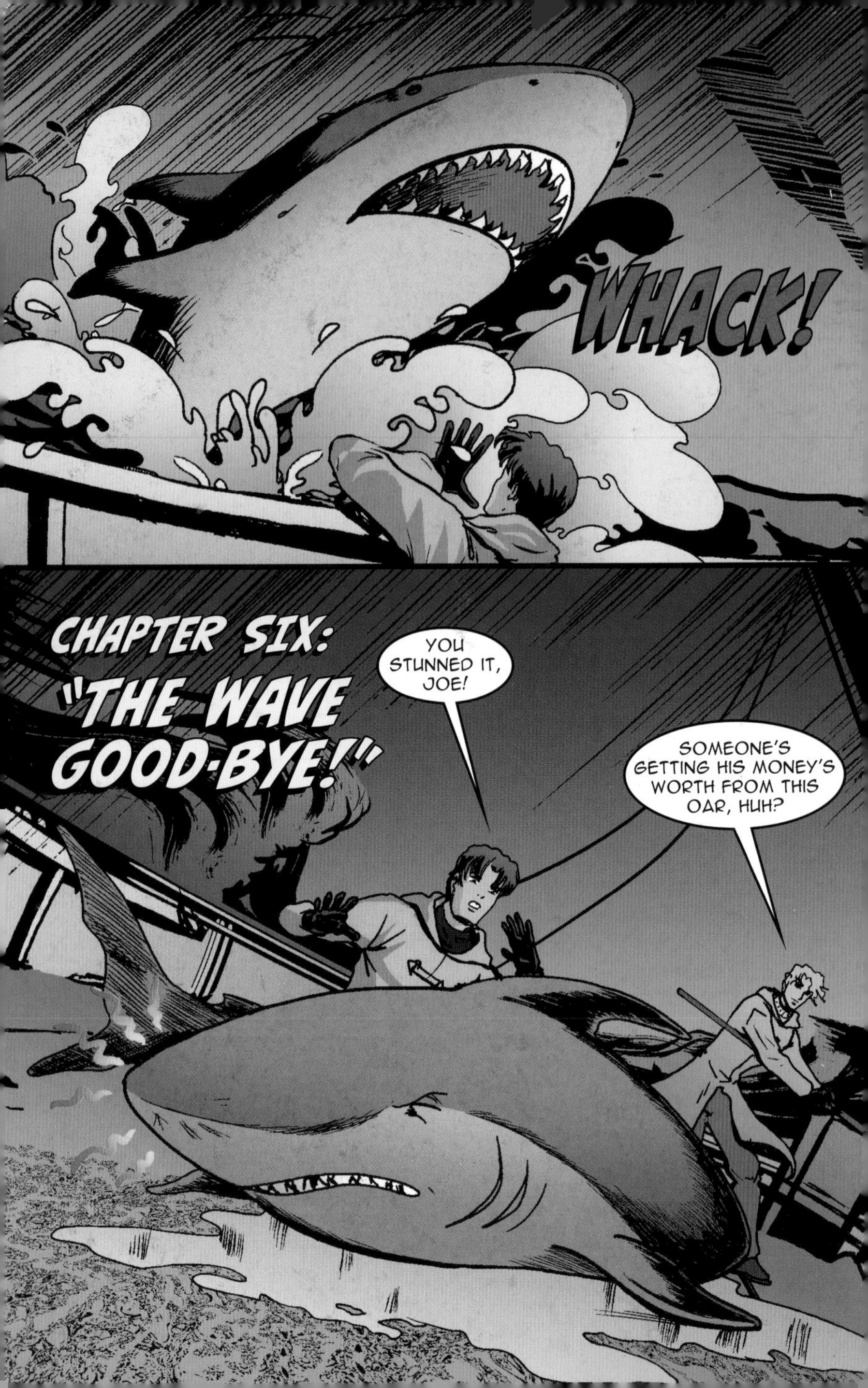
WHACK!
CHAPTER SIX:
"THE WAVE GOOD-BYE!"
YOU STUNNED IT, JOE!
SOMEONE'S GETTING HIS MONEY'S WORTH FROM THIS OAR, HUH?

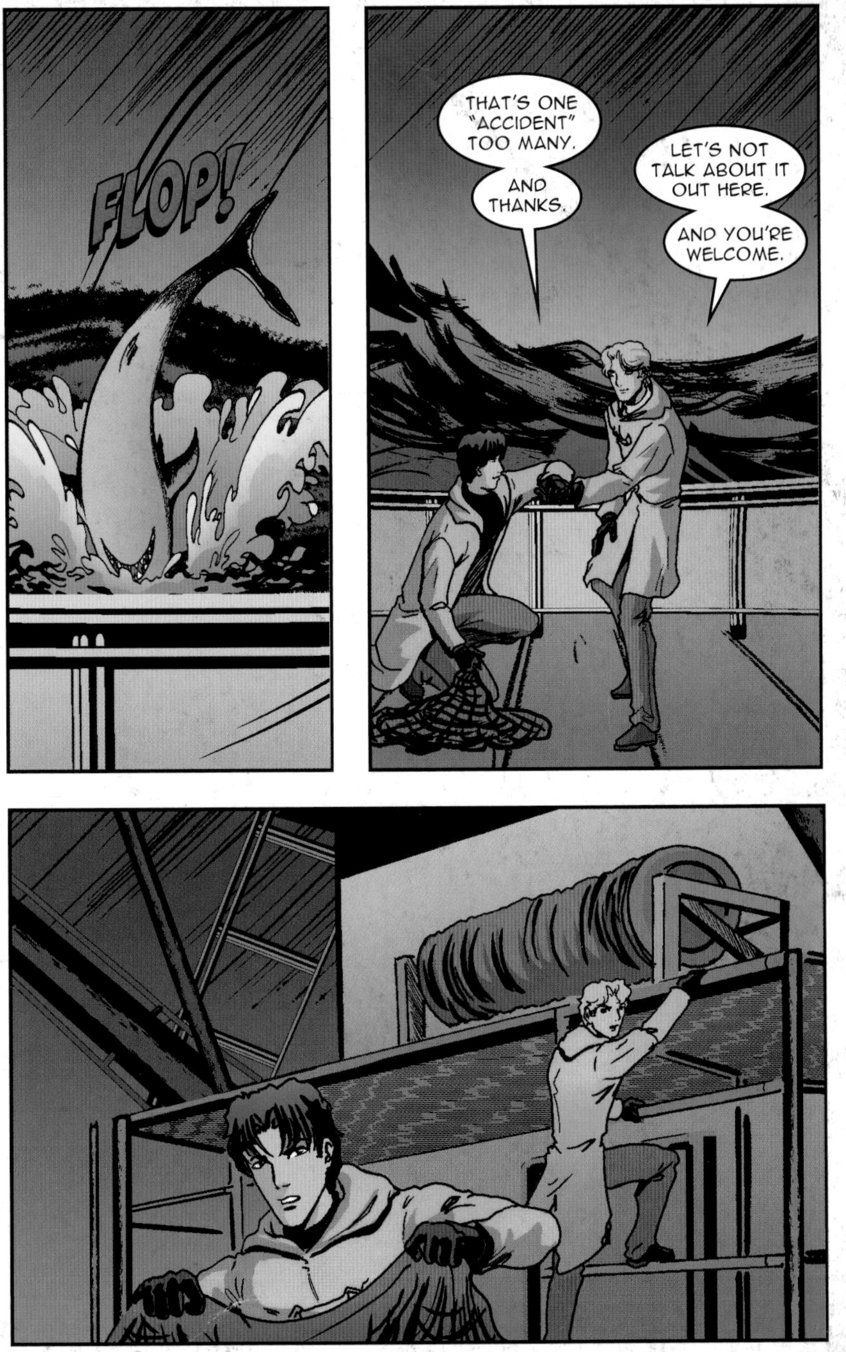
FLOP!
THAT'S ONE "ACCIDENT" TOO MANY.
AND THANKS.
LET'S NOT TALK ABOUT IT OUT HERE.
AND YOU'RE WELCOME.

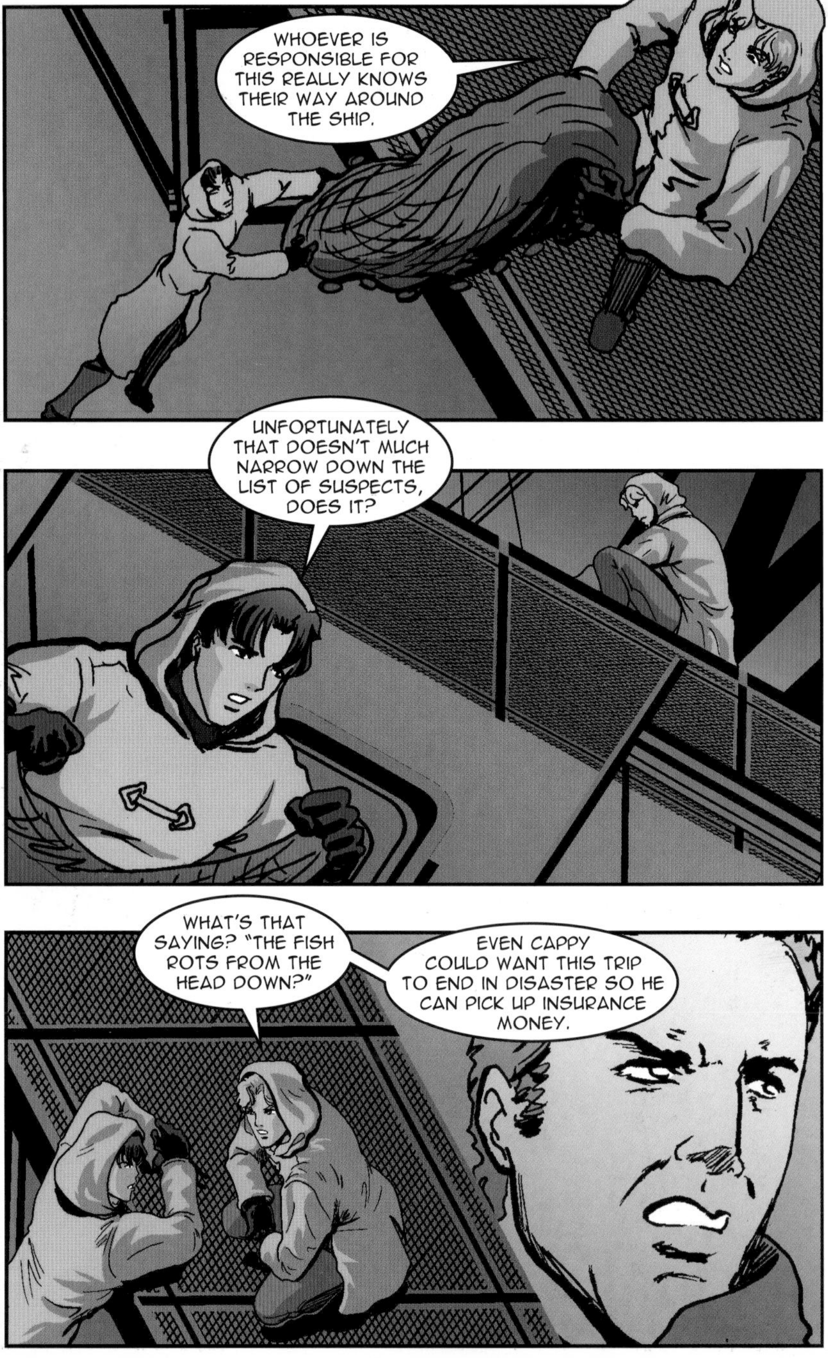
WHOEVER IS RESPONSIBLE FOR THIS REALLY KNOWS THEIR WAY AROUND THE SHIP.
UNFORTUNATELY THAT DOESN'T MUCH NARROW DOWN THE LIST OF SUSPECTS, DOES IT?
WHAT'S THAT SAYING? "THE FISH ROTS FROM THE HEAD DOWN?"
EVEN CAPPY COULD WANT THIS TRIP TO END IN DISASTER SO HE CAN PICK UP INSURANCE MONEY.

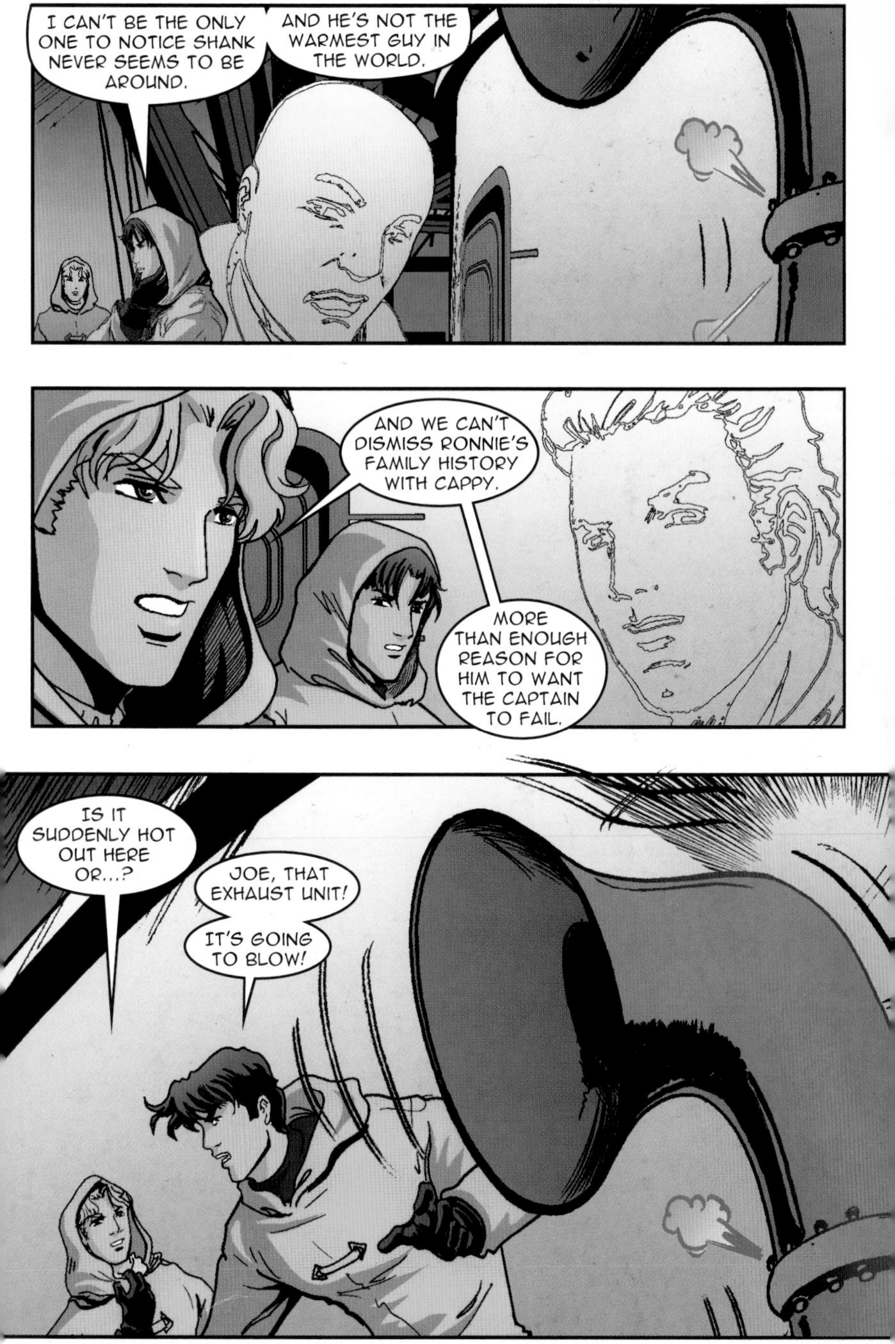
I CAN'T BE THE ONLY ONE TO NOTICE SHANK NEVER SEEMS TO BE AROUND.
AND HE'S NOT THE WARMEST GUY IN THE WORLD.
AND WE CAN'T DISMISS RONNIE'S FAMILY HISTORY WITH CAPPY.
MORE THAN ENOUGH REASON FOR HIM TO WANT THE CAPTAIN TO FAIL.
IS IT SUDDENLY HOT OUT HERE OR...?
JOE, THAT EXHAUST UNIT!
IT'S GOING TO BLOW!

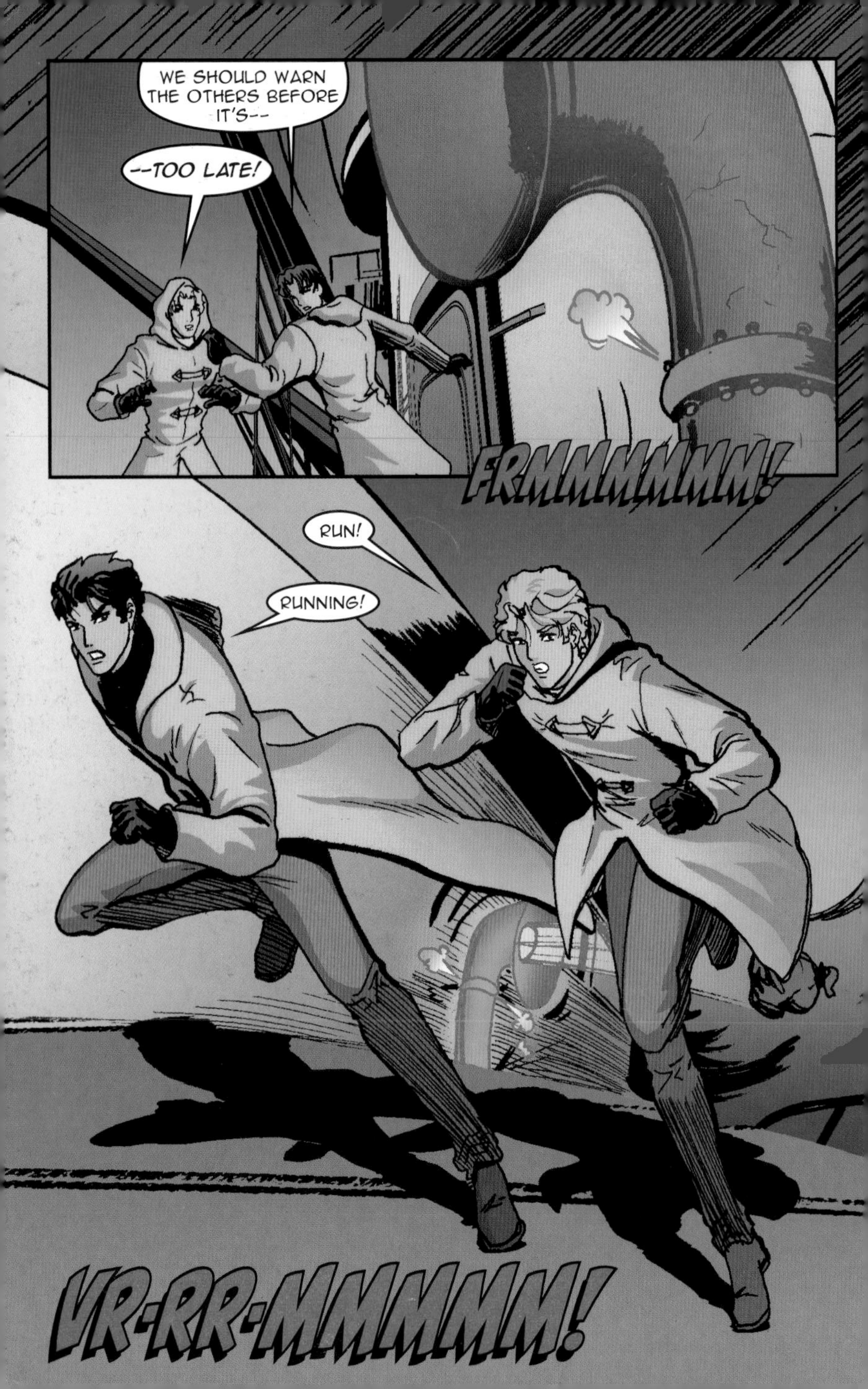
WE SHOULD WARN THE OTHERS BEFORE IT'S--
--TOO LATE!
FRMMMMMMM!
RUN!
RUNNING!
VR-RR-MMMMMM!

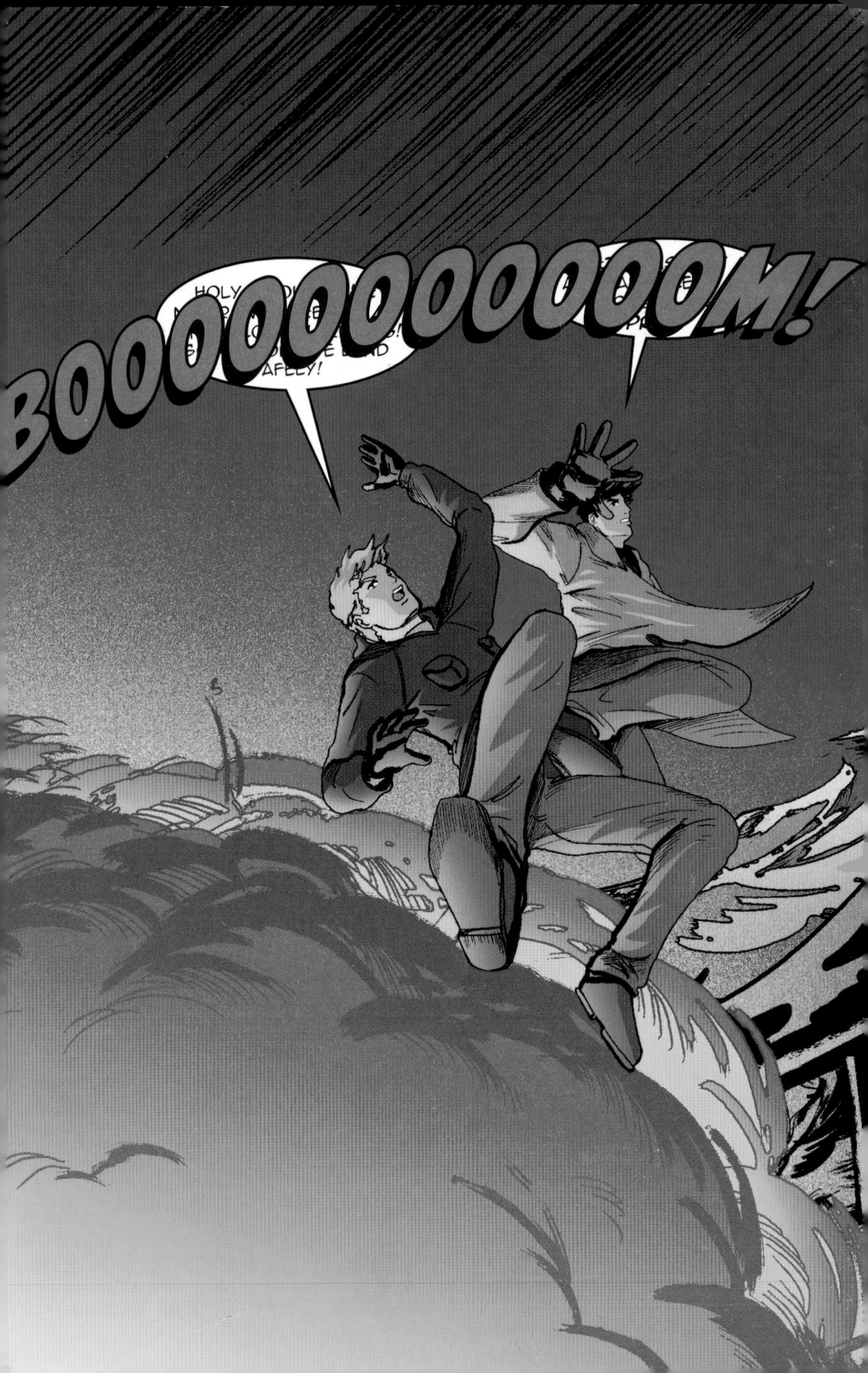
HOLY
BOOOOOOOOOOOM!

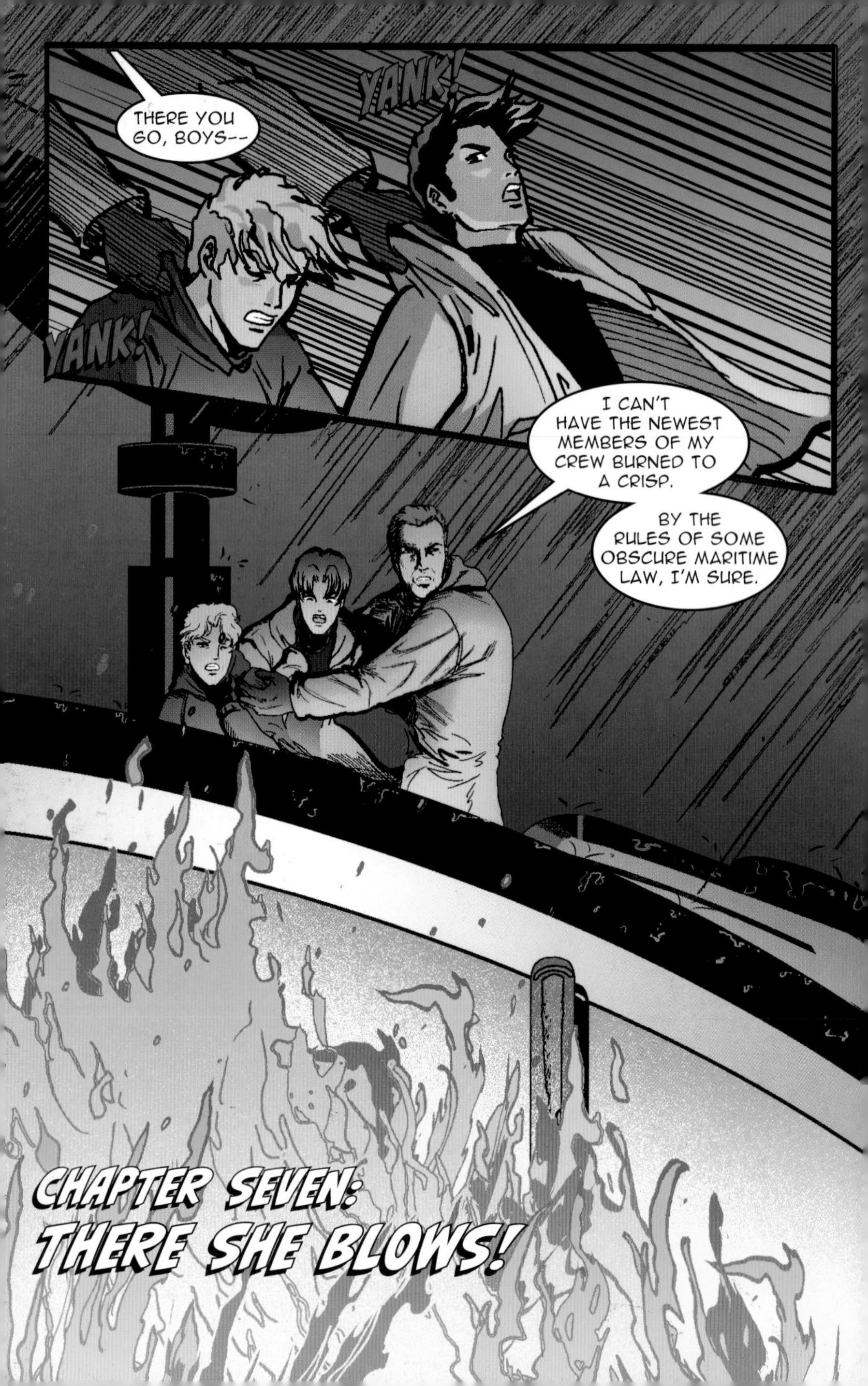
THERE YOU GO, BOYS--
YANK!
YANK!
I CAN'T HAVE THE NEWEST MEMBERS OF MY CREW BURNED TO A CRISP.
BY THE RULES OF SOME OBSCURE MARITIME LAW, I'M SURE.
CHAPTER SEVEN:
THERE SHE BLOWS!

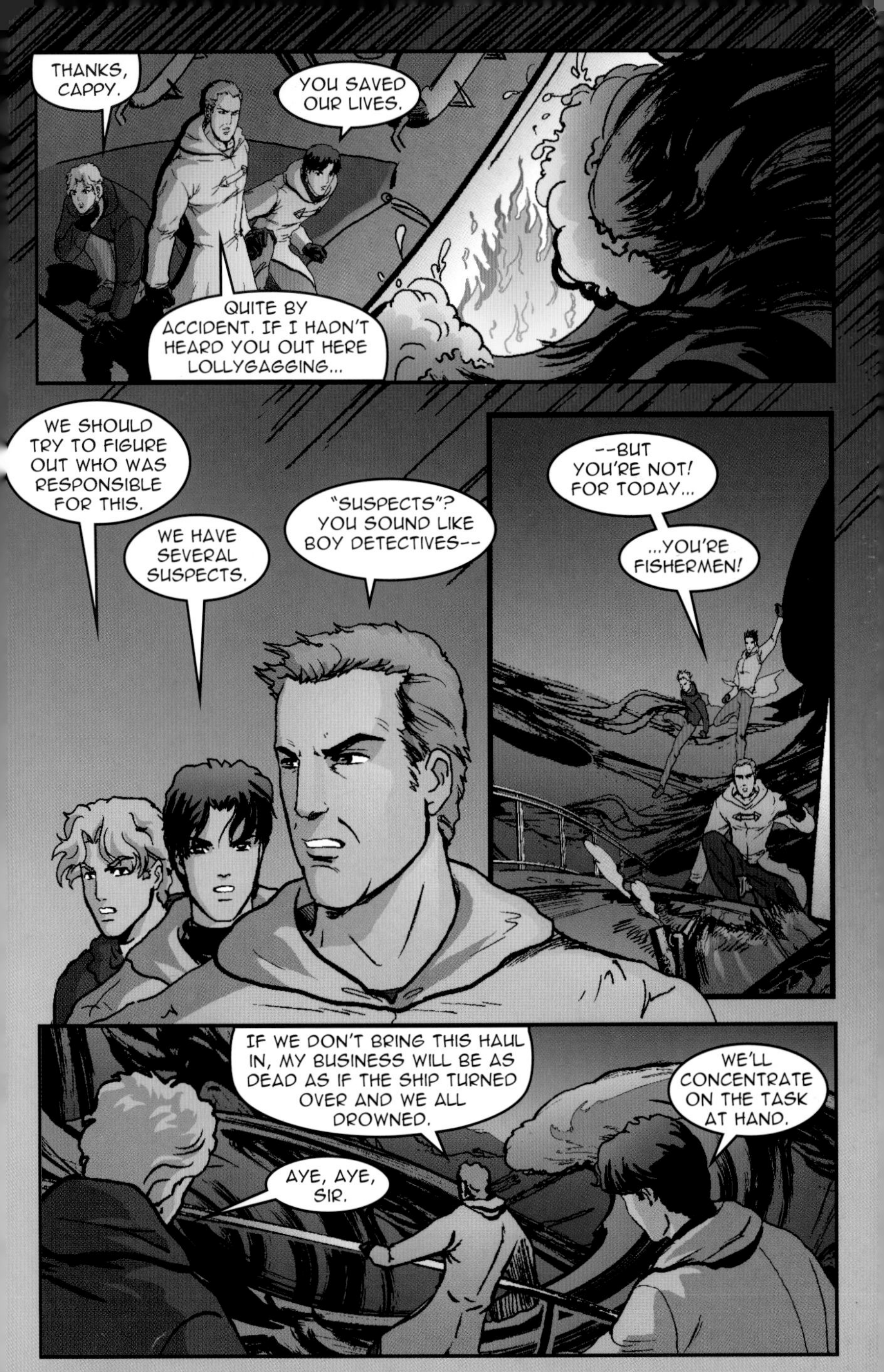

THANKS, CAPPY.
YOU SAVED OUR LIVES.
QUITE BY ACCIDENT. IF I HADN'T HEARD YOU OUT HERE LOLLYGAGGING...
WE SHOULD TRY TO FIGURE OUT WHO WAS RESPONSIBLE FOR THIS.
WE HAVE SEVERAL SUSPECTS.
"SUSPECTS"? YOU SOUND LIKE BOY DETECTIVES--
--BUT YOU'RE NOT! FOR TODAY...
...YOU'RE FISHERMEN!
IF WE DON'T BRING THIS HAUL IN, MY BUSINESS WILL BE AS DEAD AS IF THE SHIP TURNED OVER AND WE ALL DROWNED.
WE'LL CONCENTRATE ON THE TASK AT HAND.
AYE, AYE, SIR.

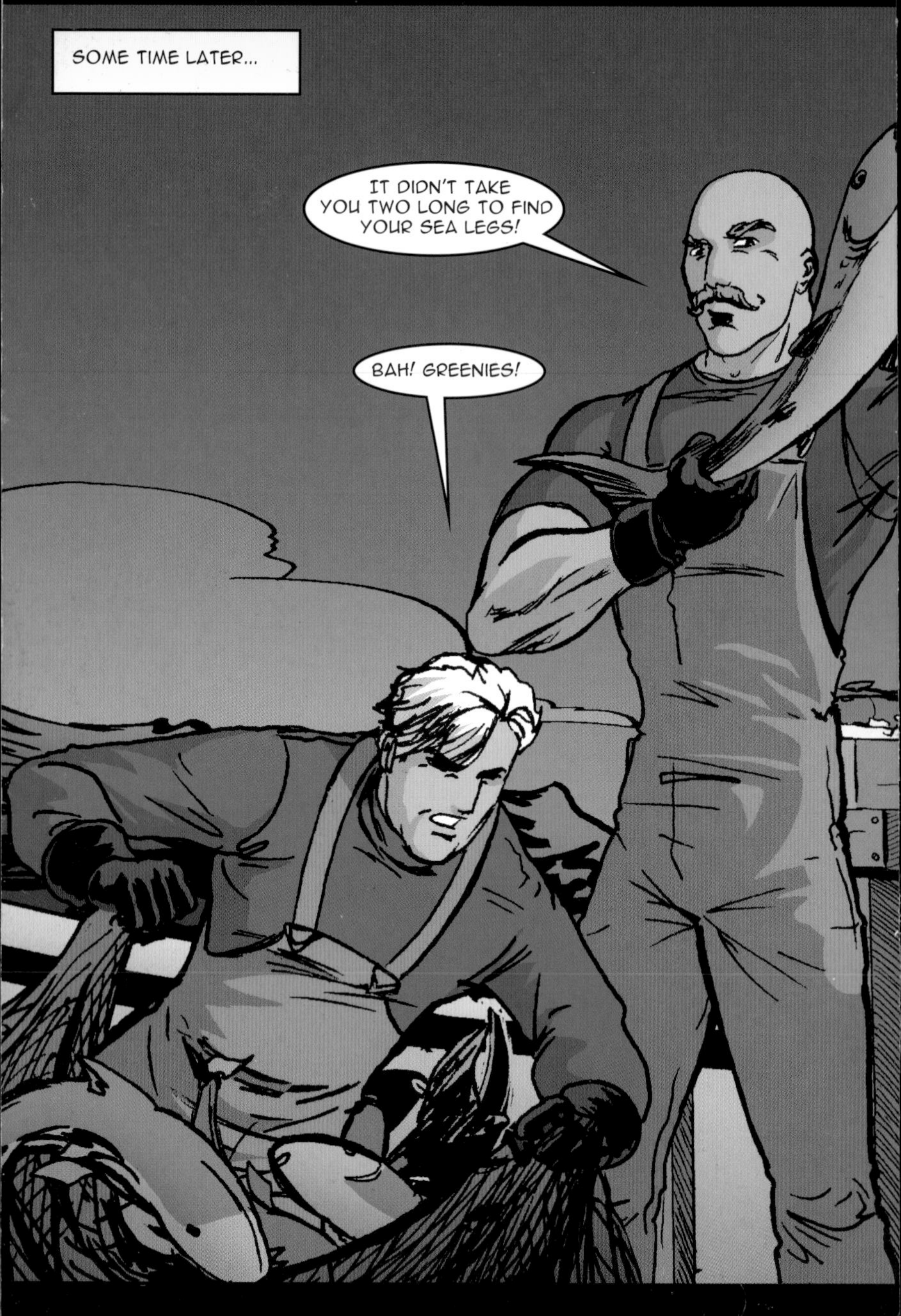
SOME TIME LATER...
IT DIDN'T TAKE YOU TWO LONG TO FIND YOUR SEA LEGS!
BAH! GREENIES!

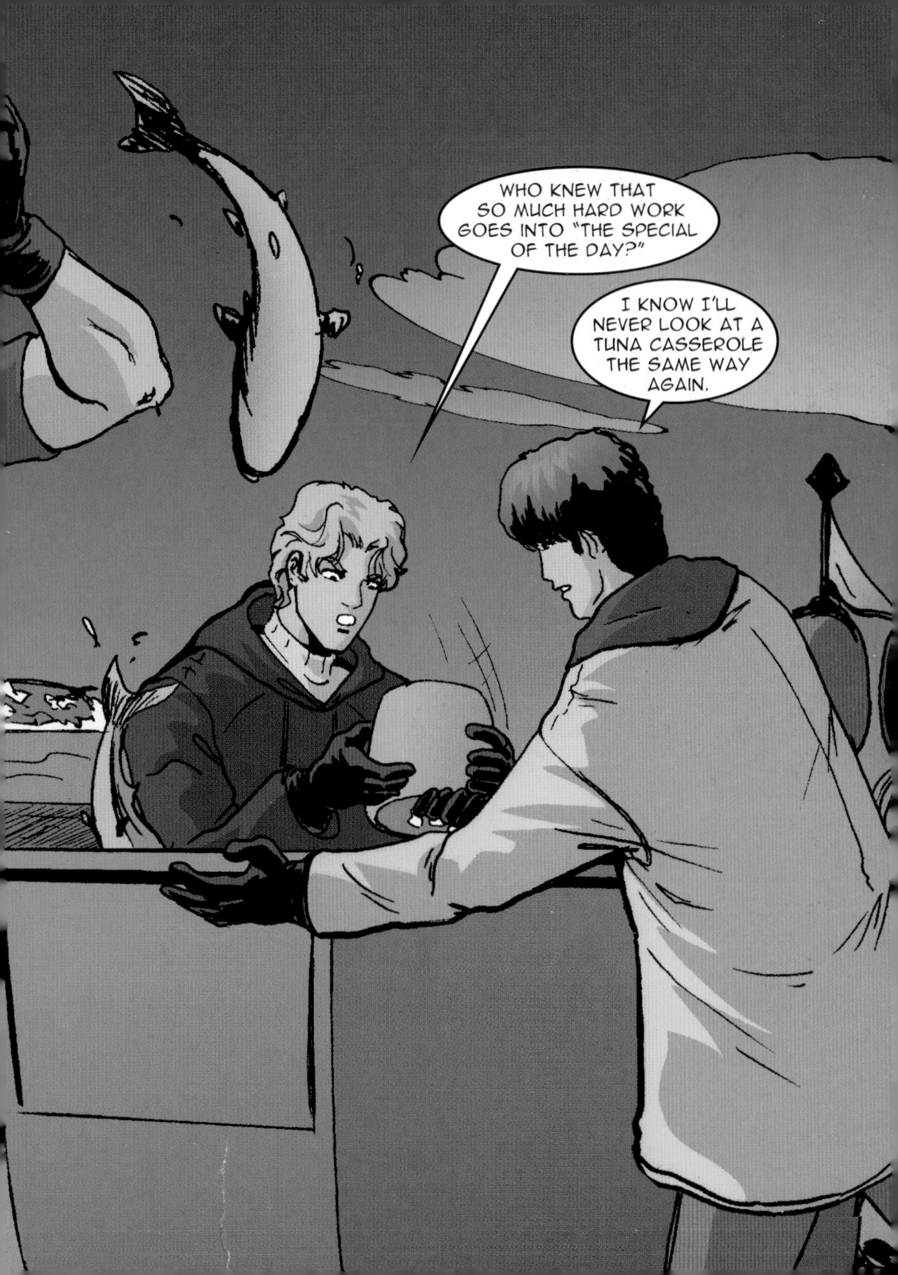
WHO KNEW THAT SO MUCH HARD WORK GOES INTO "THE SPECIAL OF THE DAY?"
I KNOW I'LL NEVER LOOK AT A TUNA CASSEROLE THE SAME WAY AGAIN.

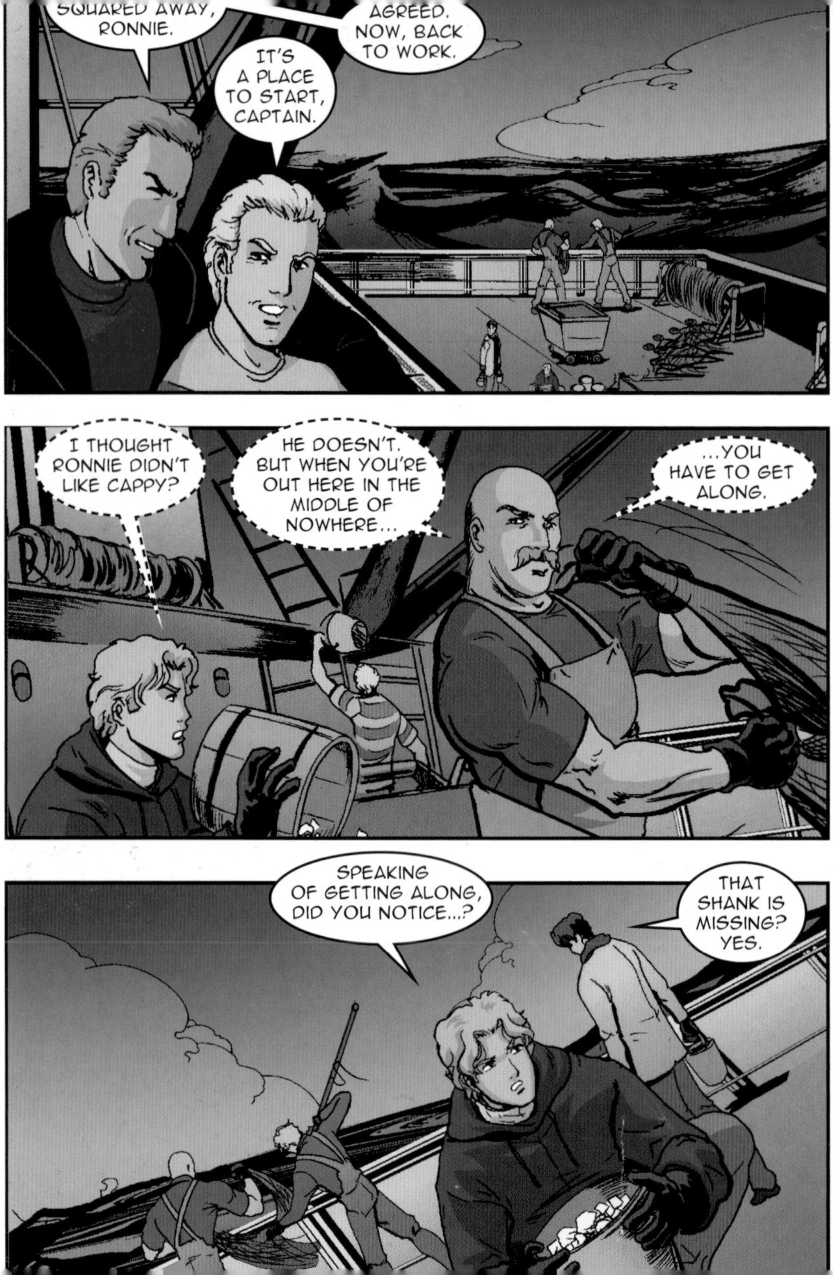
SQUARED AWAY, RONNIE.
IT'S A PLACE TO START, CAPTAIN.
AGREED. NOW, BACK TO WORK.
I THOUGHT RONNIE DIDN'T LIKE CAPPY?
HE DOESN'T. BUT WHEN YOU'RE OUT HERE IN THE MIDDLE OF NOWHERE...
...YOU HAVE TO GET ALONG.
SPEAKING OF GETTING ALONG, DID YOU NOTICE...?
THAT SHANK IS MISSING? YES.

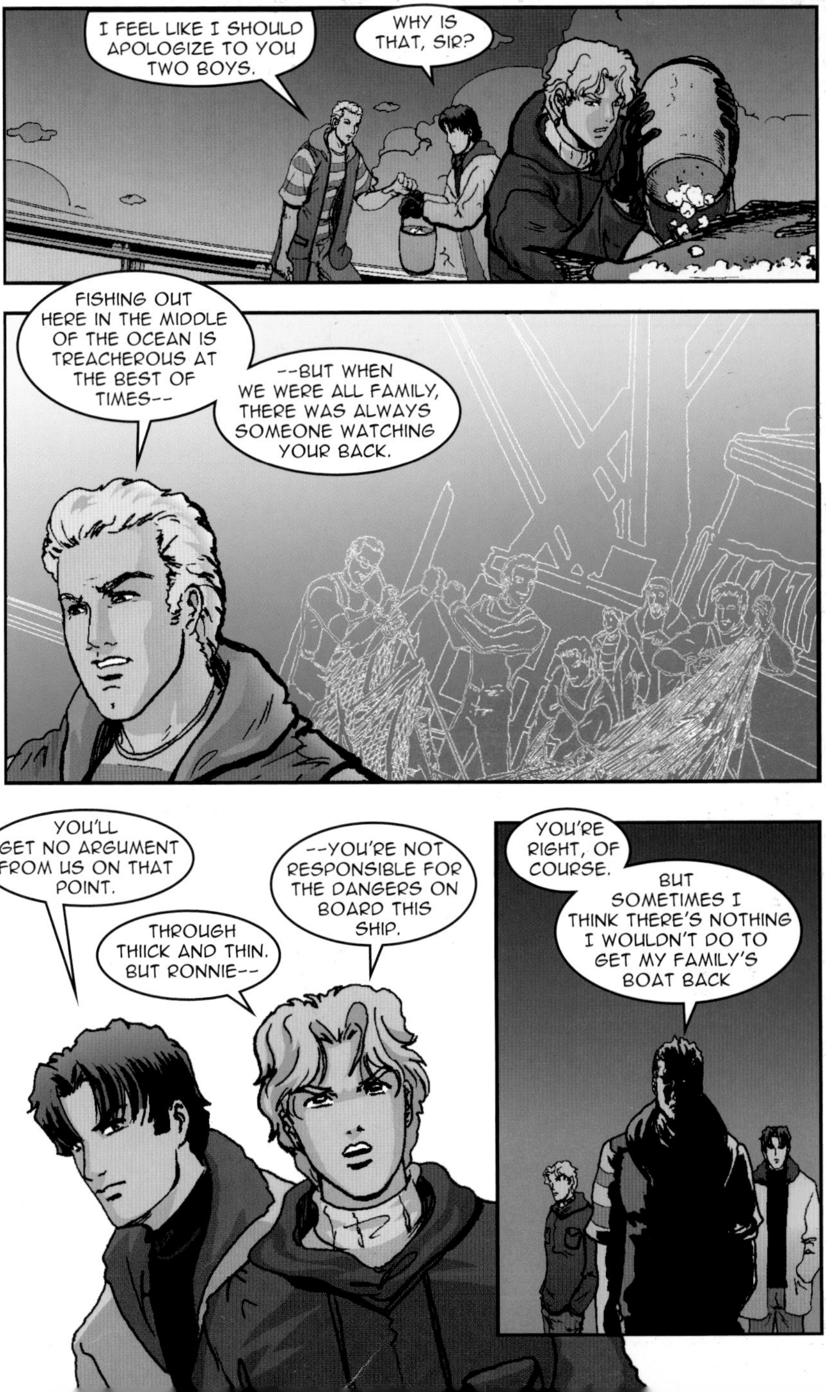
I FEEL LIKE I SHOULD APOLOGIZE TO YOU TWO BOYS.
WHY IS THAT, SIR?
FISHING OUT HERE IN THE MIDDLE OF THE OCEAN IS TREACHEROUS AT THE BEST OF TIMES--
--BUT WHEN WE WERE ALL FAMILY, THERE WAS ALWAYS SOMEONE WATCHING YOUR BACK.
YOU'LL GET NO ARGUMENT FROM US ON THAT POINT.
THROUGH THIICK AND THIN. BUT RONNIE--
--YOU'RE NOT RESPONSIBLE FOR THE DANGERS ON BOARD THIS SHIP.
YOU'RE RIGHT, OF COURSE.
BUT SOMETIMES I THINK THERE'S NOTHING I WOULDN'T DO TO GET MY FAMILY'S BOAT BACK

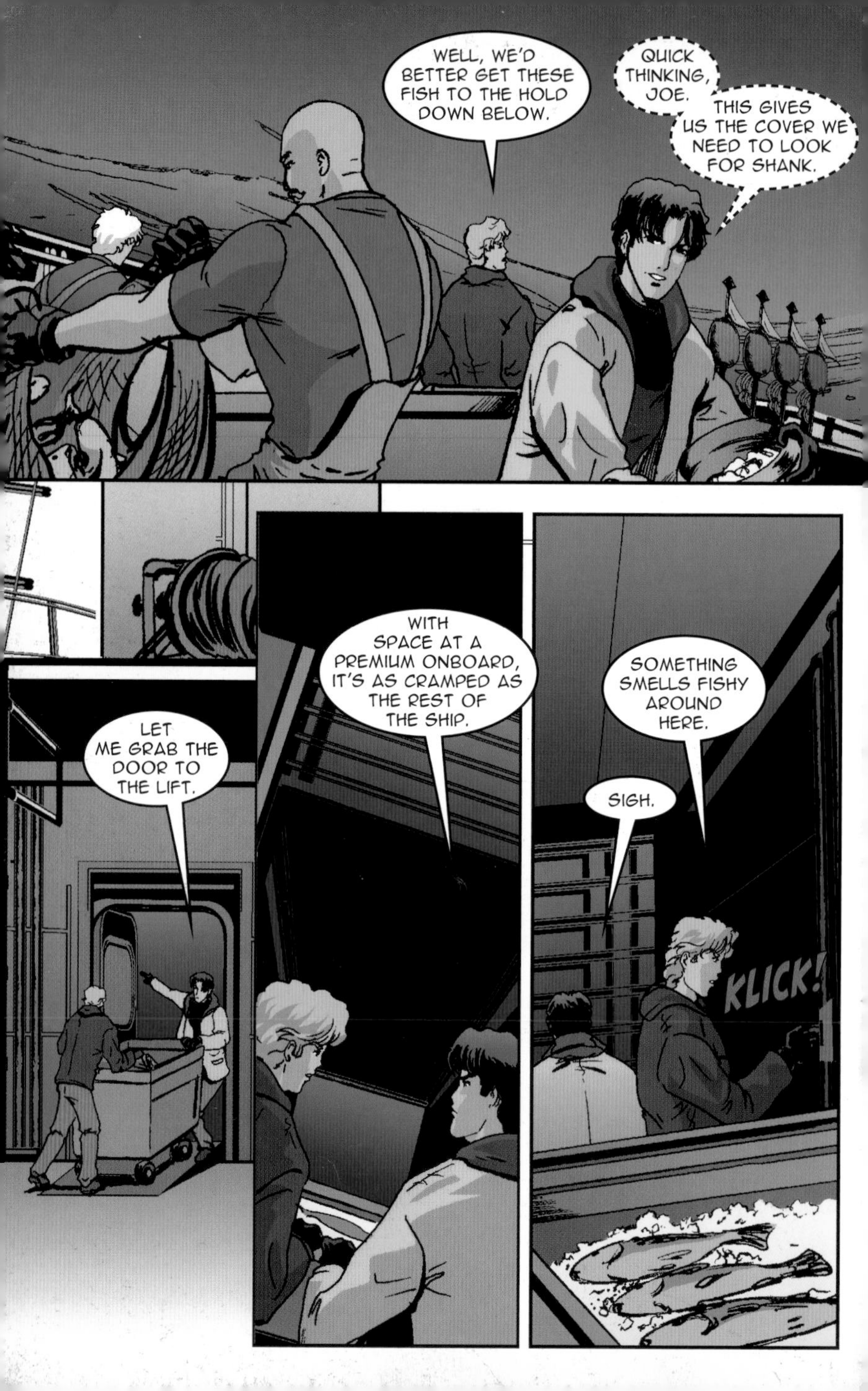
WELL, WE'D BETTER GET THESE FISH TO THE HOLD DOWN BELOW.
QUICK THINKING, JOE.
THIS GIVES US THE COVER WE NEED TO LOOK FOR SHANK.
LET ME GRAB THE DOOR TO THE LIFT.
WITH SPACE AT A PREMIUM ONBOARD, IT'S AS CRAMPED AS THE REST OF THE SHIP.
SOMETHING SMELLS FISHY AROUND HERE.
SIGH.
KLICK!

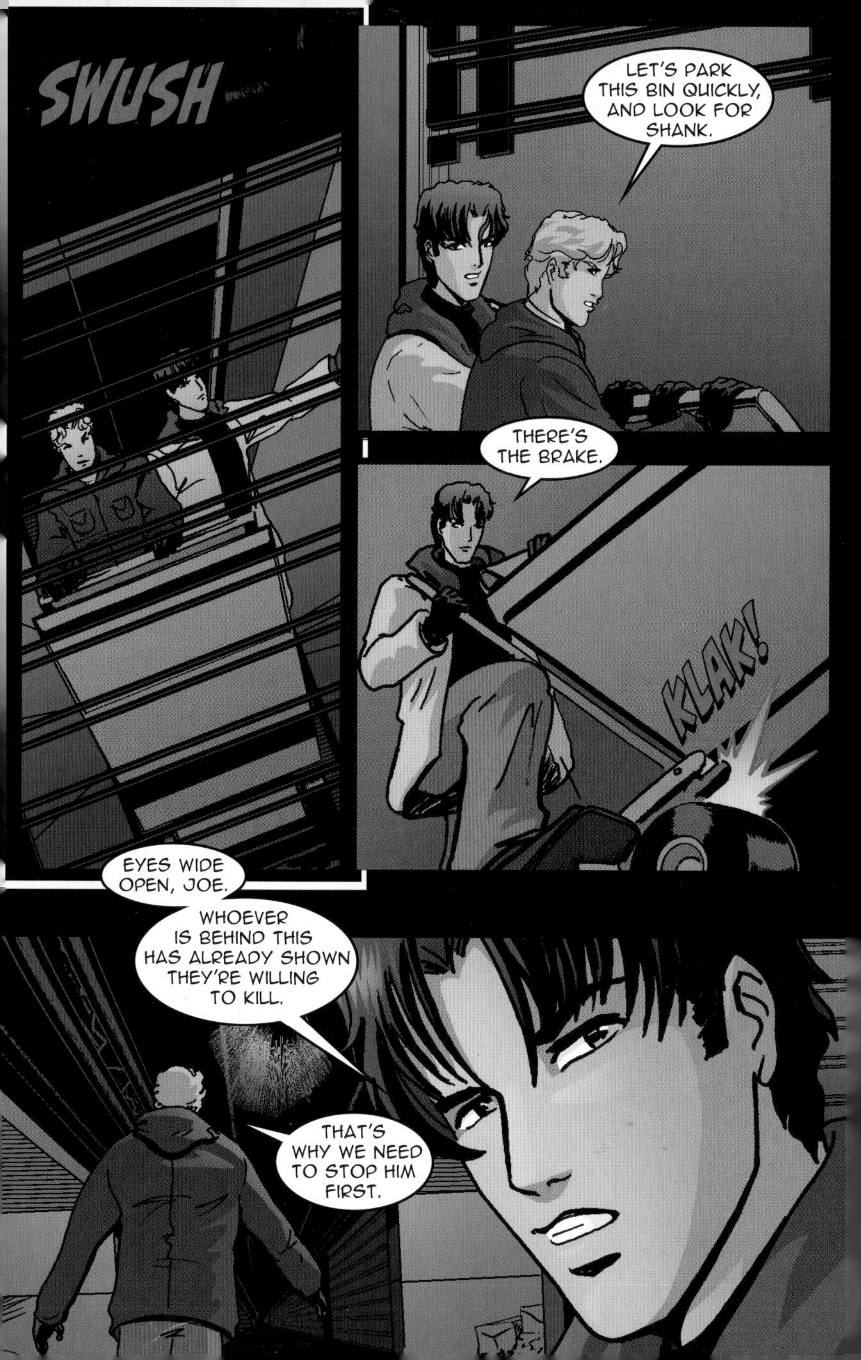
SWUSH
LET'S PARK THIS BIN QUICKLY, AND LOOK FOR SHANK.
THERE'S THE BRAKE.
KLAK!
EYES WIDE OPEN, JOE.
WHOEVER IS BEHIND THIS HAS ALREADY SHOWN THEY'RE WILLING TO KILL.
THAT'S WHY WE NEED TO STOP HIM FIRST.

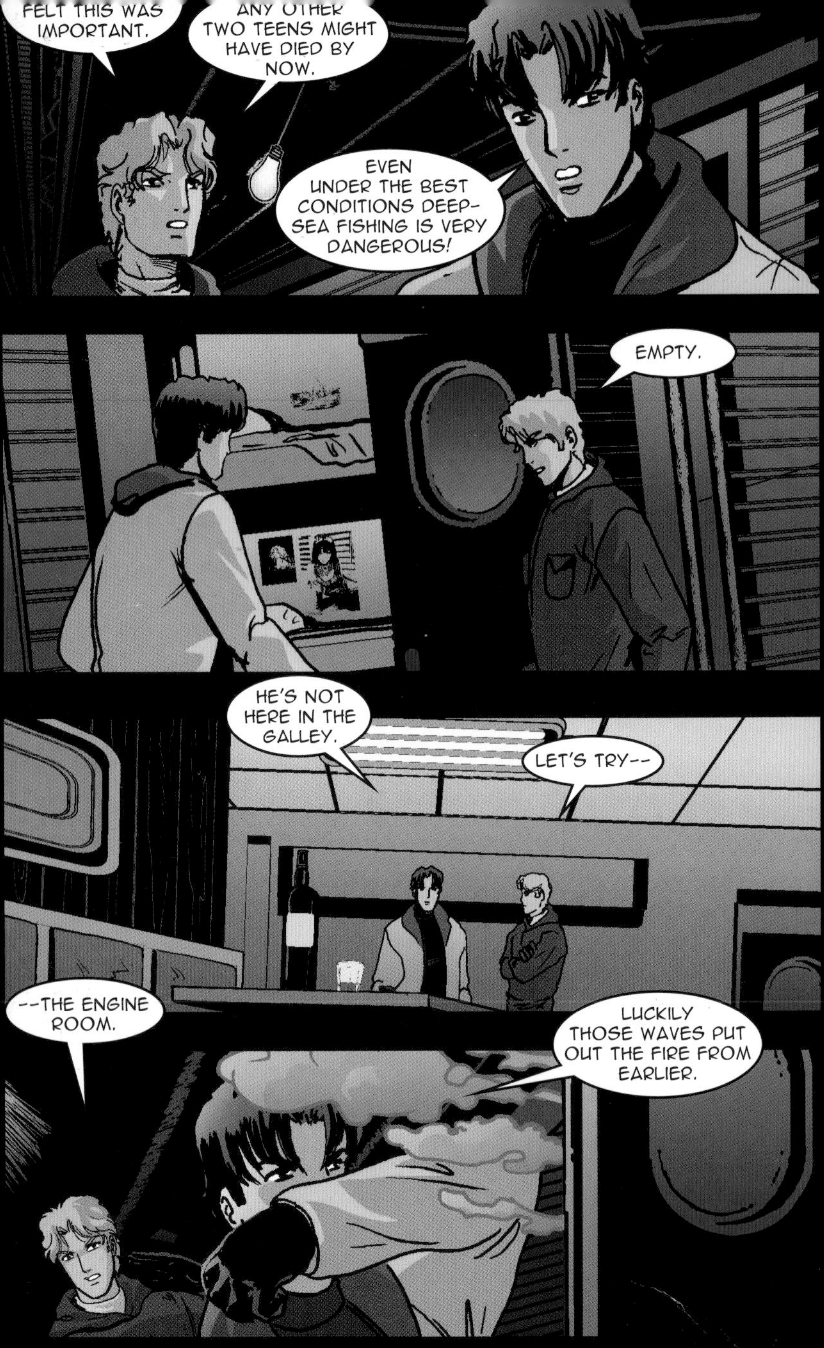
FELT THIS WAS IMPORTANT.
ANY OTHER TWO TEENS MIGHT HAVE DIED BY NOW.
EVEN UNDER THE BEST CONDITIONS DEEP-SEA FISHING IS VERY DANGEROUS!
EMPTY.
HE'S NOT HERE IN THE GALLEY.
LET'S TRY--
--THE ENGINE ROOM.
LUCKILY THOSE WAVES PUT OUT THE FIRE FROM EARLIER.

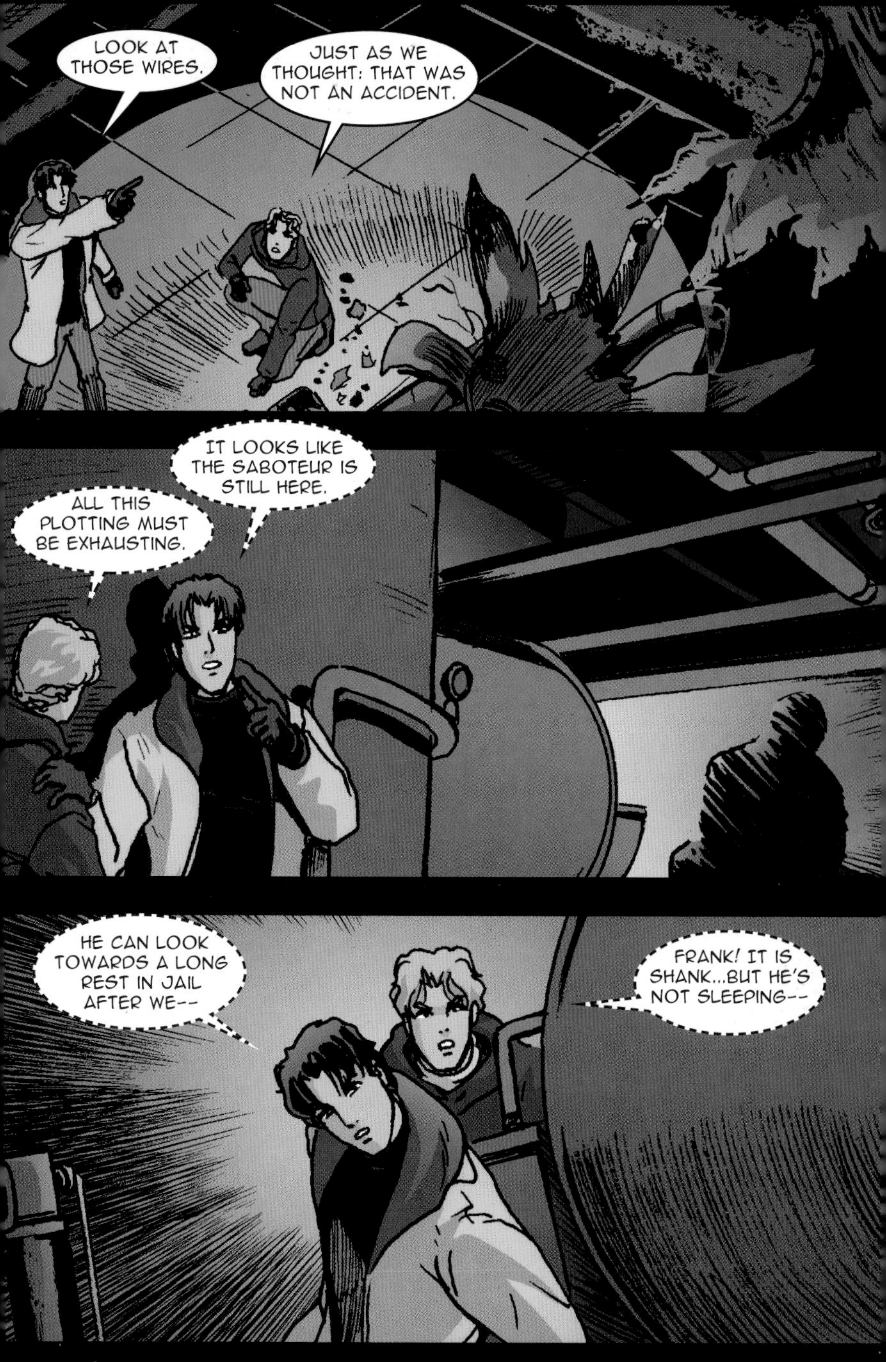
LOOK AT THOSE WIRES.
JUST AS WE THOUGHT: THAT WAS NOT AN ACCIDENT.
IT LOOKS LIKE THE SABOTEUR IS STILL HERE.
ALL THIS PLOTTING MUST BE EXHAUSTING.
HE CAN LOOK TOWARDS A LONG REST IN JAIL AFTER WE--
FRANK! IT IS SHANK...BUT HE'S NOT SLEEPING--

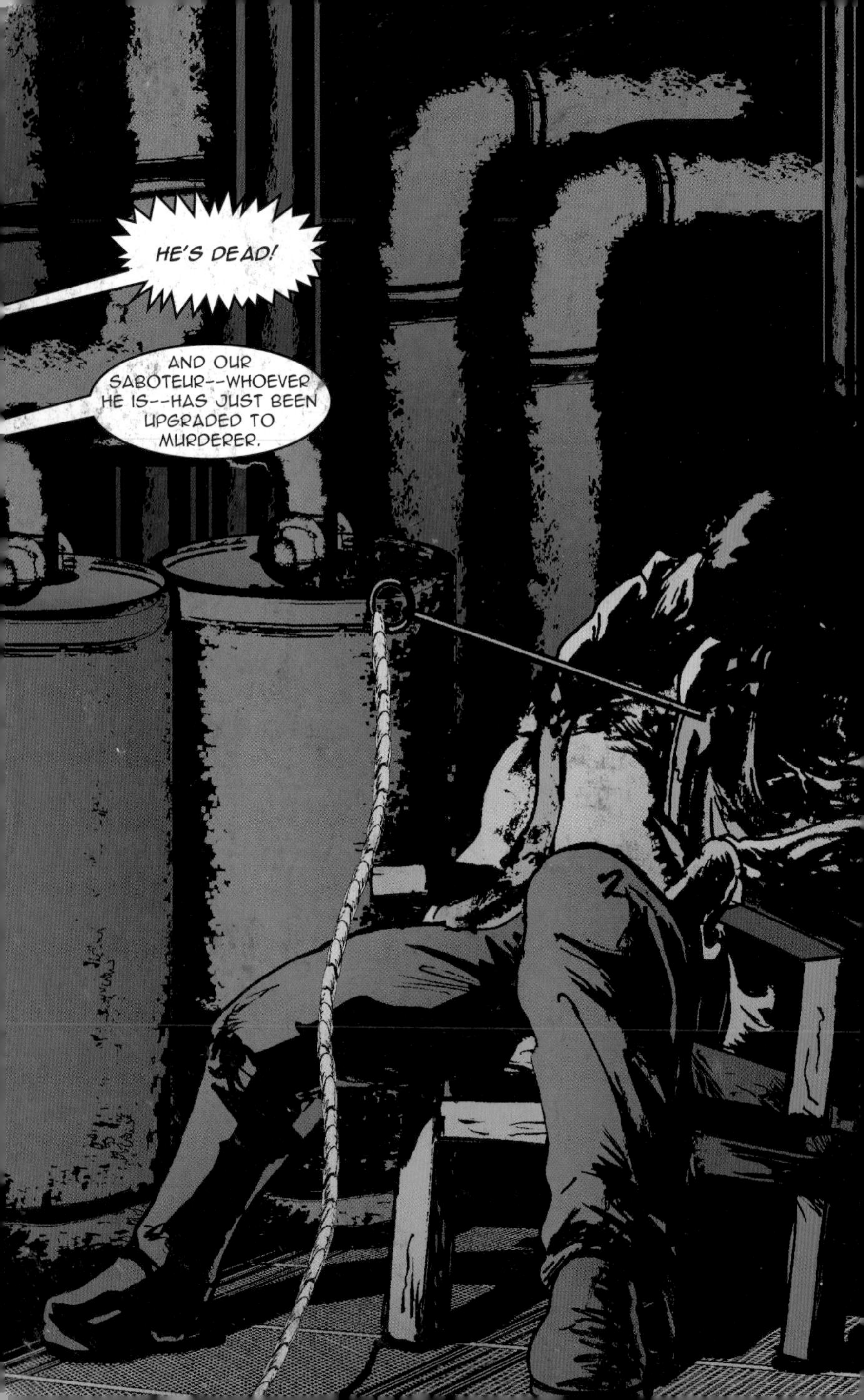
HE'S DEAD!
AND OUR SABOTEUR--WHOEVER HE IS--HAS JUST BEEN UPGRADED TO MURDERER.

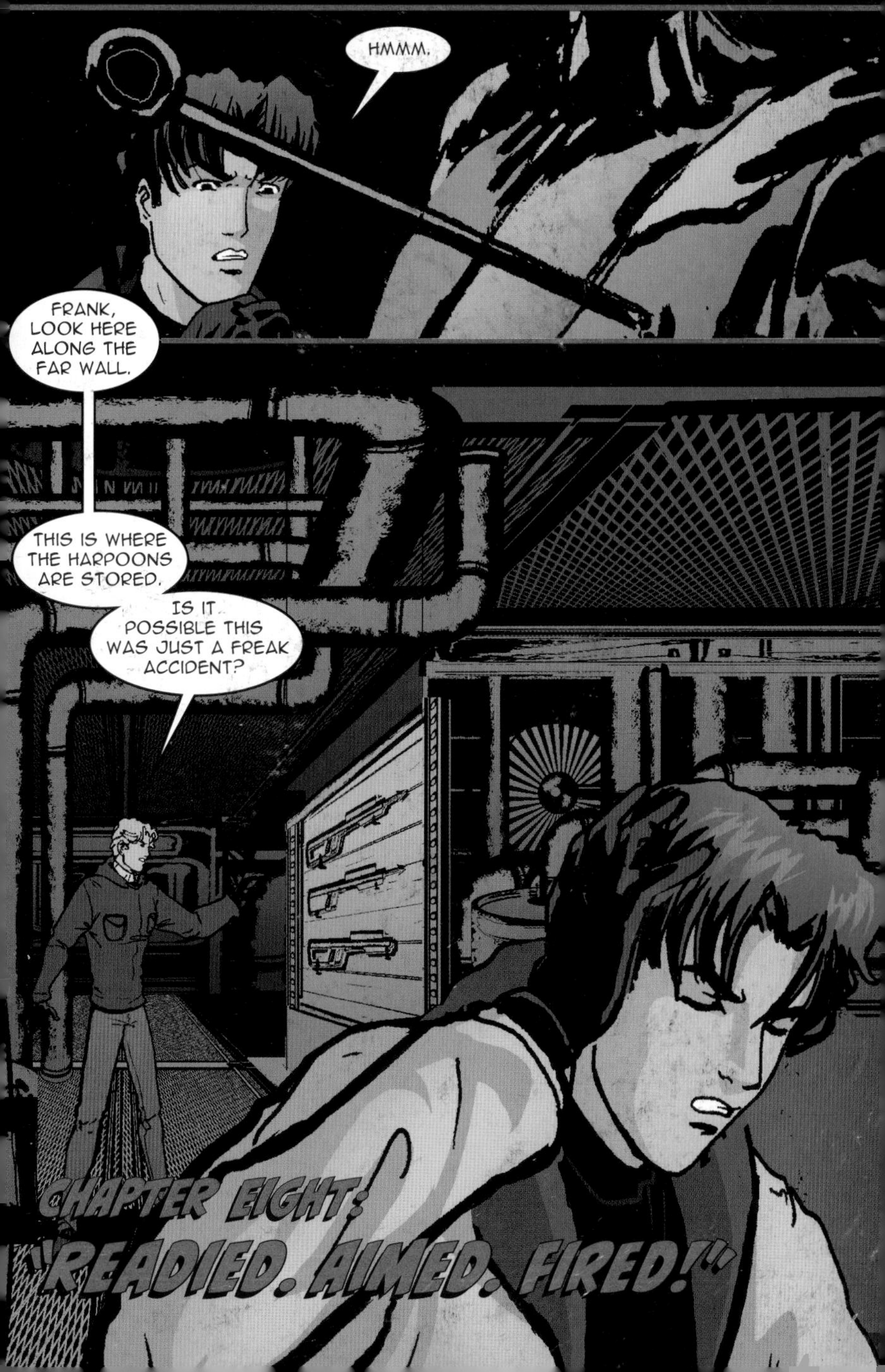
HMMM.
FRANK, LOOK HERE ALONG THE FAR WALL.
THIS IS WHERE THE HARPOONS ARE STORED.
IS IT POSSIBLE THIS WAS JUST A FREAK ACCIDENT?
CHAPTER EIGHT:
"READIED. AIMED. FIRED!"

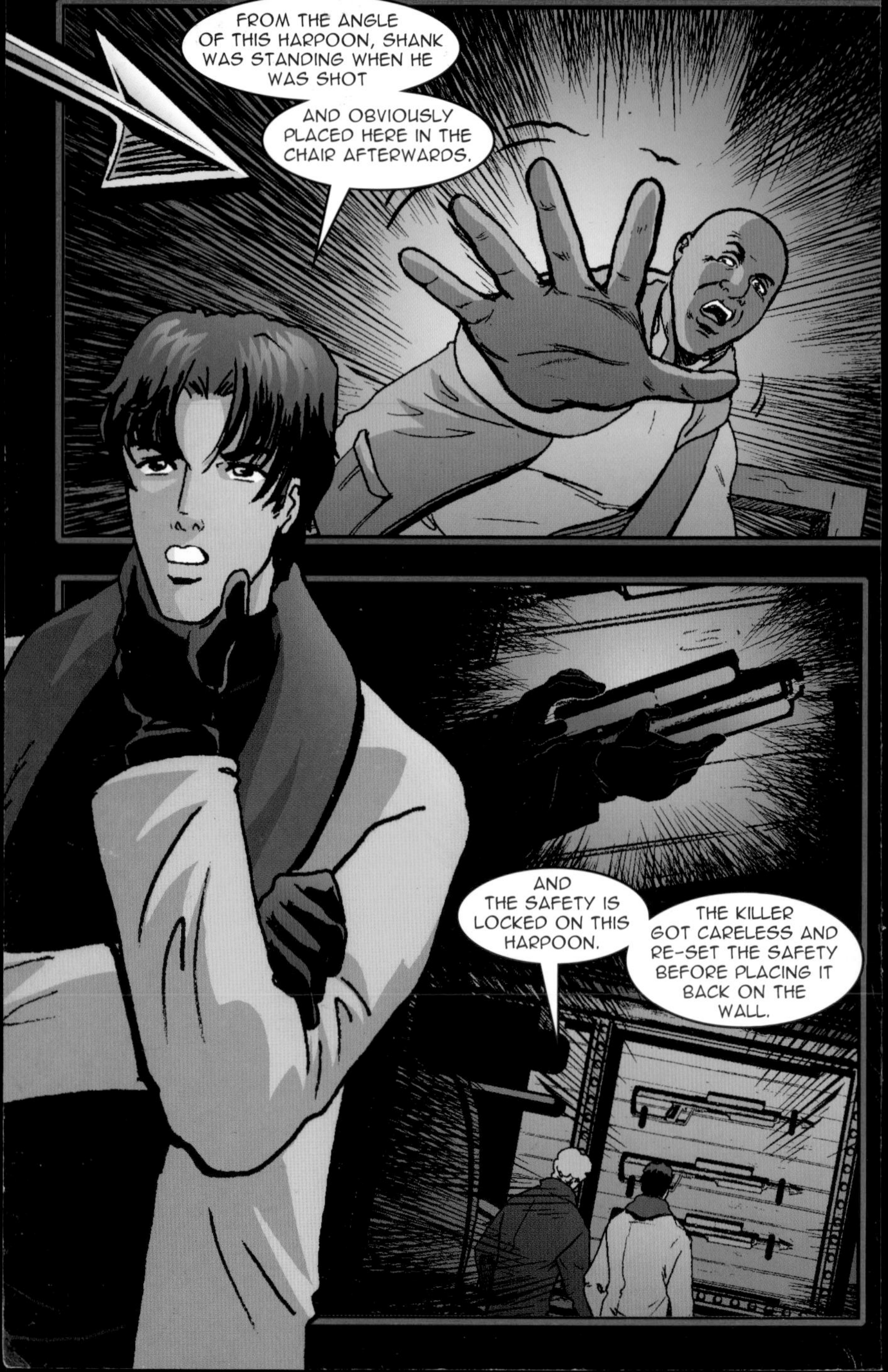
FROM THE ANGLE OF THIS HARPOON, SHANK WAS STANDING WHEN HE WAS SHOT
AND OBVIOUSLY PLACED HERE IN THE CHAIR AFTERWARDS.
AND THE SAFETY IS LOCKED ON THIS HARPOON.
THE KILLER GOT CARELESS AND RE-SET THE SAFETY BEFORE PLACING IT BACK ON THE WALL.

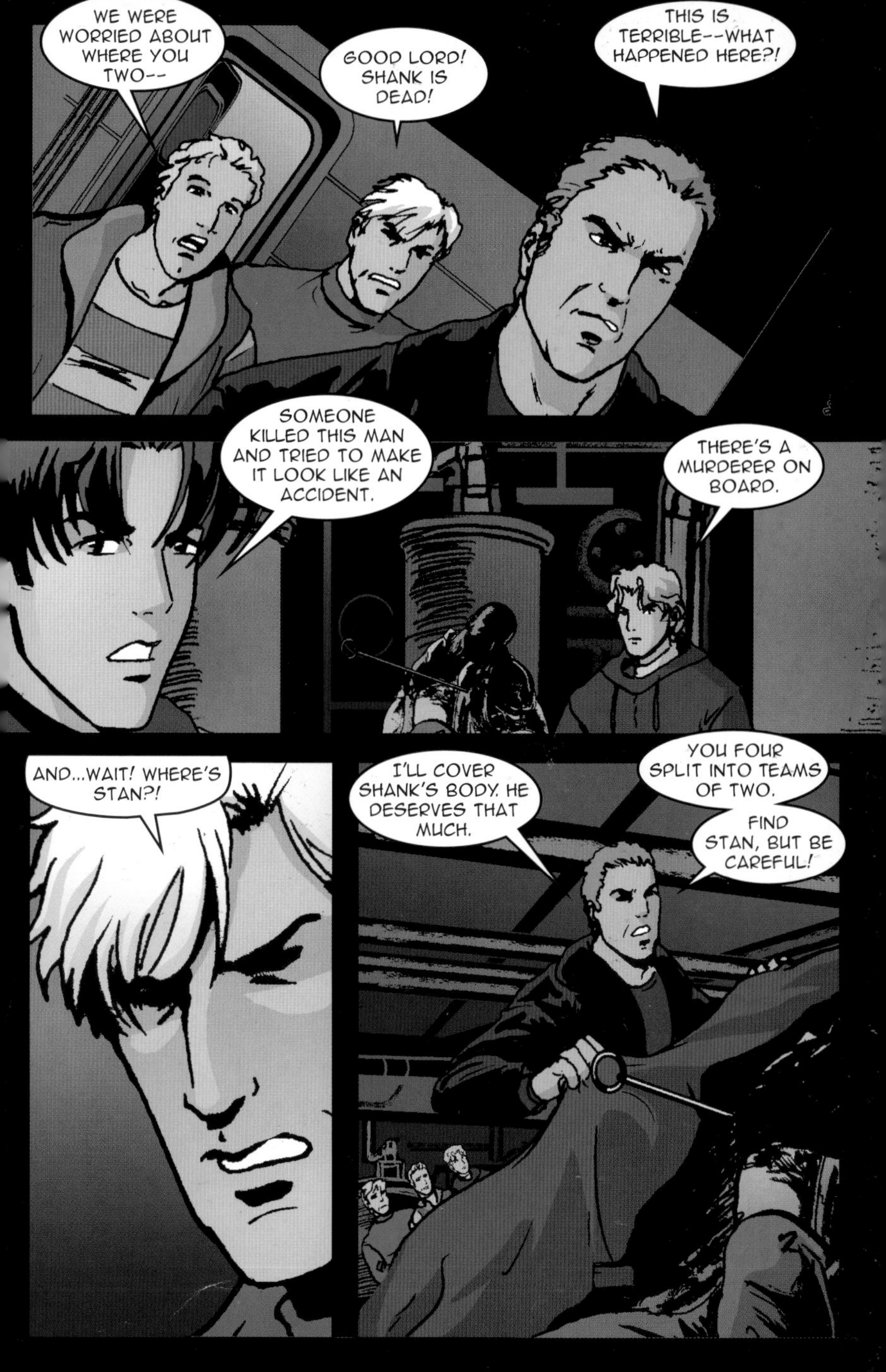
WE WERE WORRIED ABOUT WHERE YOU TWO--
GOOD LORD! SHANK IS DEAD!
THIS IS TERRIBLE--WHAT HAPPENED HERE?!
SOMEONE KILLED THIS MAN AND TRIED TO MAKE IT LOOK LIKE AN ACCIDENT.
THERE'S A MURDERER ON BOARD.
AND...WAIT! WHERE'S STAN?!
I'LL COVER SHANK'S BODY. HE DESERVES THAT MUCH.
YOU FOUR SPLIT INTO TEAMS OF TWO.
FIND STAN, BUT BE CAREFUL!

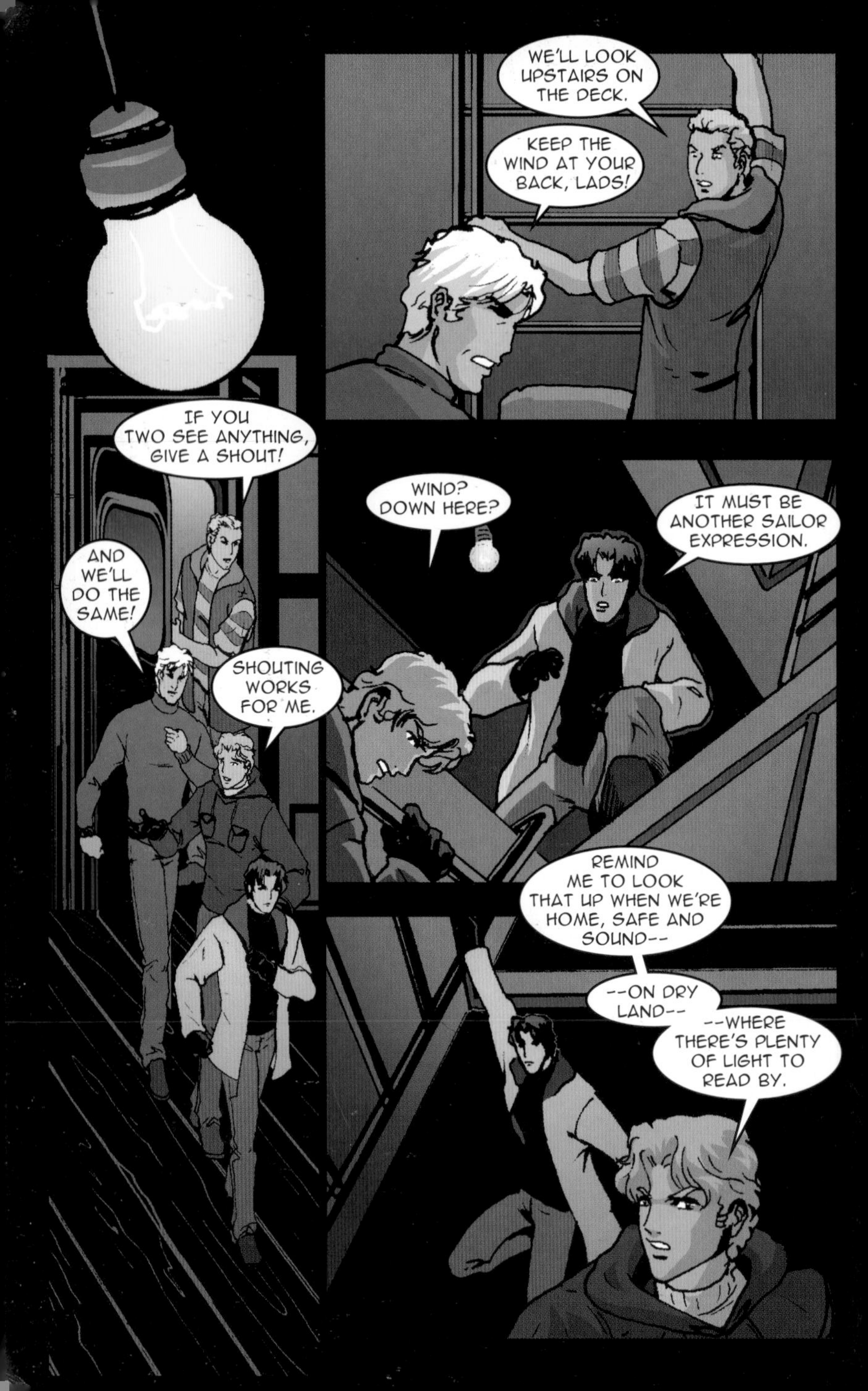
WE'LL LOOK UPSTAIRS ON THE DECK.
KEEP THE WIND AT YOUR BACK, LADS!
IF YOU TWO SEE ANYTHING, GIVE A SHOUT!
AND WE'LL DO THE SAME!
SHOUTING WORKS FOR ME.
WIND? DOWN HERE?
IT MUST BE ANOTHER SAILOR EXPRESSION.
REMIND ME TO LOOK THAT UP WHEN WE'RE HOME, SAFE AND SOUND--
--ON DRY LAND--
--WHERE THERE'S PLENTY OF LIGHT TO READ BY.

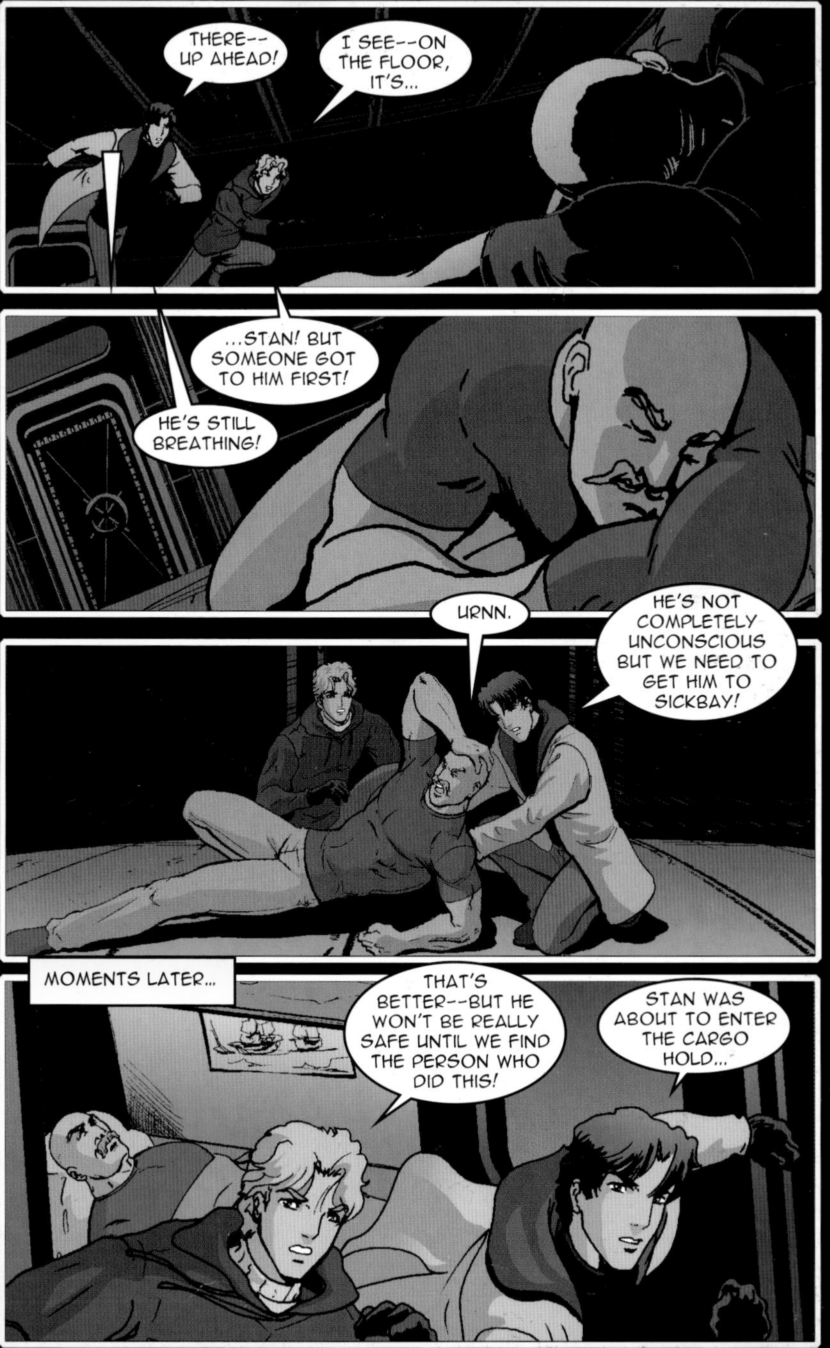
THERE--UP AHEAD!
I SEE--ON THE FLOOR, IT'S...
...STAN! BUT SOMEONE GOT TO HIM FIRST!
HE'S STILL BREATHING!
URNN.
HE'S NOT COMPLETELY UNCONSCIOUS BUT WE NEED TO GET HIM TO SICKBAY!
MOMENTS LATER...
THAT'S BETTER--BUT HE WON'T BE REALLY SAFE UNTIL WE FIND THE PERSON WHO DID THIS!
STAN WAS ABOUT TO ENTER THE CARGO HOLD...

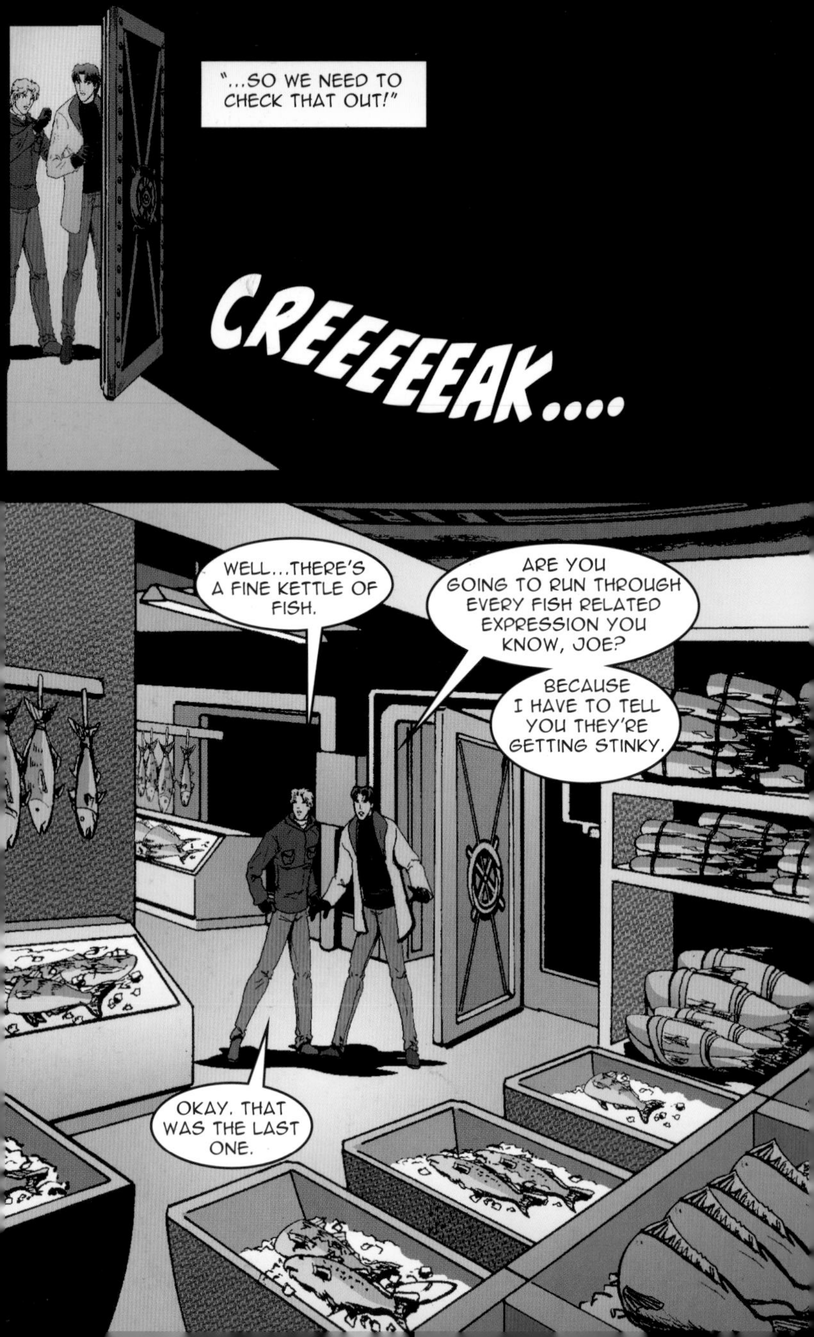
"...SO WE NEED TO CHECK THAT OUT!"
CREEEEEAK....
WELL...THERE'S A FINE KETTLE OF FISH.
ARE YOU GOING TO RUN THROUGH EVERY FISH RELATED EXPRESSION YOU KNOW, JOE?
BECAUSE I HAVE TO TELL YOU THEY'RE GETTING STINKY.
OKAY. THAT WAS THE LAST ONE.

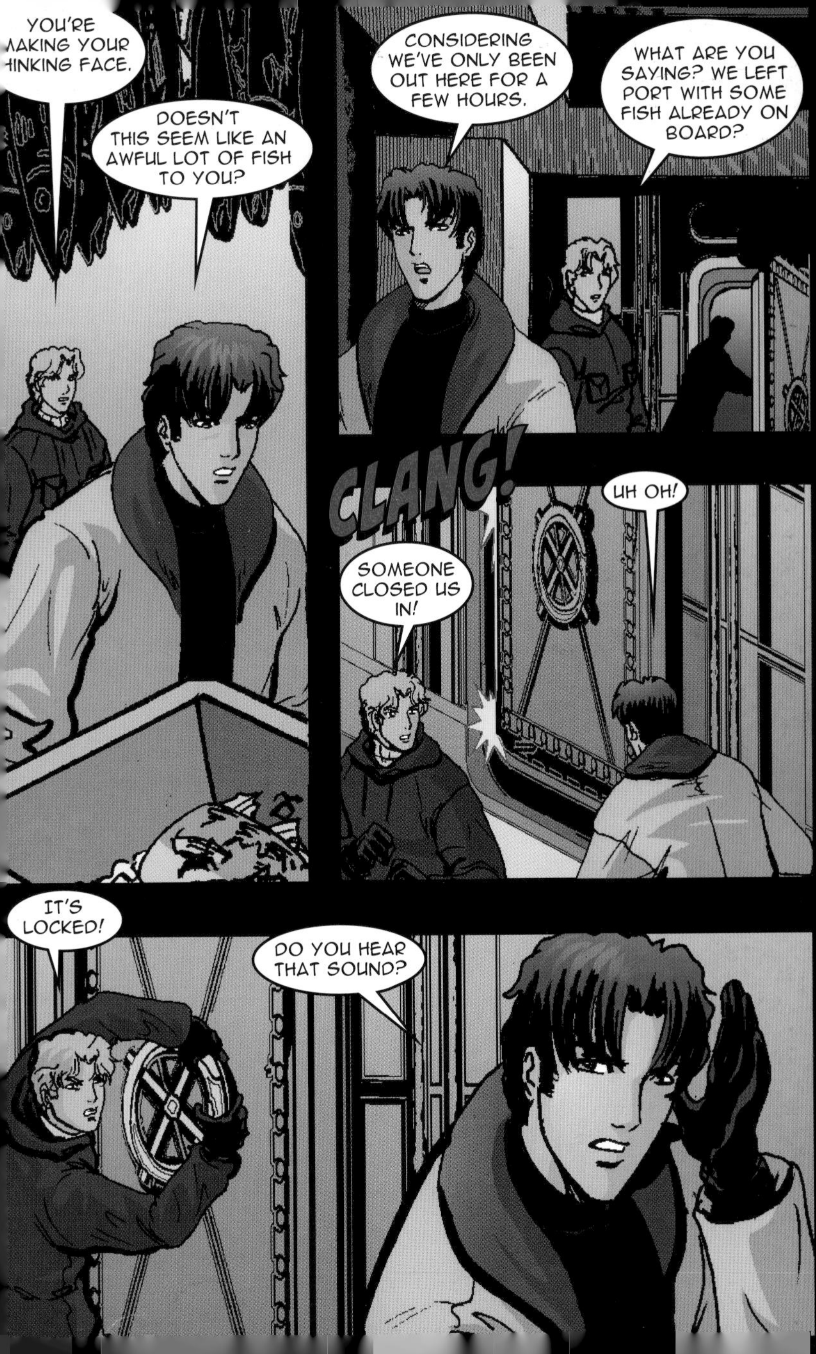
YOU'RE
MAKING YOUR
THINKING FACE.
DOESN'T THIS SEEM LIKE AN AWFUL LOT OF FISH TO YOU?
CONSIDERING WE'VE ONLY BEEN OUT HERE FOR A FEW HOURS.
WHAT ARE YOU SAYING? WE LEFT PORT WITH SOME FISH ALREADY ON BOARD?
CLANG!
UH OH!
SOMEONE CLOSED US IN!
IT'S LOCKED!
DO YOU HEAR THAT SOUND?

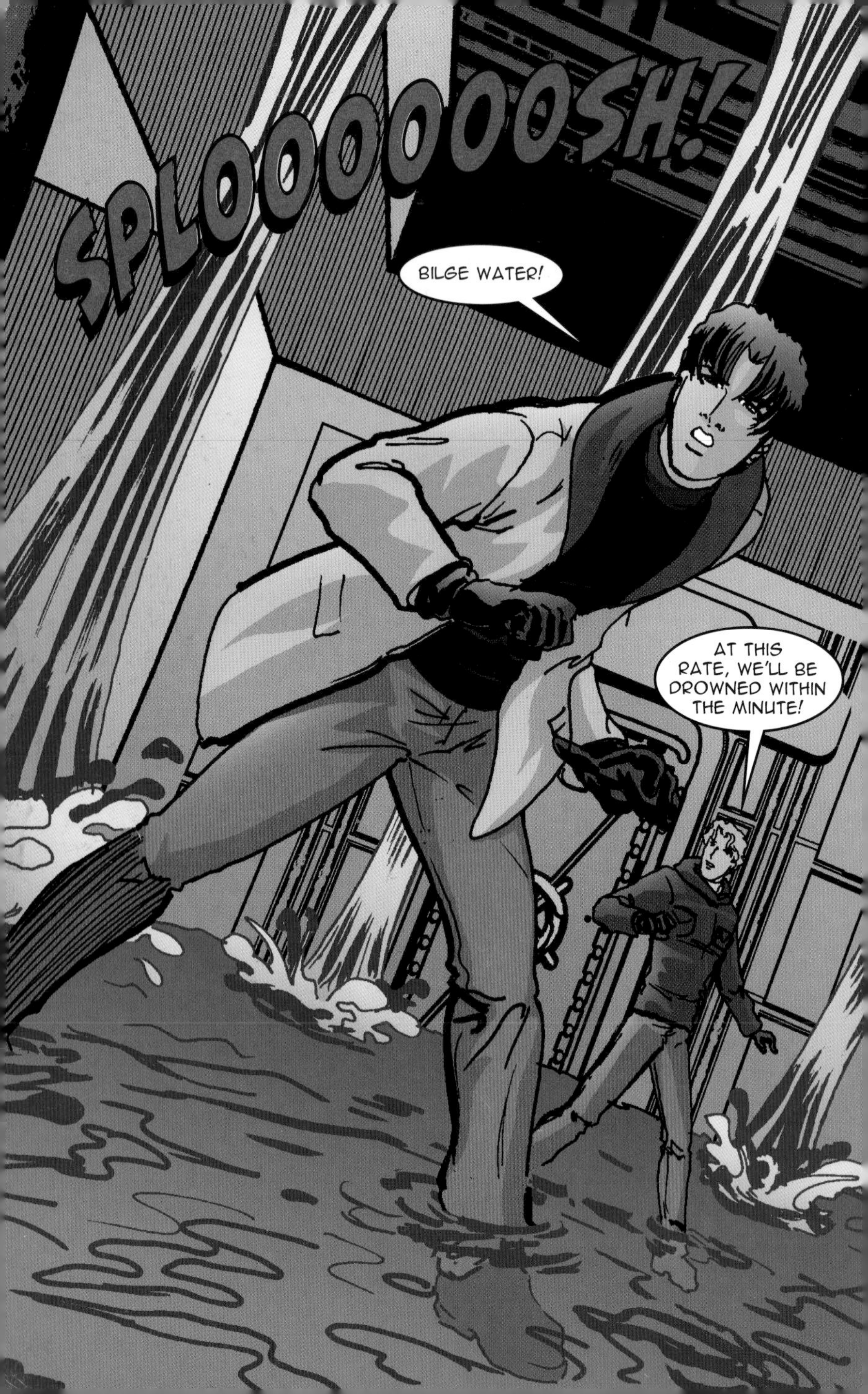
SPLOOOOOOOSH!
BILGE WATER!
AT THIS RATE, WE'LL BE DROWNED WITHIN THE MINUTE!

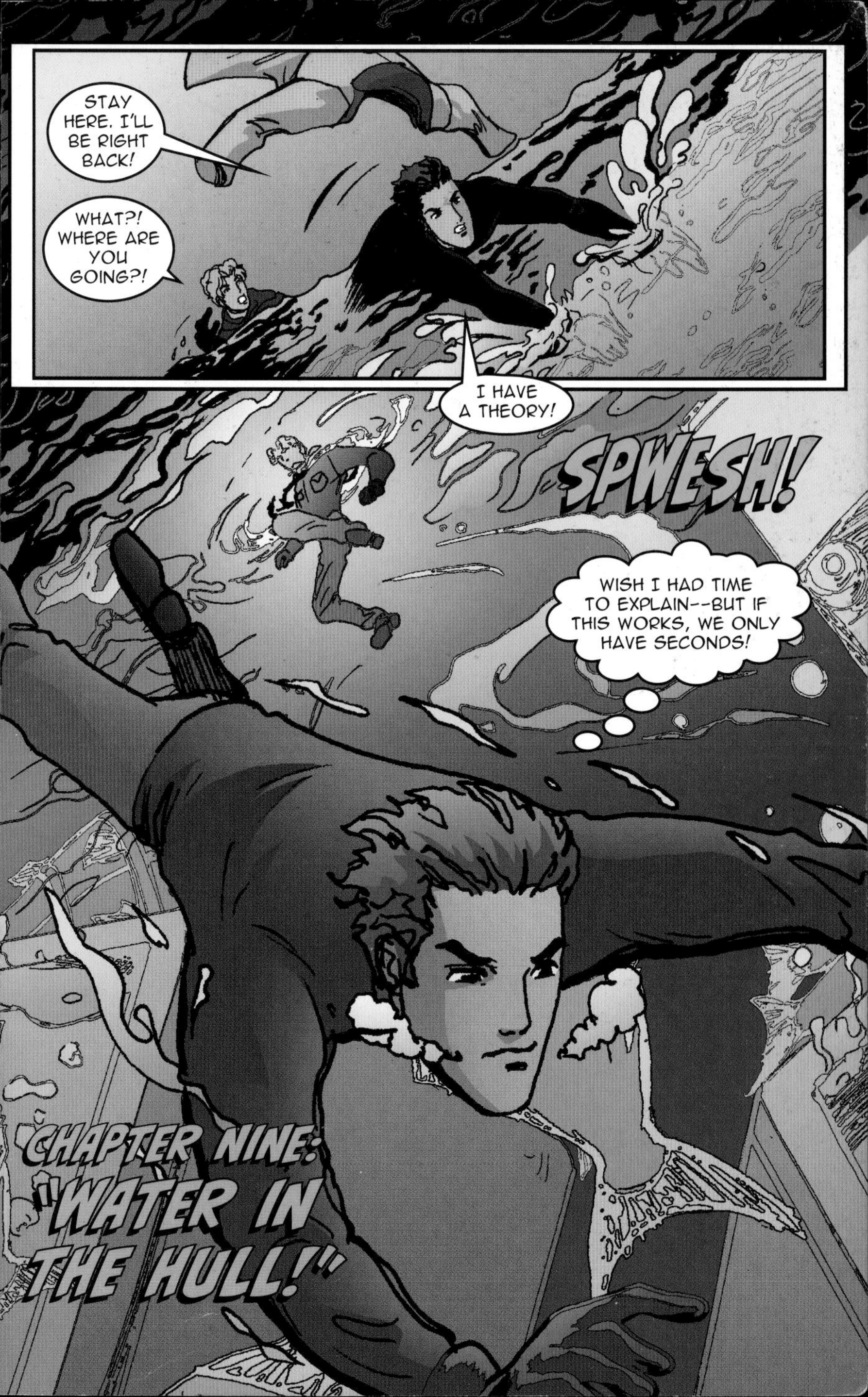
STAY HERE. I'LL BE RIGHT BACK!
WHAT?! WHERE ARE YOU GOING?!
I HAVE A THEORY!
SPWESH!
WISH I HAD TIME TO EXPLAIN--BUT IF THIS WORKS, WE ONLY HAVE SECONDS!
CHAPTER NINE: "WATER IN THE HULL!"

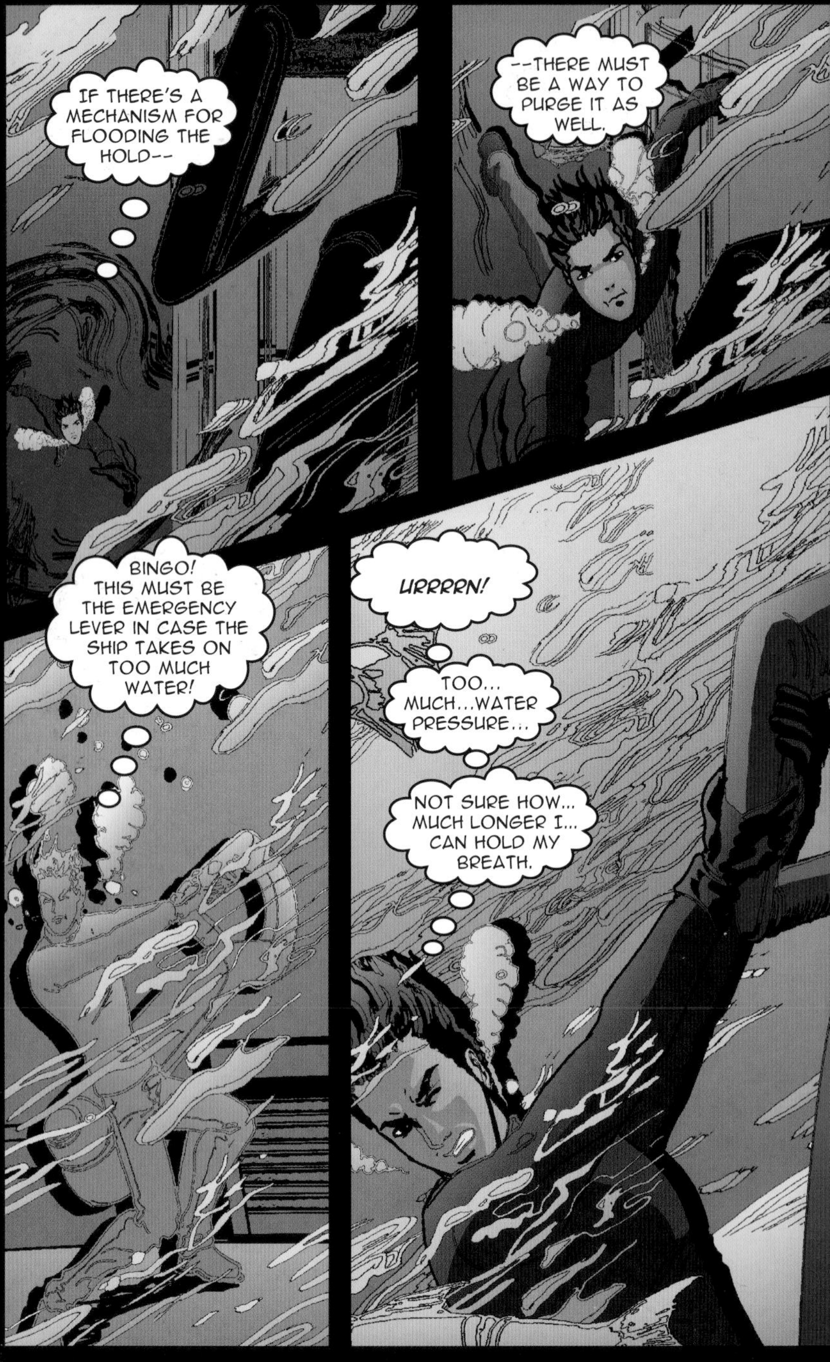
IF THERE'S A MECHANISM FOR FLOODING THE HOLD--
--THERE MUST BE A WAY TO PURGE IT AS WELL.
BINGO! THIS MUST BE THE EMERGENCY LEVER IN CASE THE SHIP TAKES ON TOO MUCH WATER!
URRRRN!
TOO... MUCH...WATER PRESSURE...
NOT SURE HOW... MUCH LONGER I... CAN HOLD MY BREATH.

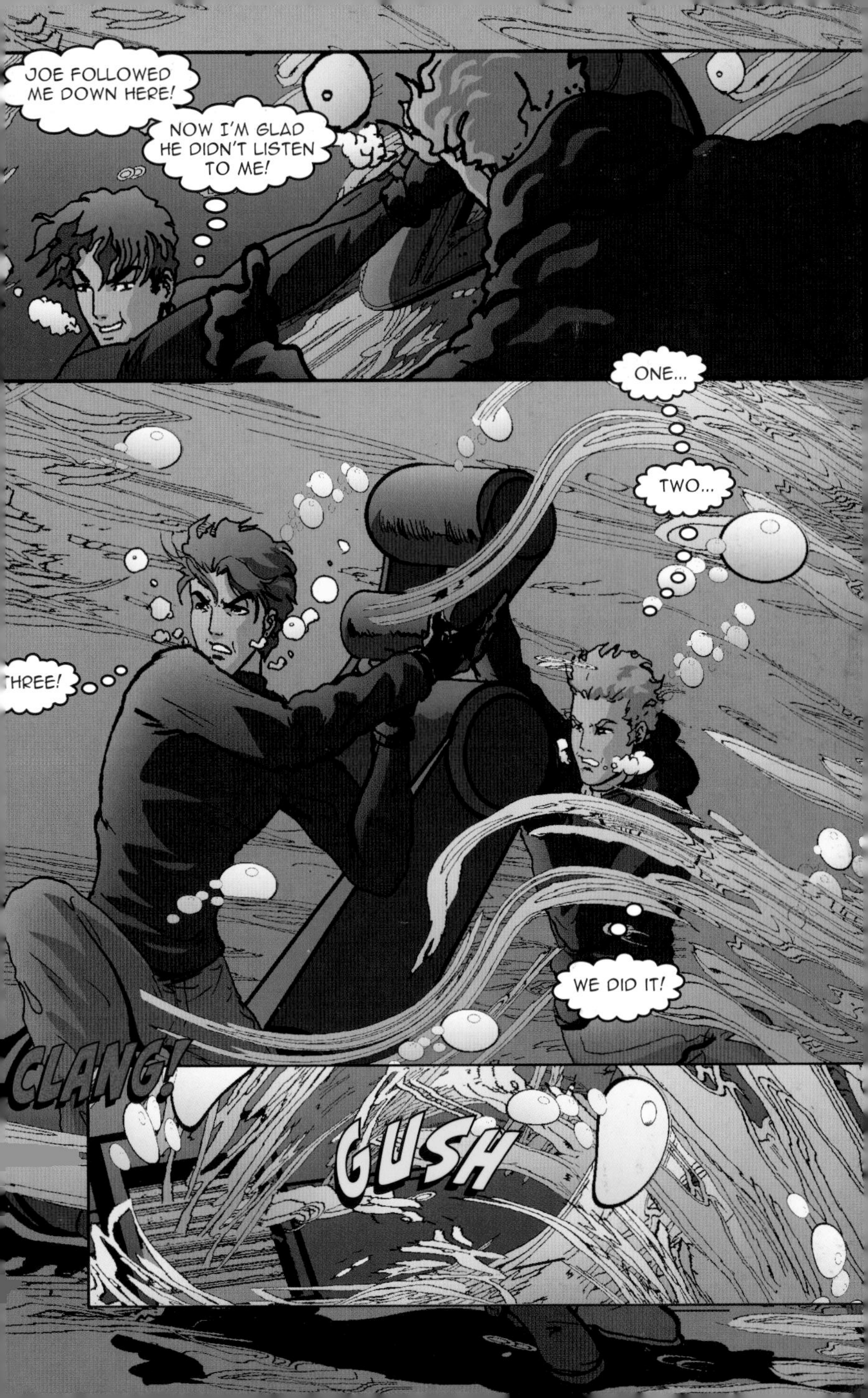
JOE FOLLOWED ME DOWN HERE!
NOW I'M GLAD HE DIDN'T LISTEN TO ME!
ONE...
TWO...
THREE!
WE DID IT!
CLANG!
GUSH

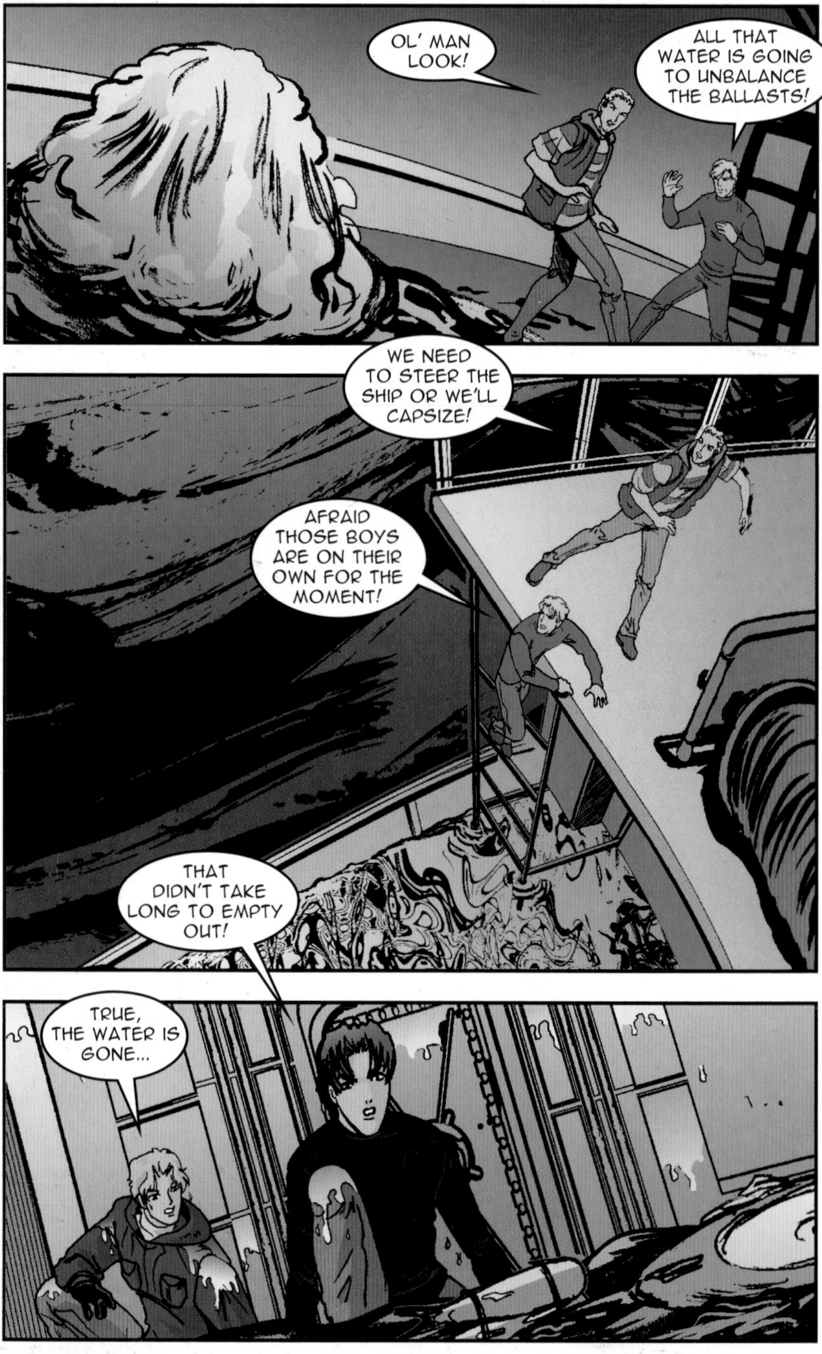
OL' MAN LOOK!
ALL THAT WATER IS GOING TO UNBALANCE THE BALLASTS!
WE NEED TO STEER THE SHIP OR WE'LL CAPSIZE!
AFRAID THOSE BOYS ARE ON THEIR OWN FOR THE MOMENT!
THAT DIDN'T TAKE LONG TO EMPTY OUT!
TRUE, THE WATER IS GONE...

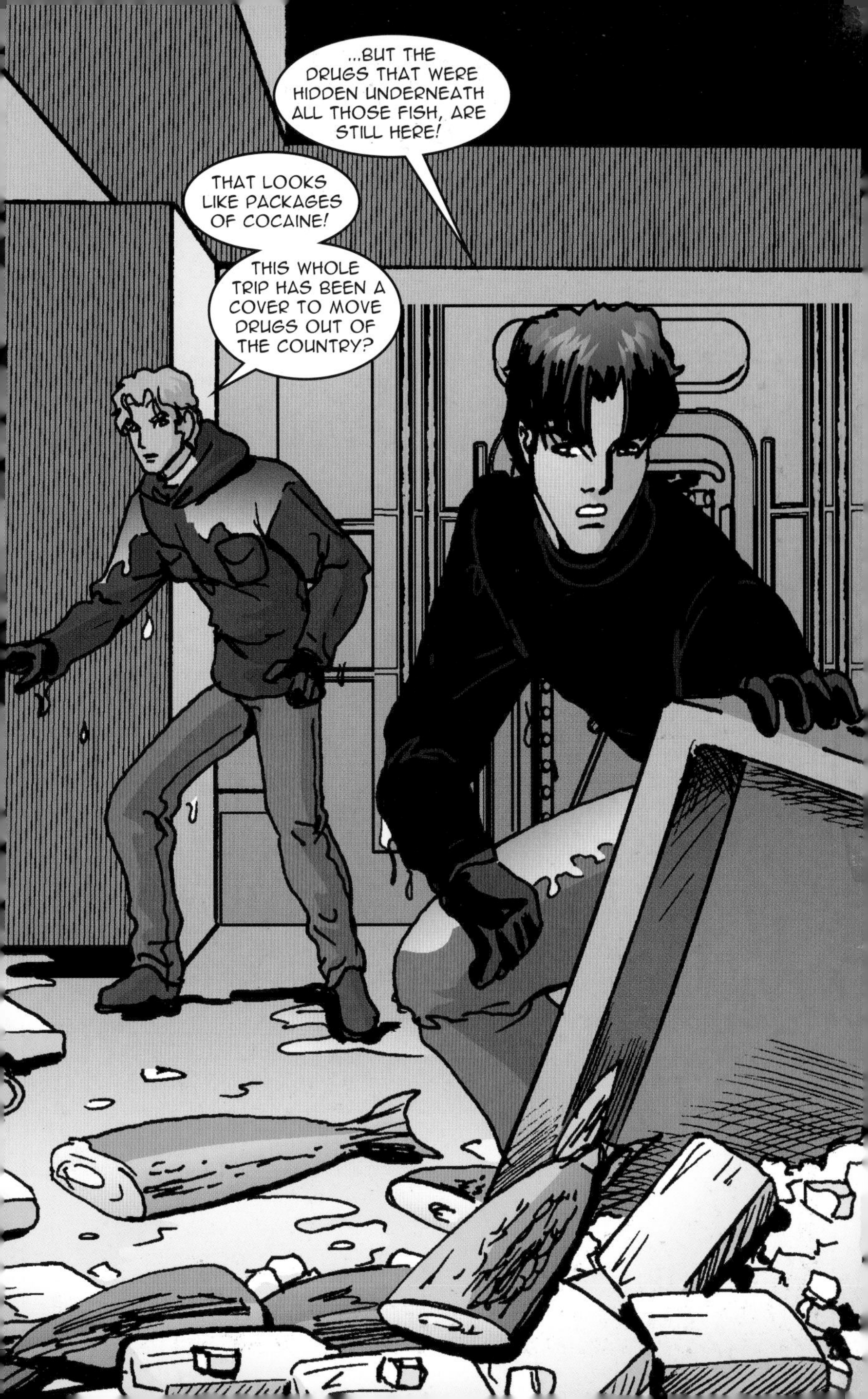
...BUT THE DRUGS THAT WERE HIDDEN UNDERNEATH ALL THOSE FISH, ARE STILL HERE!
THAT LOOKS LIKE PACKAGES OF COCAINE!
THIS WHOLE TRIP HAS BEEN A COVER TO MOVE DRUGS OUT OF THE COUNTRY?

DRUG TRAFFICKING IS A LOT MORE PROFITABLE THAN FISHING...

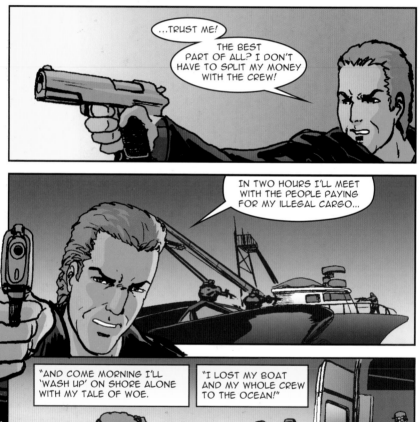

...TRUST ME!

THE BEST PART OF ALL? I DON'T HAVE TO SPLIT MY MONEY WITH THE CREW!

IN TWO HOURS I'LL MEET WITH THE PEOPLE PAYING FOR MY ILLEGAL CARGO...

"AND COME MORNING I'LL 'WASH UP' ON SHORE ALONE WITH MY TALE OF WOE.

"I LOST MY BOAT AND MY WHOLE CREW TO THE OCEAN!"

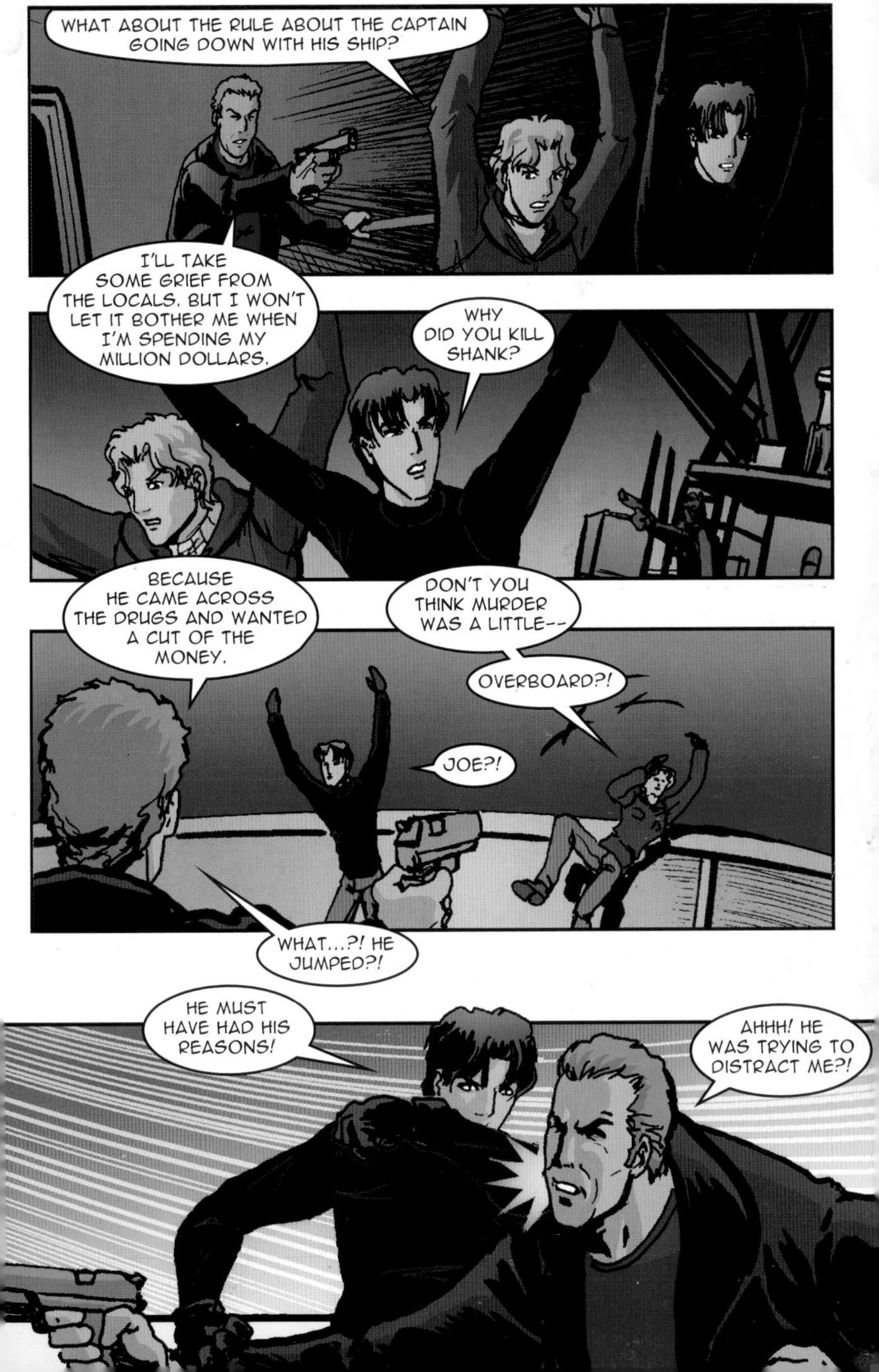
WHAT ABOUT THE RULE ABOUT THE CAPTAIN GOING DOWN WITH HIS SHIP?
I'LL TAKE SOME GRIEF FROM THE LOCALS. BUT I WON'T LET IT BOTHER ME WHEN I'M SPENDING MY MILLION DOLLARS.
WHY DID YOU KILL SHANK?
BECAUSE HE CAME ACROSS THE DRUGS AND WANTED A CUT OF THE MONEY.
DON'T YOU THINK MURDER WAS A LITTLE--
OVERBOARD?!
JOE?!
WHAT...?! HE JUMPED?!
HE MUST HAVE HAD HIS REASONS!
AHHH! HE WAS TRYING TO DISTRACT ME?!

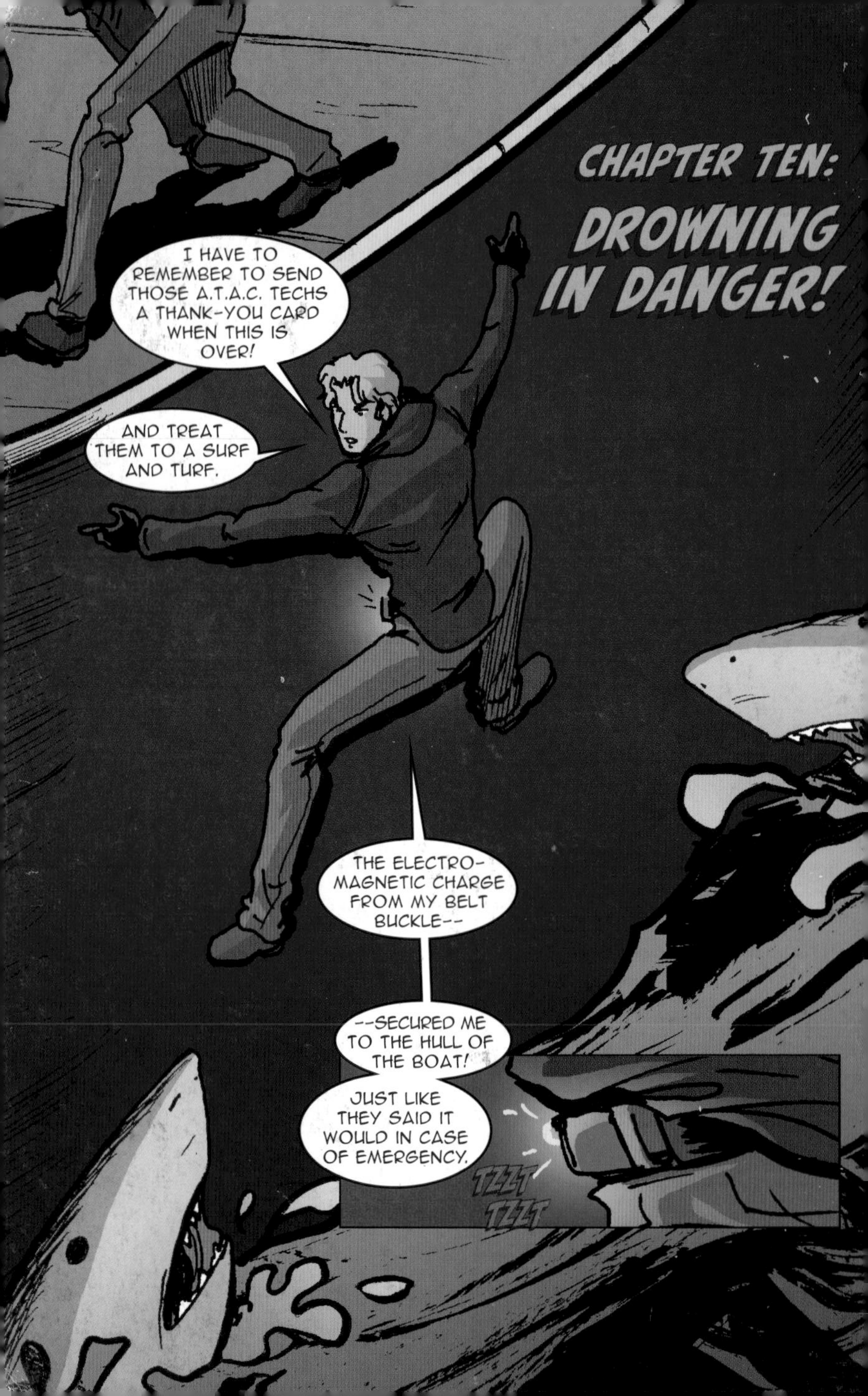
CHAPTER TEN:
DROWNING IN DANGER!
I HAVE TO REMEMBER TO SEND THOSE A.T.A.C. TECHS A THANK-YOU CARD WHEN THIS IS OVER!
AND TREAT THEM TO A SURF AND TURF.
THE ELECTRO-MAGNETIC CHARGE FROM MY BELT BUCKLE--
--SECURED ME TO THE HULL OF THE BOAT!
JUST LIKE THEY SAID IT WOULD IN CASE OF EMERGENCY.
TZZT
TZZT

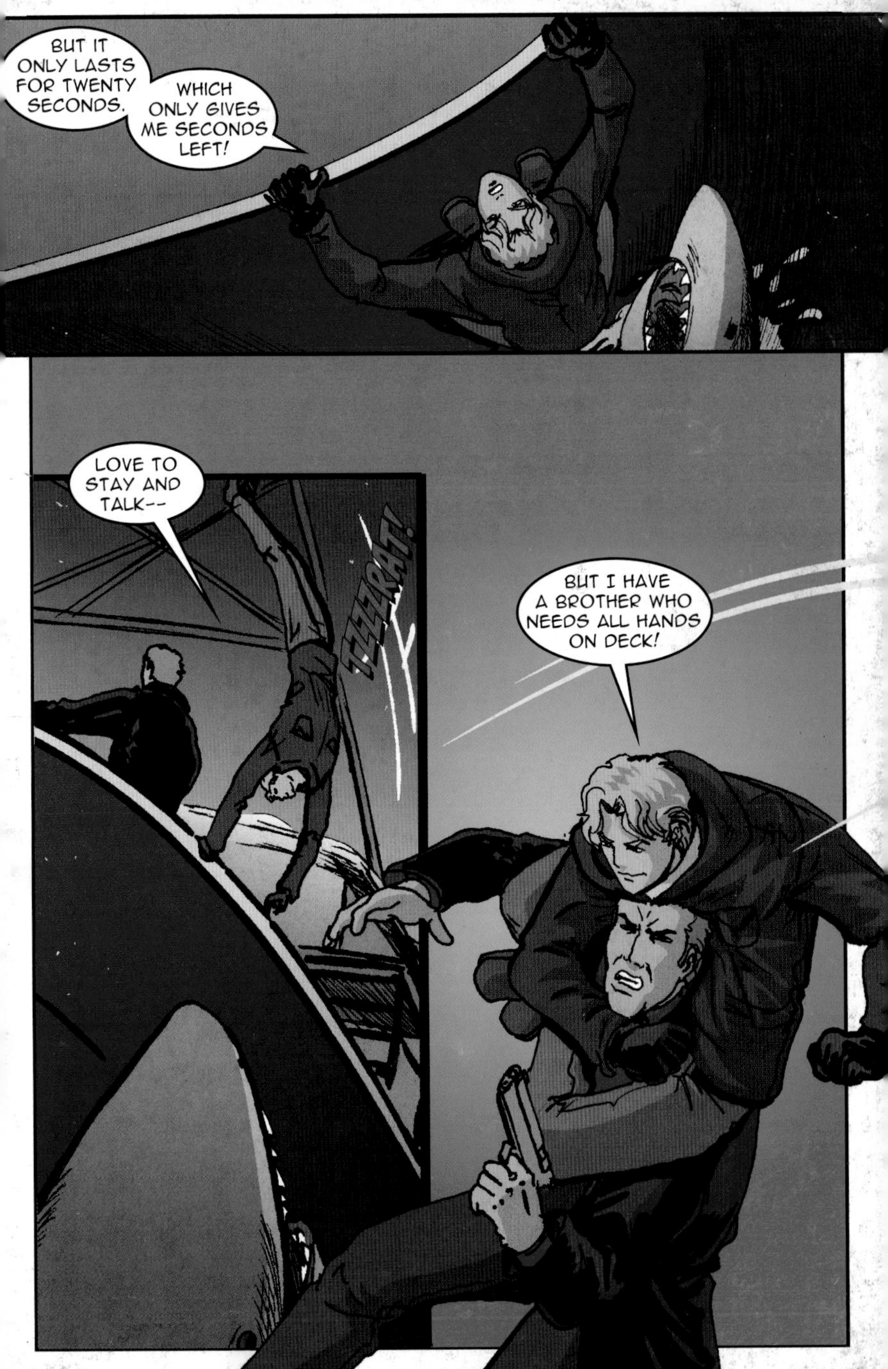
BUT IT ONLY LASTS FOR TWENTY SECONDS.
WHICH ONLY GIVES ME SECONDS LEFT!
LOVE TO STAY AND TALK--
TZZZRAT!
BUT I HAVE A BROTHER WHO NEEDS ALL HANDS ON DECK!

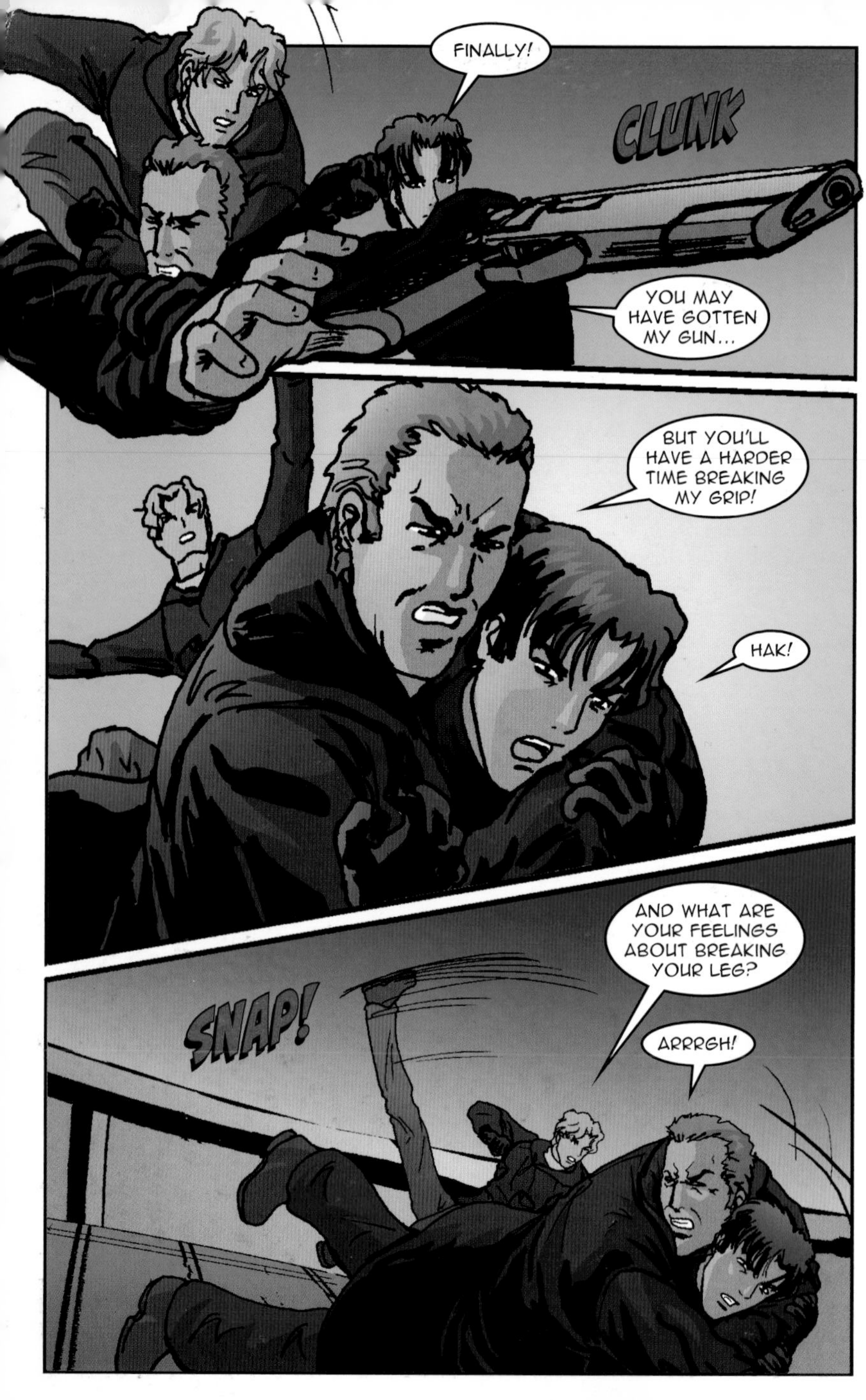
FINALLY!
CLUNK
YOU MAY HAVE GOTTEN MY GUN...
BUT YOU'LL HAVE A HARDER TIME BREAKING MY GRIP!
HAK!
AND WHAT ARE YOUR FEELINGS ABOUT BREAKING YOUR LEG?
SNAP!
ARRRGH!

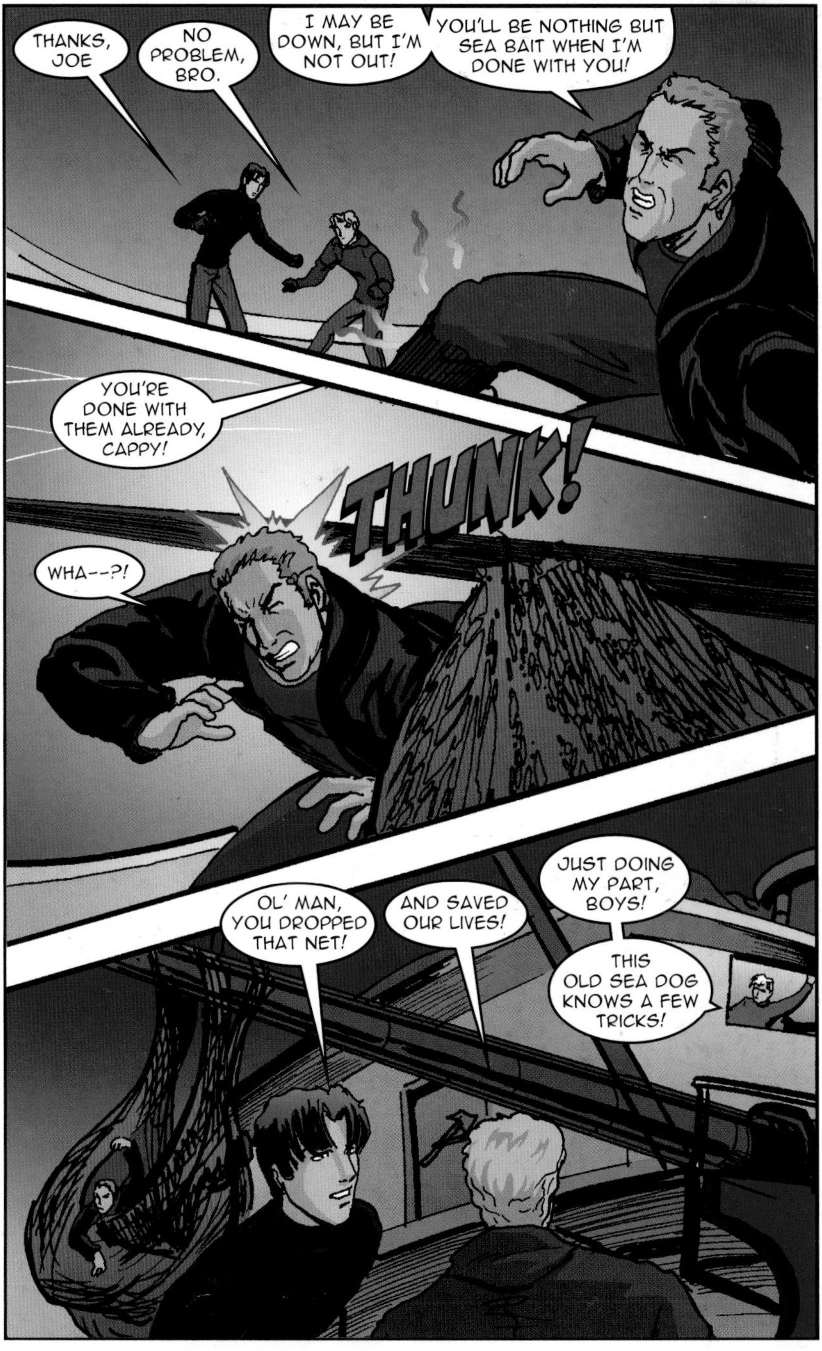
THANKS, JOE
NO PROBLEM, BRO.
I MAY BE DOWN, BUT I'M NOT OUT!
YOU'LL BE NOTHING BUT SEA BAIT WHEN I'M DONE WITH YOU!
YOU'RE DONE WITH THEM ALREADY, CAPPY!
THUNK!
WHA--?!
OL' MAN, YOU DROPPED THAT NET!
AND SAVED OUR LIVES!
JUST DOING MY PART, BOYS!
THIS OLD SEA DOG KNOWS A FEW TRICKS!

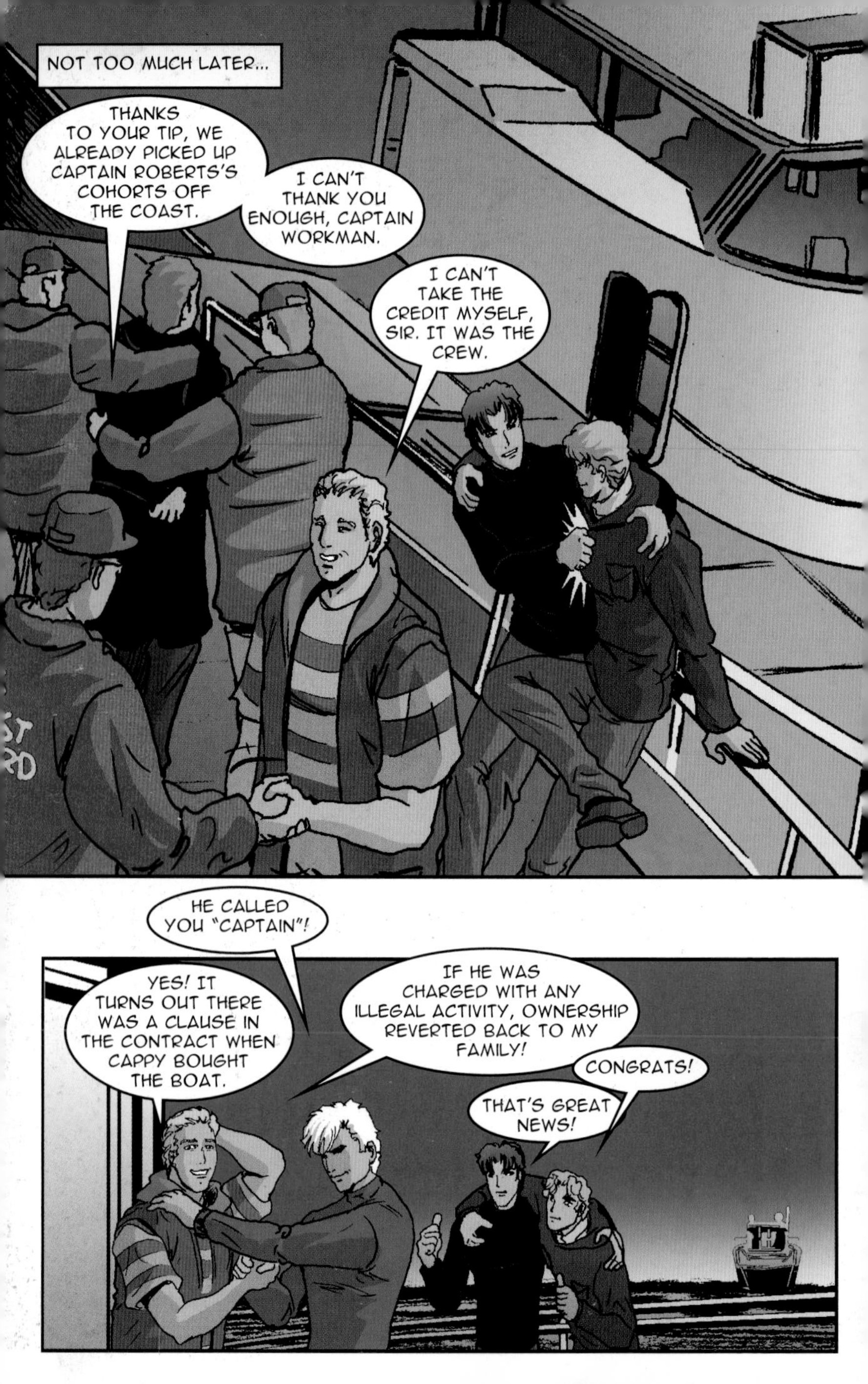
NOT TOO MUCH LATER...
THANKS TO YOUR TIP, WE ALREADY PICKED UP CAPTAIN ROBERTS'S COHORTS OFF THE COAST.
I CAN'T THANK YOU ENOUGH, CAPTAIN WORKMAN.
I CAN'T TAKE THE CREDIT MYSELF, SIR. IT WAS THE CREW.
HE CALLED YOU "CAPTAIN"!
YES! IT TURNS OUT THERE WAS A CLAUSE IN THE CONTRACT WHEN CAPPY BOUGHT THE BOAT.
IF HE WAS CHARGED WITH ANY ILLEGAL ACTIVITY, OWNERSHIP REVERTED BACK TO MY FAMILY!
CONGRATS!
THAT'S GREAT NEWS!

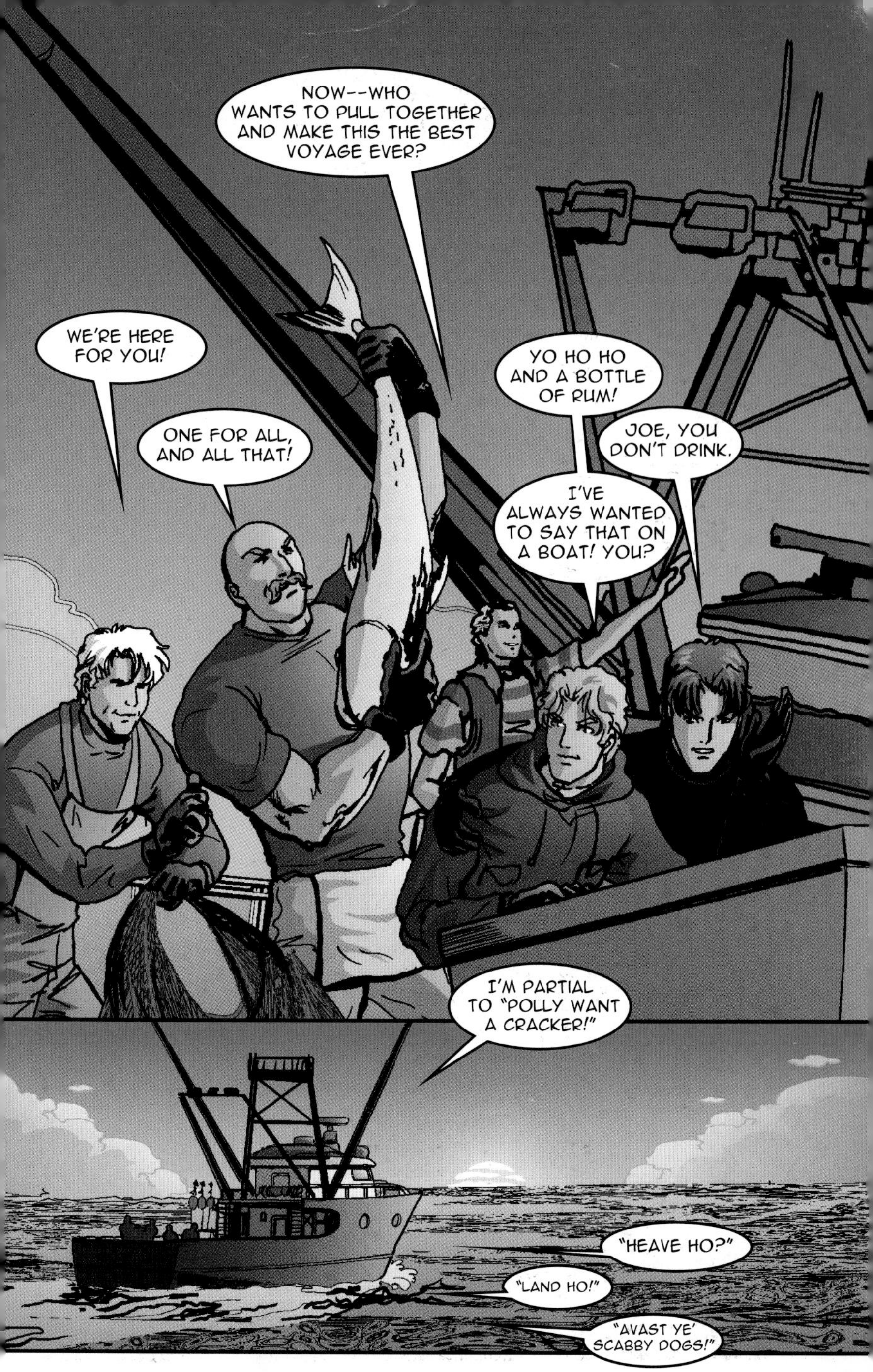
NOW--WHO WANTS TO PULL TOGETHER AND MAKE THIS THE BEST VOYAGE EVER?
WE'RE HERE FOR YOU!
ONE FOR ALL, AND ALL THAT!
YO HO HO AND A BOTTLE OF RUM!
JOE, YOU DON'T DRINK.
I'VE ALWAYS WANTED TO SAY THAT ON A BOAT! YOU?
I'M PARTIAL TO "POLLY WANT A CRACKER!"
"HEAVE HO?"
"LAND HO!"
"AVAST YE' SCABBY DOGS!"

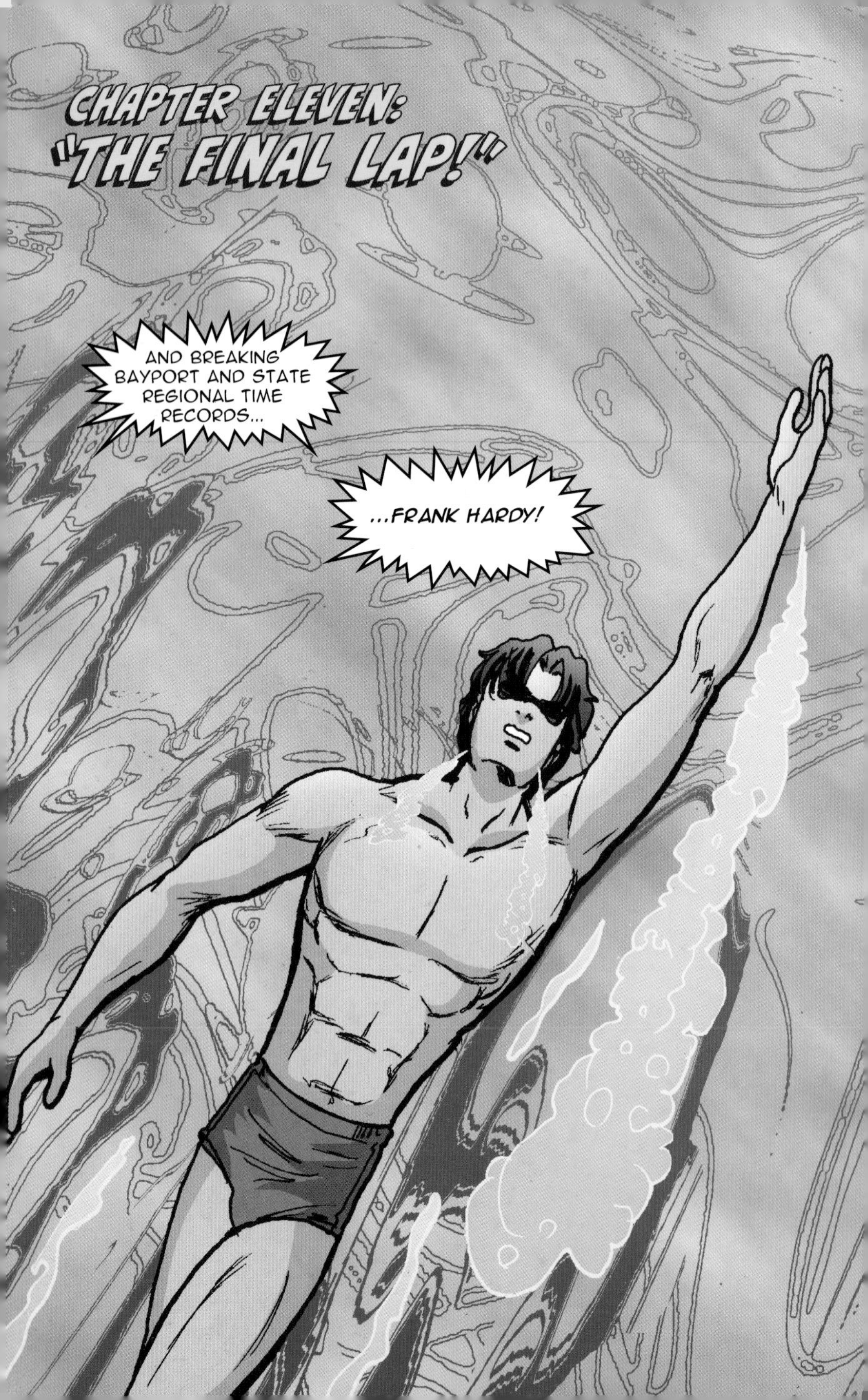
CHAPTER ELEVEN:
"THE FINAL LAP!"
AND BREAKING BAYPORT AND STATE REGIONAL TIME RECORDS...
...FRANK HARDY!

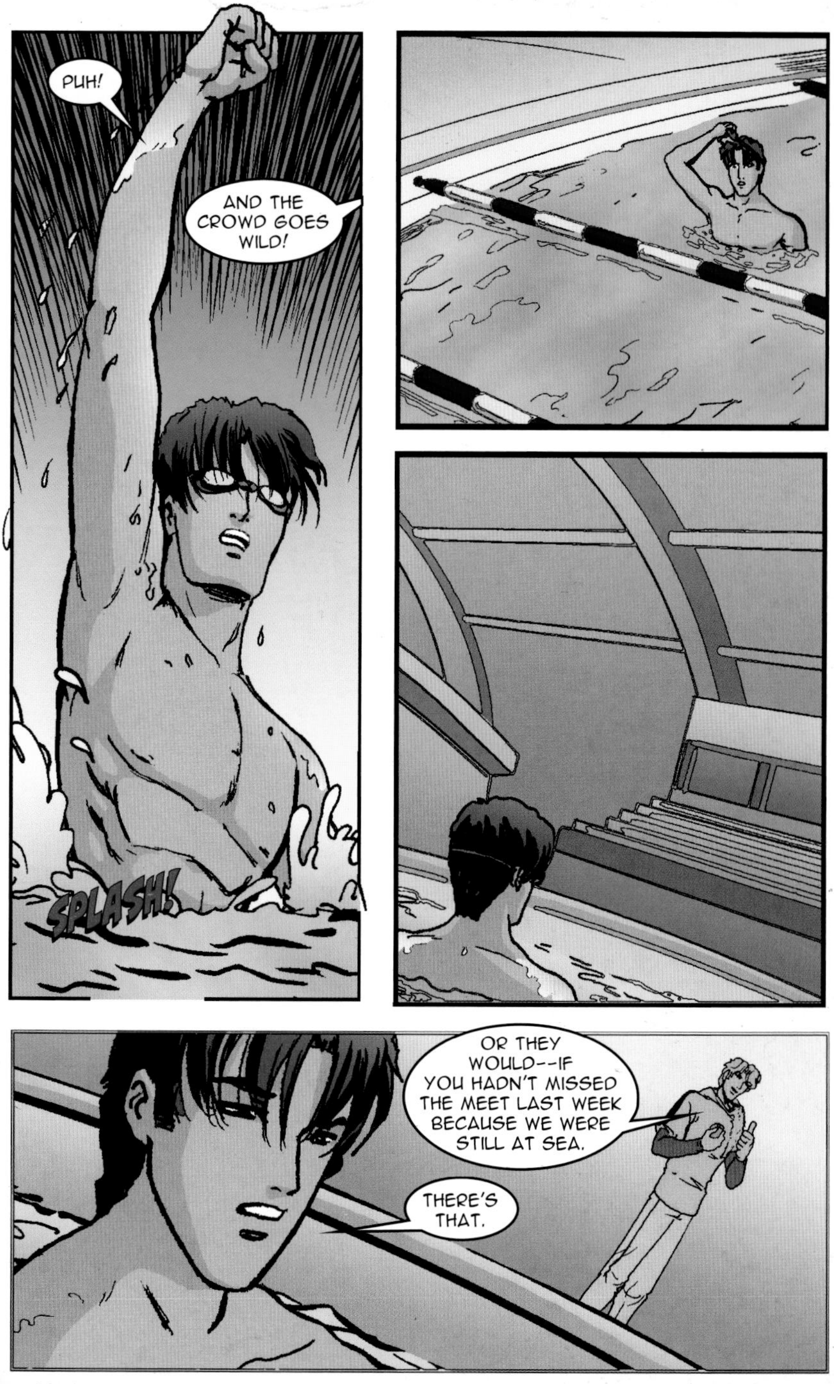
PUH!
AND THE CROWD GOES WILD!
SPLASH!
OR THEY WOULD--IF YOU HADN'T MISSED THE MEET LAST WEEK BECAUSE WE WERE STILL AT SEA.
THERE'S THAT.

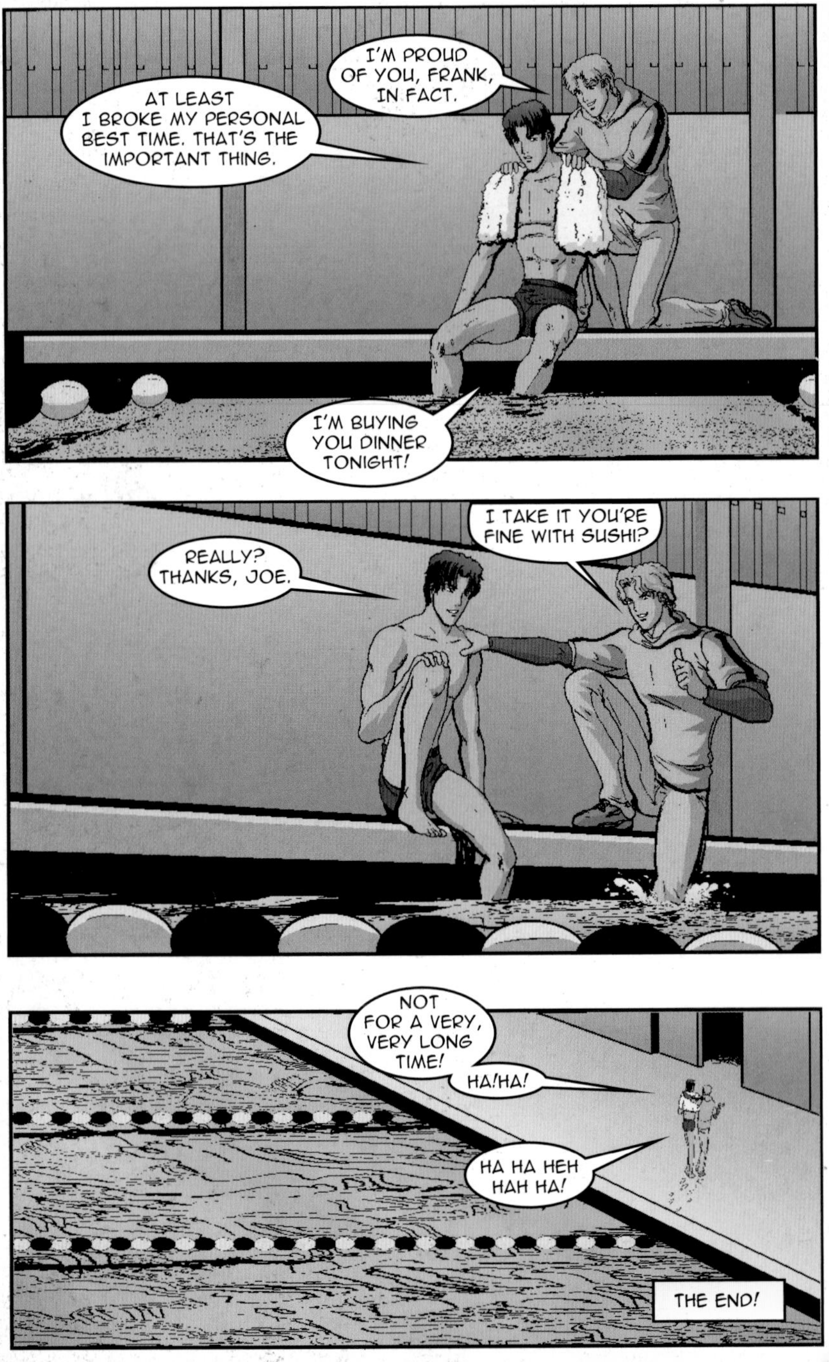
I'M PROUD OF YOU, FRANK, IN FACT.
AT LEAST I BROKE MY PERSONAL BEST TIME. THAT'S THE IMPORTANT THING.
I'M BUYING YOU DINNER TONIGHT!
REALLY? THANKS, JOE.
I TAKE IT YOU'RE FINE WITH SUSHI?
NOT FOR A VERY, VERY LONG TIME!
HA!HA!
HA HA HEH HAH HA!
THE END!

Special Advance Preview of THE HARDY BOYS Graphic Novel # 6 – "Hyde & Shriek"

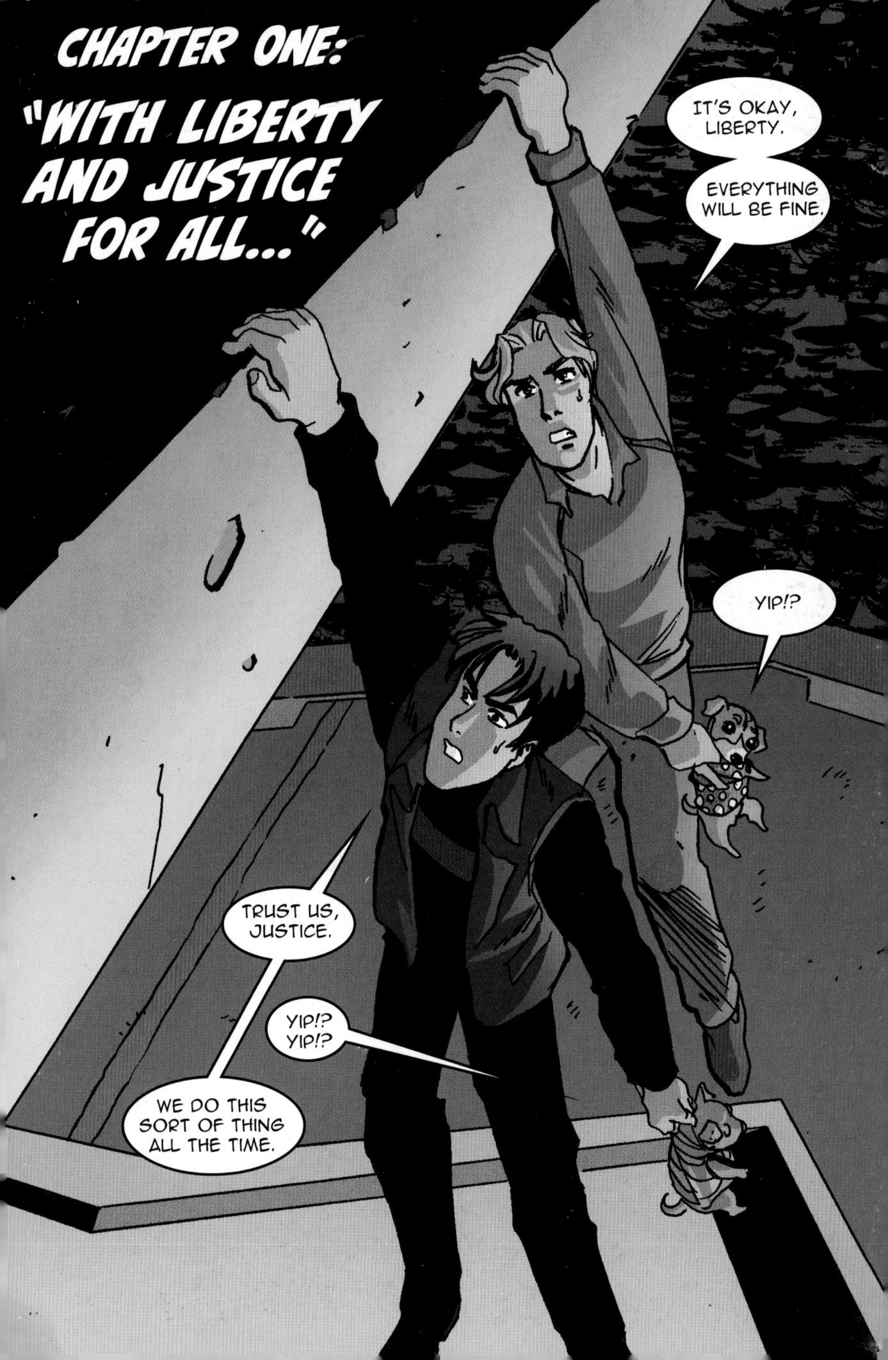
CHAPTER ONE:
"WITH LIBERTY AND JUSTICE FOR ALL..."
IT'S OKAY, LIBERTY.
EVERYTHING WILL BE FINE.
YIP!?
TRUST US, JUSTICE.
YIP!? YIP!?
WE DO THIS SORT OF THING ALL THE TIME.

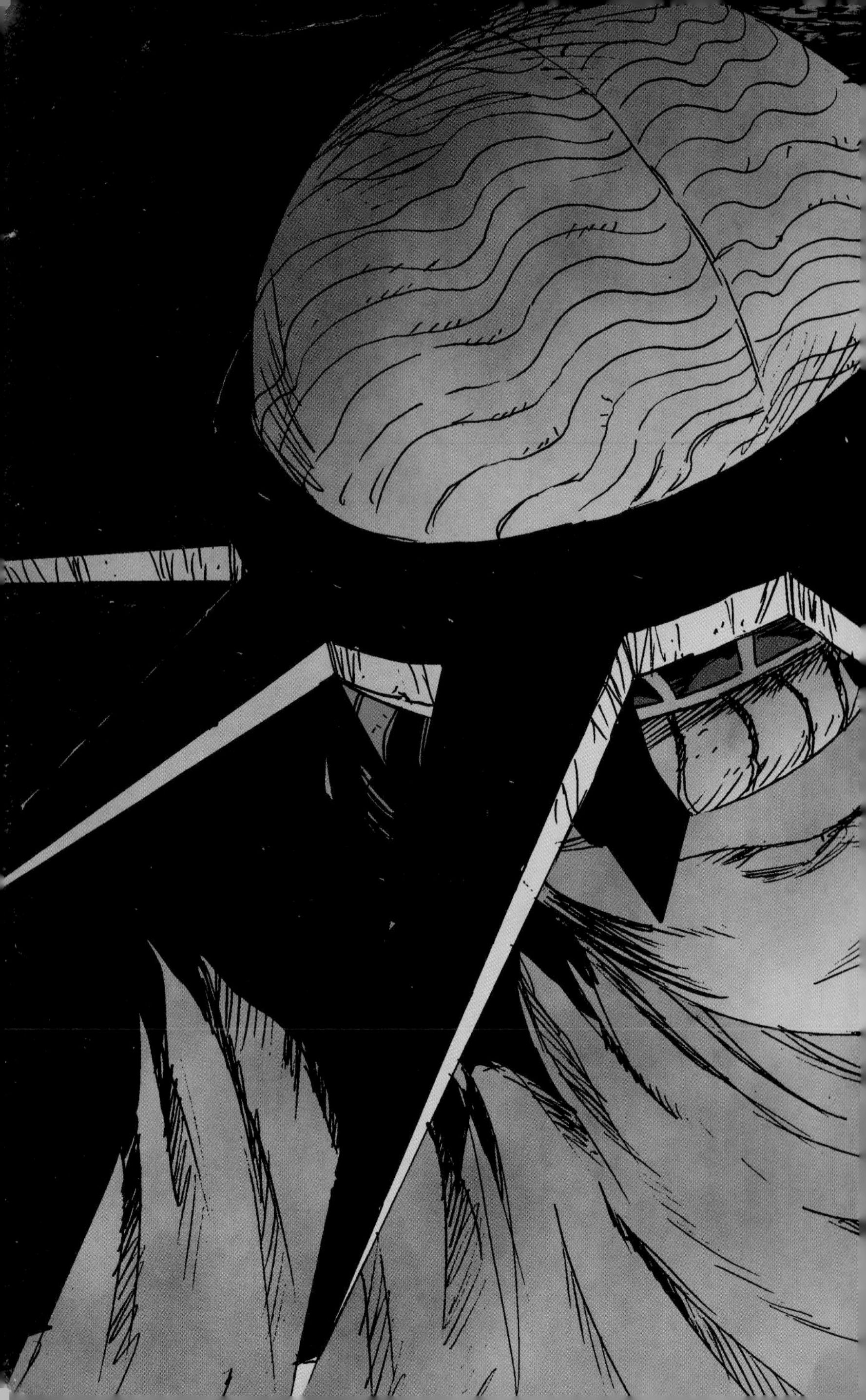

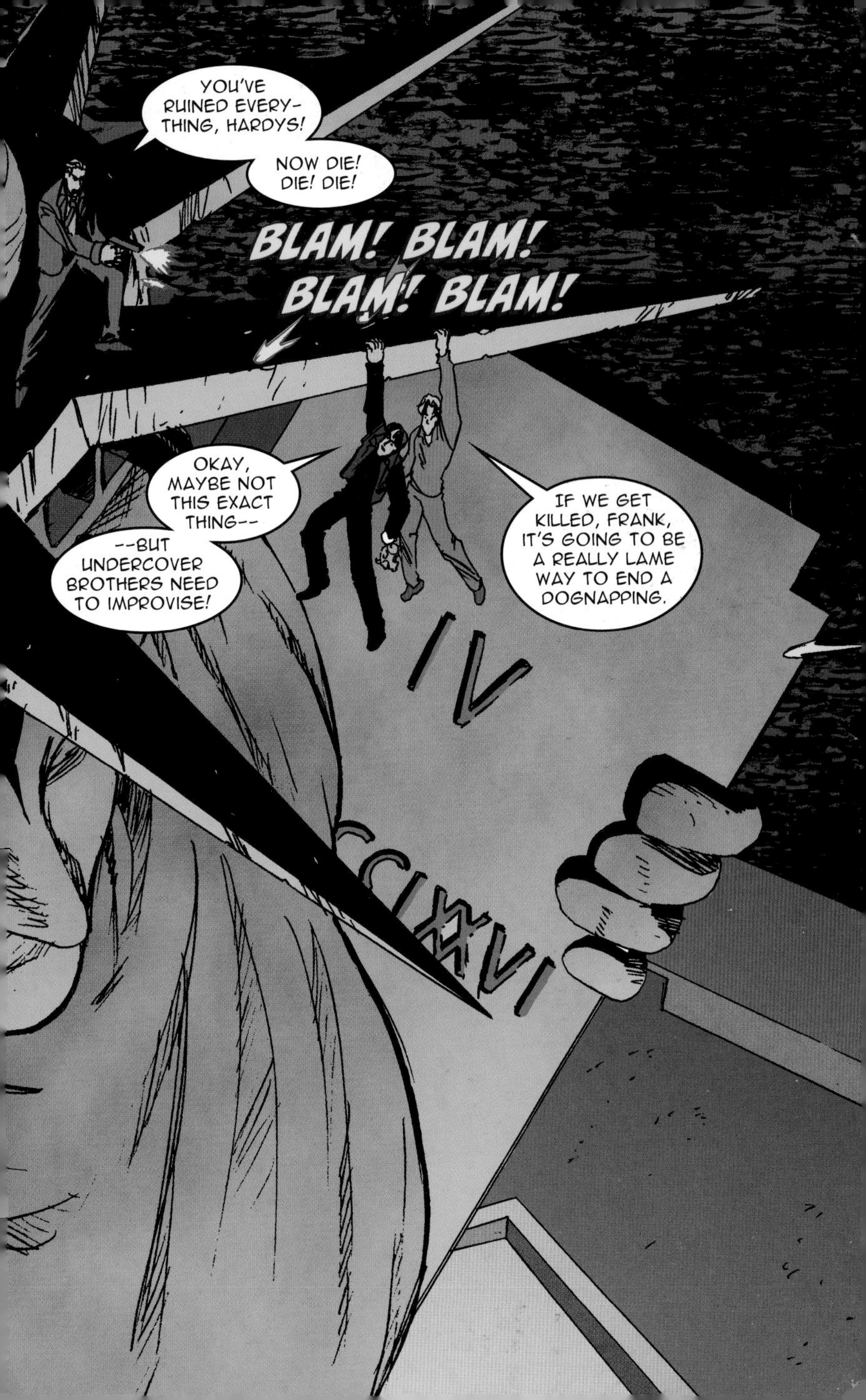
YOU'VE RUINED EVERY- THING, HARDYS!
NOW DIE! DIE! DIE!
BLAM! BLAM! BLAM! BLAM!
OKAY, MAYBE NOT THIS EXACT THING--
--BUT UNDERCOVER BROTHERS NEED TO IMPROVISE!
IF WE GET KILLED, FRANK, IT'S GOING TO BE A REALLY LAME WAY TO END A DOGNAPPING.
IV
CLXXVI

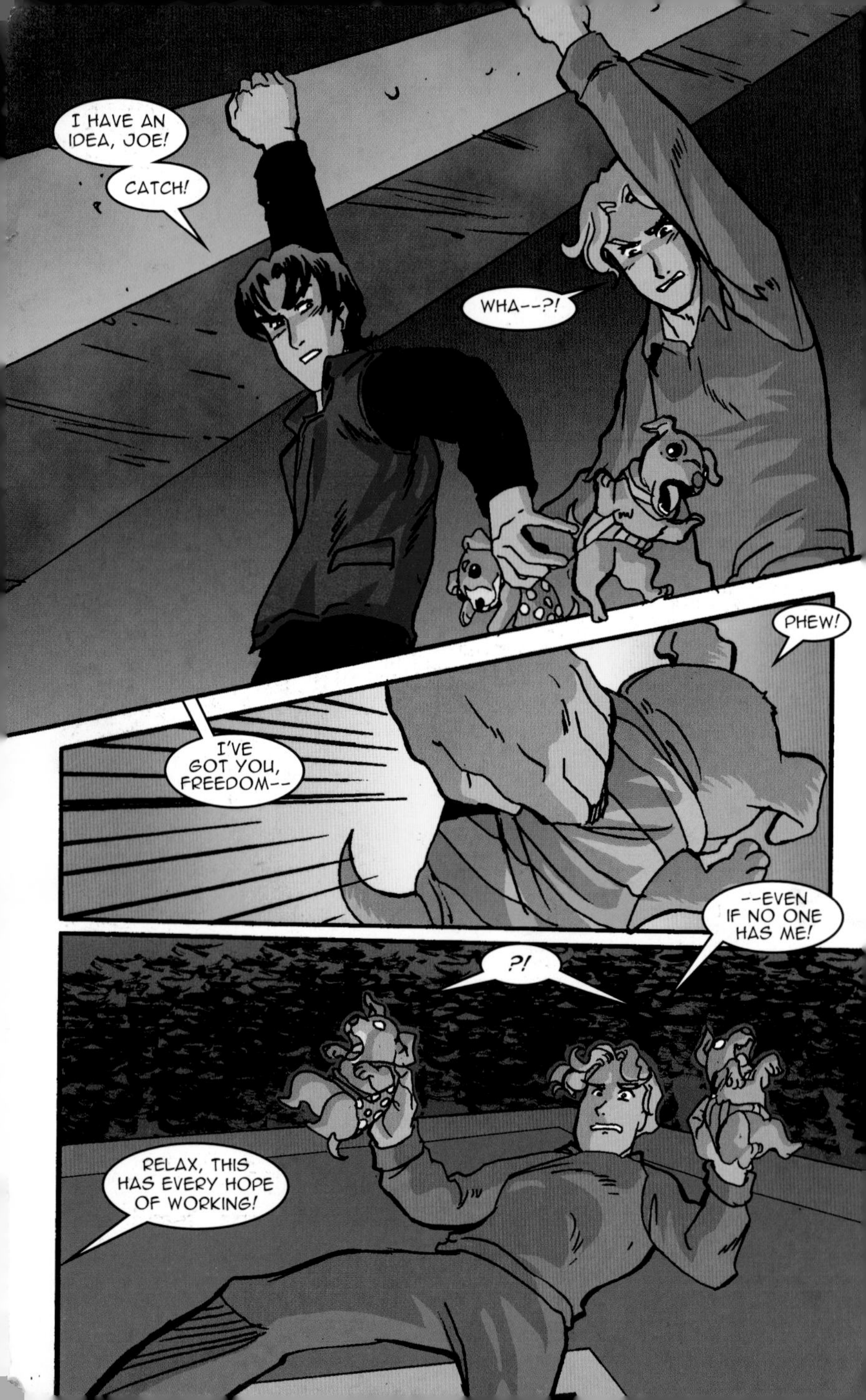
I HAVE AN IDEA, JOE!
CATCH!
WHA--?!
PHEW!
I'VE GOT YOU, FREEDOM--
--EVEN IF NO ONE HAS ME!
?!
RELAX, THIS HAS EVERY HOPE OF WORKING!

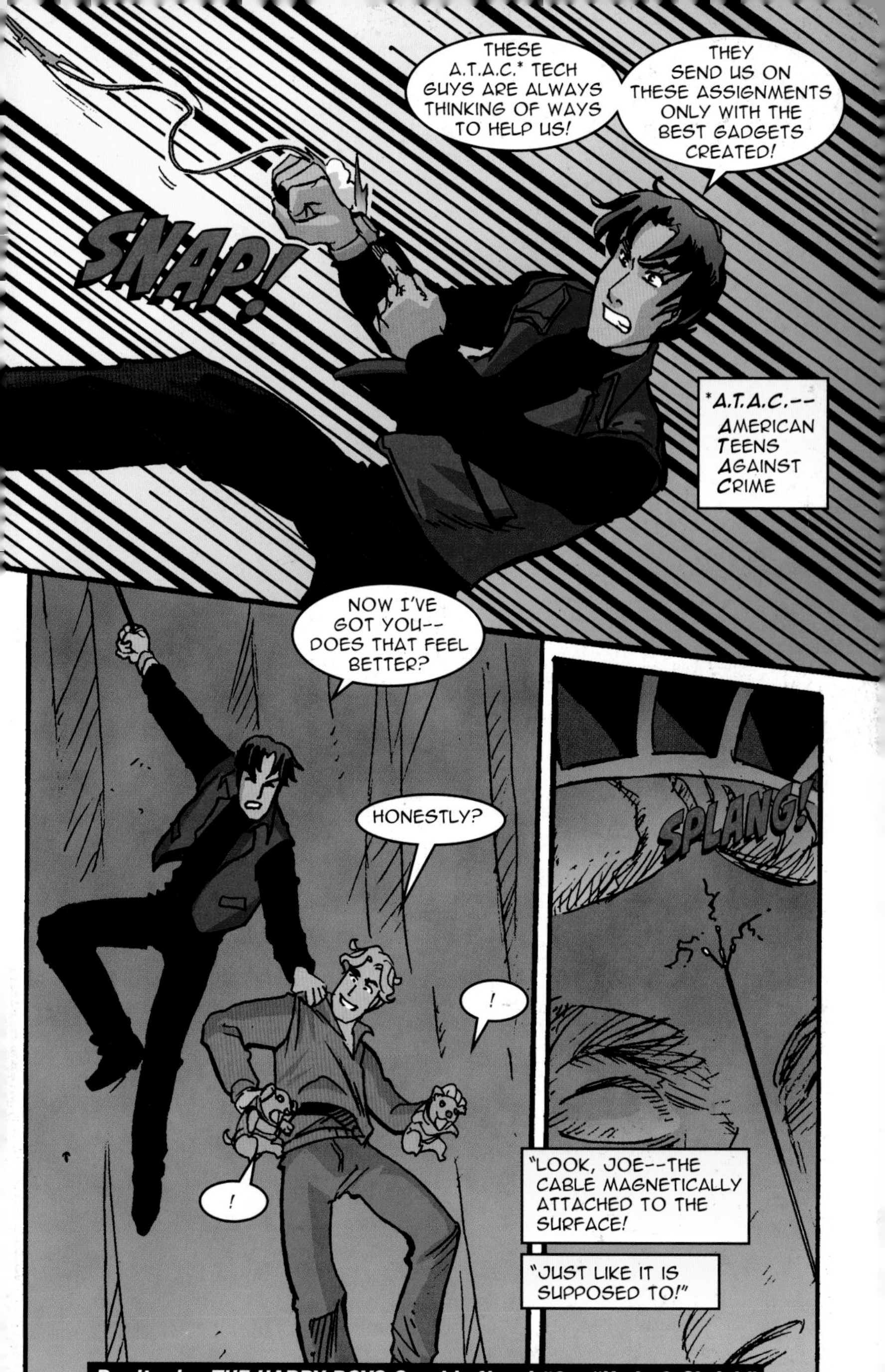

THESE A.T.A.C.* TECH GUYS ARE ALWAYS THINKING OF WAYS TO HELP US!
THEY SEND US ON THESE ASSIGNMENTS ONLY WITH THE BEST GADGETS CREATED!
SNAP!
*A.T.A.C.-- AMERICAN TEENS AGAINST CRIME
NOW I'VE GOT YOU-- DOES THAT FEEL BETTER?
HONESTLY?
!
!
SPLANG!
"LOOK, JOE--THE CABLE MAGNETICALLY ATTACHED TO THE SURFACE!
"JUST LIKE IT IS SUPPOSED TO!"

Don't miss THE HARDY BOYS Graphic Novel #6 – "Hyde & Shriek"

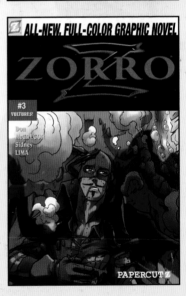

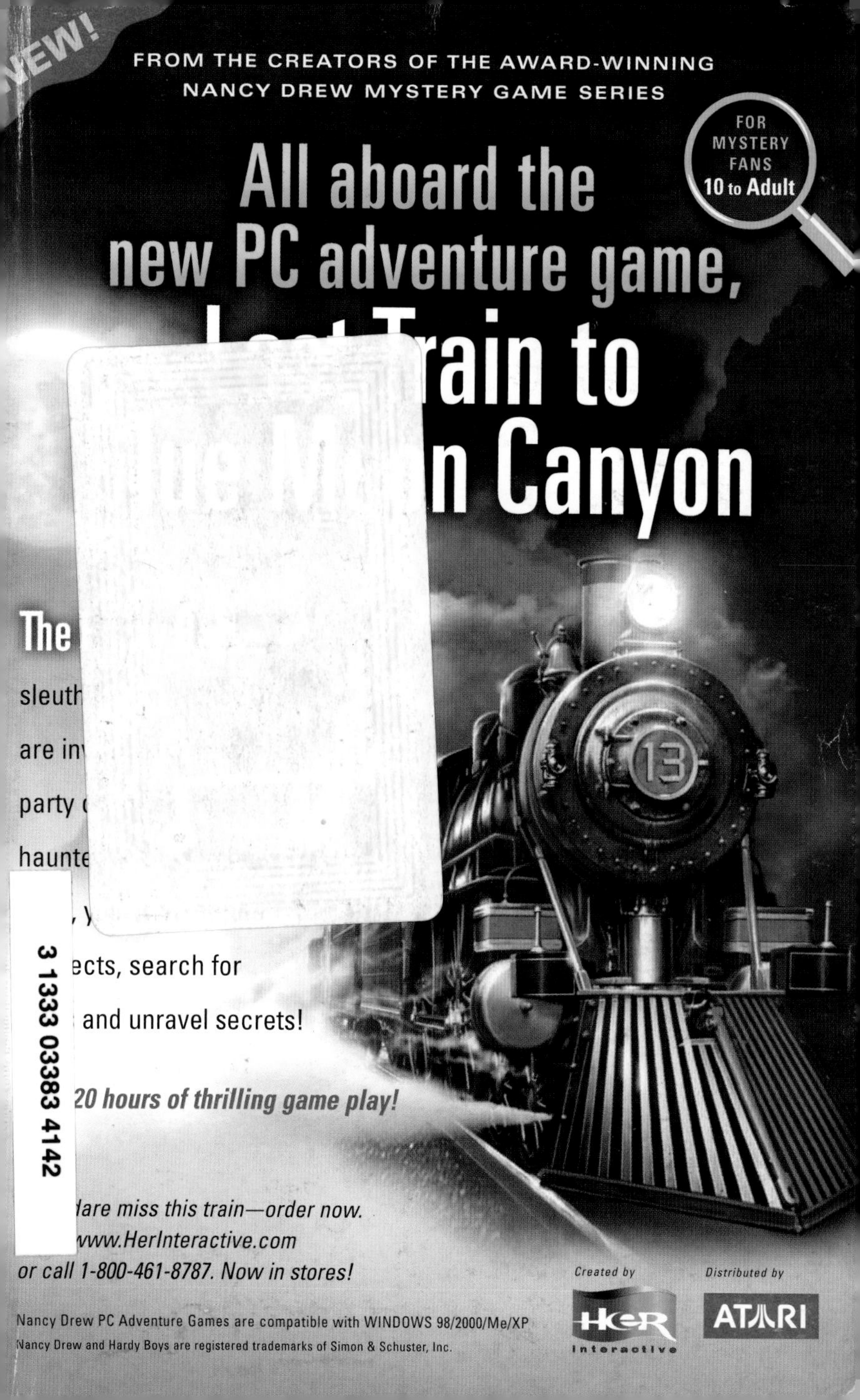
NEW!
FROM THE CREATORS OF THE AWARD-WINNING
NANCY DREW MYSTERY GAME SERIES
FOR MYSTERY FANS
10 to Adult
All aboard the
new PC adventure game,
rain to
n Canyon
The
sleuth
are in
party
haunte
ects, search for
and unravel secrets!
20 hours of thrilling game play!
dare miss this train—order now.
www.HerInteractive.com
or call 1-800-461-8787. Now in stores!
Created by
HeR Interactive
Distributed by
ATARI
Nancy Drew PC Adventure Games are compatible with WINDOWS 98/2000/Me/XP
Nancy Drew and Hardy Boys are registered trademarks of Simon & Schuster, Inc.
3 1333 03383 4142